KU-544-287

Meet me Under the Mistletoe

Abby Clements

Quercus

First published in Great Britain in 2012 by
Quercus
55 Baker Street
7th Floor, South Block
London W1U 8EW

Copyright © 2012 Abby Clements

The moral right of Abby Clements to be
identified as the author of this work has been
asserted in accordance with the Copyright,
Designs and Patents Act, 1988.

All rights reserved. No part of this publication
may be reproduced or transmitted in any form
or by any means, electronic or mechanical,
including photocopy, recording, or any
information storage and retrieval system,
without permission in writing from the publisher.

A CIP catalogue record for this book is available
from the British Library

PB ISBN 978 1 78087 662 7
EBOOK ISBN 978 1 78087 663 4

This book is a work of fiction. Names, characters,
businesses, organizations, places and events are
either the product of the author's imagination
or are used fictitiously. Any resemblance to
actual persons, living or dead, events or
locales is entirely coincidental.

10 9 8 7 6 5 4 3 2

Printed and bound in Great Britain by Clays Ltd, St Ives plc

Typeset by Ellipsis Digital Limited, Glasgow

For Eloise

CHAPTER 1

Monday 20th November

'Not even half seven yet, Laurie,' the young security guard teased her. 'Don't you ever get a lie-in?'

'Big day today,' she said, swinging open the glass door of her office, latte held tight in her other hand. 'If I'm lucky I might get some sleep next week.'

Laurie crossed the empty entrance hall, winter sunlight streaming in through the floor-to-ceiling windows, and stepped into the waiting lift. She pressed the button for the second floor, then turned towards the mirror and tidied the blunt-cut fringe of her dark bob. As the doors closed, she took a deep breath, then exhaled slowly, glad she'd arrived early before the building got busy. After just three hours' sleep, her capacity for small-talk was minimal today – she wanted to focus on the job at hand, and nothing more.

'Floor One . . . Two – DING!'

'Morning, Laurie,' Jacques said from behind the Seamless reception desk as Laurie walked out of the lift.

Newly employed at the upmarket fashion brand,

Jacques, a snappily dressed Frenchman, had been getting in early for the last couple of weeks, keen to make a good impression. Laurie nodded hello politely, then walked on, passing the rows of unoccupied desks on the way to her corner office. She glanced around. Her boss Danny wasn't in yet, and it looked as if the only other person on the floor was Gillian, their steely-willed CEO. Laurie could make her out behind the frosted-glass dividing walls, talking on the phone.

Laurie closed the door to her own office behind her, and glanced out at the view from her windows. Double-decker buses and cabs crawled down the Strand, past glittering Christmas shop-window displays, and the pavements were crowded with commuters and tourists walking to Trafalgar Square. But inside, apart from the faint hum of traffic, her office was an oasis of calm.

Laurie put her bag down, sat on her swivel chair and switched on her computer. As it powered up, she got settled at her immaculate, clear desk, the surface cool to the touch and smelling faintly of lemon cleaning fluid. After a few days abroad – another whirl of airports, new faces and anonymous hotel rooms – it felt good to be back in London.

Her computer started up with its familiar jingle of electronic notes and her eyes drifted to her pinboard – on it were a couple of fabric swatches, ideas for the Seamless spring accessories palette, and her calendar. One date stood out: Monday 20th November: today.

Navajo bags! was ringed in red and had been marked there for months. Laurie smiled. Navajo was Seamless' exclusive new line of wintertime accessories, and she was in charge of it – the handbag she was launching today was their leading design, embodying the understated elegance of the whole product line. She had lived, breathed and dreamed about this launch day since the summer, when she'd started her first sketches of the bag. If everything went smoothly, today could be the making of her. The publicity around the launch was unprecedented – features and mentions were lined up across all the glossies and the Seamless marketing department was primed to mail out freebies to a raft of A-list celebrities.

Laurie took a sip of her coffee as her emails opened on screen. After months of work designing and overseeing production on the bag, the first shipment was finally due in from China. On Friday she'd returned from two days in the factory outside Beijing, where she'd been checking the tassels on the bags as they sped off the production line. Her plan for today was simple: she'd check the newly delivered handbags swiftly, give the green light for them to be sent on to the shops ready for the pre-Christmas rush – then cross town to promote the whole Navajo range at a dedicated launch party. It was the highest-profile product line she'd handled since she'd stepped up to the role of Head of Accessories, and she was ready for her big moment.

She'd dressed for the part in a fitted slate-grey dress

3

and black knee-high boots, her chestnut bob blow-dried straight and glossy, with plenty of liquid eyeliner and smoky grey eyeshadow to hide the fact her eyes were red-rimmed from lack of sleep. She'd been awake for most of the night, frequently checking her iPhone for the shipment's progress. A technical issue at the factory had already set them back three days, so the timing was tight – there was absolutely no room for error.

The first delivery of a thousand bags was due in at 8 a.m. She tapped her nails on the desk as she watched the minutes tick by.

'Are you sure there's nothing down there?' Laurie said, holding the phone receiver with one hand and clicking on the courier's website with the other. 'Would you mind checking again?' She bit her lip. 'They should have come in half an hour ago.'

Her heart raced. From the online tracking details it looked as if the packages should already have arrived.

'There's nothing down here,' the boy in the post room replied. 'Unless . . . you work for Danny Graham, don't you? Always a chance they could have gone straight up to him.'

Laurie heard some noise from the open-plan area, a conversation going on in raised voices outside her office walls, then a knock came at her door. She saw through the frosted glass that it was her boss, Danny. She thanked the post-room boy and put the phone down.

'Come in,' she called out.

Danny opened the door and peeked around it. With his Just for Men black hair, ill-fitting suits and wild eyebrows, she marvelled once again at how he'd ever made it through the doors of the Seamless office – let alone become a director. Business sense had, in a rare moment at Seamless, triumphed over fashion sense.

'Hi, Laurie.'

'Danny, hi,' Laurie said, spotting right away that he had one of the boxes from the shipment in his hands.

He put the cardboard box on the table between them. 'They're in.'

Laurie put a hand to her mouth in anticipation as he held up one of the tan woven-leather handbags she'd spent the last six months working on. The curves were elegant, the leather had a delicate sheen and the small tassel hanging at the side added a final dash of style. Laurie reached over to touch the bag and couldn't help smiling – it was perfect.

'Wow. Beautiful, isn't it?' she said, running a finger over the small gold clasp. 'And you said using kangaroo leather was a no-no? Come on, Danny, this stuff is amazing. Soft and hardwearing. Those roos are going to be immortalised by the Navajo range.'

'Well,' Danny said, the colour rising in his face. Somehow he didn't look as relaxed or excited as she had expected. 'I don't know about that.' He pointed down at the Seamless logo.

Or rather, where it should have been. As Laurie peered in to take a close look at the lettering, the realisation hit her like a jolt. Her breath caught. No. No. Way.

The Seamless logo – the distinctive 'S' in a large swirl – should have been pressed into the leather in the bottom left-hand corner, as it was across all their accessories. But it wasn't.

Instead, imprinted indelibly in expensive, imported kangaroo leather on the Navajo bag, were the words: STAMP LOGO HERE.

'Can you fill me in, Laurie?' Danny asked, his eyebrows meeting as concern creased his brow.

Laurie angled her desk lamp to illuminate the lettering on the bag, and tucked her dark hair behind her ear. She looked at the printing more closely and reminded herself to breathe. Shit. It was far too big to stamp over.

'It can't be on all of them,' she said, her chest tight. She put down the bag she was holding and reached into the box. But as she brought each identical bag out into the light, all she saw was the mistake repeated, again, and again, crushingly obvious.

How could this have happened? Laurie had been right there, she'd actually gone to China. She thought back to the fourteen-hour days she'd spent in the fume-filled factory, communicating as best she could with the staff, ensuring the right materials were being used, walking up and down the conveyer belt, checking the tassels on the pilot versions, doing and undoing buckles at random to make sure they all worked.

Then a memory flashed back to her. The email she'd sent to the Chinese factory owner on her last day out there, with final tweaks for the bulk Christmas order. Her stomach contracted. Unable to locate the relevant jpeg, she had hastily typed in the logo instructions instead.

Her eyes met Danny's – a wave of shame crept over her as she realised her error. Laurie knew the owner only spoke limited English. She'd made an utterly stupid mistake. Worse than that – an extremely expensive one. Yes, she'd been jet-lagged. Yes, it had taken time renegotiating costs, and that had taken her away from keeping an eye on the production line. But she'd managed to juggle similar tasks without any issues on previous projects. The full picture slowly became clear to her. There'd just been one difference on this trip. She'd been thinking about Jay.

She'd been distracted from the moment she left Heathrow. Jay, her friend, her neighbour – the man she'd thought until recently could be a lot more than that – had dominated her thoughts. On the plane, in the factory, in the hotel, her mind had whirred, trying to work out where it had all gone so wrong. She looked down at the unusable stack of leather accessories in the box in front of her. Getting this bag order right had been her responsibility. The buck stopped right where she was standing.

'We've got a thousand faulty bags here already,' Danny said. 'Gillian's seen them, and she's spitting bricks. I've put a hold on the rest of the delivery and called the factory to tell them to stop production. We'll have to arrange for a new batch to be made and sent immediately. As you know, these bags were meant to be on the shelves last Friday.' Danny dropped his head into his hands, exposing the thinning patch on the top of his head, then looked back up. 'We were already running late, Laurie, and – God – we risk missing the Christmas shoppers at this rate.'

'OK,' Laurie said slowly, as the full impact of her oversight began to sink in. 'Leave it to me,' she said, trying hard to retain a calm façade, despite her rising panic. 'I'll sort this out today, Danny. I'll talk to the factory, design a . . .' She tried to think up a workable solution. 'I don't know, a patch, or . . .' She stumbled. A lump rose in her throat and her words dried up.

'Laurie,' Danny looked at her directly, a questioning look in his eye. 'The thing is, this isn't like you. Is something up?'

'No, I'm fine,' she said, tears springing to her eyes as she looked at the boss she'd let down. 'I mean. I can fix this. And Gillian.' She thought then of the CEO's fury – Gillian, the woman she'd been going all out for years trying to impress – and felt a stab of guilt, realising that Danny must already have caught the brunt of it. 'She can't stay this angry for long. I mean, she'll

8

remember the bronze belts, won't she? The ones we sold last summer, that broke retail records?'

'I'm sure she remembers the belts,' Danny said, but the strain on his face hadn't eased.

A wave of fear took hold of Laurie. She knew – had seen with her own eyes over the last year – that no one at Seamless was indispensable. With the shareholders demanding better returns, the pressure to deliver had never been higher. Every employee was expected to add value, and during the recent round of redundancies they'd all been made aware of that. Laurie knew that this was exactly the kind of costly mistake that could see her out the door, with a cheaper, fresh-faced fashion graduate like Jacques hopping into her still-warm seat.

Danny's expression softened. 'Laurie, what's really going on?'

Flashes of her life over the last few months returned to her: China, New York, Paris, Berlin, Rome. Since the summer she'd gone from one bout of jet-lag to the next, frantically sketching and emailing on her iPad on red-eye flights to prepare for meetings. But while she usually thrived on pressure, this time round she'd struggled, lost focus. And there was a reason for that – when she'd seen that blonde girl going into Jay's flat two weeks ago, drawing a line under anything they might have had – it had taken all her strength not to fall apart.

'Danny, I know you took a chance on me with the

promotion. But I've shown my dedication to the company, haven't I? The last couple of weeks have just been . . .'

Her sentence fell away, unfinished. The job she'd worked so hard to get was hanging by a thread, but what could she say in her defence – that knowing the man she cared about, maybe even loved, had moved on was breaking her heart? That Jay was in her head the whole time and she couldn't think straight about logos, or buckles, or anything else for that matter?

'Laurie,' Danny said, after a pause. 'No one's doubting your commitment, but all the same, I'm going to have to take you off the Navajo line.'

'No,' Laurie cried desperately. 'Seriously, you can't. Come on, Danny. I know I messed up, but let me fix this. It was a one-off.'

'Navajo is our highest-profile product line, Laurie, and we can't risk any more mistakes.' His eyes were cast down. 'We need someone we can rely on one hundred per cent.'

'You can rely on me,' she insisted. 'You know that.'

'Laurie, look, I'm sorry,' he said, looking back up at her. 'I know you're talented – I've seen what you can do – but I'm afraid this isn't a one-off. While you were away in China our customer services department received a string of complaints.'

Danny's words hit Laurie with a jolt. Complaints? She worked around the clock to make sure her accessories were perfect. She sourced the finest materials. She oversaw every aspect of the production. She prided herself on the quality of her Seamless designs. She didn't ... her products never got anything but positive feedback.

'What kind of complaints?' she said, forcing the words out.

'The Sinaloa boots – the heels come loose.' Danny put a hand to his forehead, as if it pained him to go into the details. 'One customer sprained her ankle wearing them.'

'Right ...' Laurie stumbled, trying to mentally unpick the production trail. She felt numb. Her mind was blocked. 'I can find a way ...'

This couldn't be happening. Seamless was her life. Designing was what she did, what she was good at. What would she do if they sacked her?

'Laurie, Gillian admires your work as much as I do, but she feels the brand is being damaged. I managed to convince her that you need a break, that with two months off to regain your focus you'll be back to your best.'

'Two months?' she said, tears springing to her eyes.

He reached over and put a hand on her arm. 'Laurie, do me a favour here. A couple of months of rest. What do you say? Please prove me right on this one.'

'But I don't need a break,' she said, emotion weakening her voice.

He glanced back at the door. 'Listen, I'll get Jacques to order you a cab,' he said. 'Make sure you get home OK.'

'What, you want me to go home now?' Laurie said, incredulous.

'It's for the best. You don't want to be running into Gillian today, believe me.'

Laurie picked up her coat in a daze, and Danny opened her office door. As they crossed the office floor together, the familiar buzz quietened and a heavy silence took its place. Designers, interns and assistants glanced over at her, and then back at their computers. With a rush of shame, she realised what had happened. Everyone in the office must have heard Gillian's tirade. Everyone she worked with knew how badly she'd messed up.

By the time she reached reception, she was wiping away the hot tears falling on to her cheeks.

'Laurie darling,' Laurie's Aunt Clara said, in a heavy Spanish accent, sweeping her niece up in a huge hug and a cloud of Chanel. 'What a lovely surprise to see you.'

She stood back for a moment, holding Laurie at arm's length to take in her appearance. 'But . . . what's happened? You look dreadful! Tired – too thin. And you need to wear more colour, sweetheart.'

Laurie was too tired and upset to protest. But even in her weary state, she knew that Aunt Clara, in a leopard-print top and pink jeans, diamanté-studded nails and overstyled dark hair, wasn't one to be dishing out style advice. At fifty-three, she was two years older than Carolina, Laurie's mum, but while Carolina had gracefully accepted middle age, her elder sister was fighting it on all fronts.

'You need a holiday, sweetheart. How about a trip to Spain? You could visit your mother, she's always saying . . .'

Laurie tuned out as Clara led her into the hallway, and thought back on how she had come to be here. She had refused Danny's offer of a cab, and instead had walked straight out of the Seamless offices into the bitterly cold November wind. Pulling her wool coat around her, she'd walked down the Strand until she got to Charing Cross, then found herself standing in the middle of the train station gazing at the departure board.

Unable to face going home alone to her flat in Brixton, staring at her four walls and waiting for her neighbour Siobhan to get back from work, she'd decided to go and see her aunt and cousin instead. Acting quickly, so she wouldn't be able to change her mind, she'd dried her tears and caught a train to Bromley.

'Laurie!' Andrea dashed towards the door and offered a warm embrace. Laurie hugged her back.

'I didn't know if you'd be here,' Laurie said.

'Night shift last night,' Andrea explained, pointing to her discarded nurse's uniform in the laundry basket.

Andrea was more like a sister than a cousin to Laurie. They were both in their mid-thirties now and had grown up together. They'd both inherited dark hair and olive skin from their Spanish mothers, but the resemblance between Andrea and Aunt Clara ended there – everything about Andrea was natural, from her womanly curves to her make-up-free dark eyes.

'Come and sit down,' Andrea said, clearing a place for Laurie to sit on the sofa – there were so many fluffy cushions that the floral-print furniture underneath was barely visible.

'So what's up? What brings you here, at –' she checked her watch – 'ten-thirty in the morning? I thought I was the one working weird hours.'

Laurie leaned back into the squishy floral sofa and the morning's events flooded back. 'I did a terrible thing at work.'

'But I thought things were going really well?'

'So did I,' Laurie said, biting her lip. 'But they aren't.' The sting of humiliation was still fresh. Four years Laurie had worked at Seamless, steadily building her reputation, and now, because of a couple of foolish mistakes, it all seemed to be crumbling.

'What happened?' Andrea asked, with a concerned look in her eyes.

'I messed up, big time,' Laurie said. When Andrea

14

put a comforting arm around her, the tears she'd been fighting to hold back came and she started to sob.

'It's OK,' Andrea said comfortingly. 'It'll be OK.' In the warmth of her cousin's arms she cried until her throat was raw. Finally, she pulled back.

'Do you want to talk about it?' Andrea asked.

'I don't know,' Laurie said. 'Not yet. It's horrible.'

Andrea nodded. 'Of course. Whatever you want. You're with family now. Why don't you stay over tonight?'

'Thanks,' Laurie said, sitting up straighter and wiping her eyes. 'I might take you up on that, just this once.' She forced a smile and tried to lighten the atmosphere. 'What about you, how have you been?'

'Ha, well this will make you feel better,' Andrea said, with a laugh. 'Back living here again, saving for a flat deposit. All day, every day: Mum.' She nodded to the kitchen, where Clara was preparing tea, and feigned exhaustion. 'Can you imagine? Dad's snuck out to walk the dog – for the second time today – really can't blame him.'

Laurie smiled, then looked around the room. Photos lined the shelves and mantelpiece – she could even see one of Andrea and Laurie together up there, posing as pop stars when they were kids. It was so different to her own stylish, minimal flat.

Clara came back into the room with tea and biscuits, then placed them on the table. 'I spoke to your mother at the weekend,' she said.

'Oh yes?' Laurie responded, realising it had been a couple of weeks, at least, since she and her mother had last been in touch. 'How's she doing?'

'Oh, Laurie, these men she chooses,' Clara said, her voice despairing. 'I mean, your father – he was bad enough, with his big exit. What that man put your mother through, it's a miracle she's still here – but now it's getting even worse, darling.'

'Don't exaggerate, Mum,' Andrea said, taking a biscuit from the plate and then looking at Laurie. 'She sounded fine when I talked to her.'

'Fine?' Clara said. 'She obviously didn't give you the full story, Andrea. Believe me, she's far from fine. She and Javier broke up, she's very lonely.'

'Javier?' Laurie asked.

'Yes – an old flame. They'd only been together a few months. But you know, for your mother – another heartbreak, for the collection,' Clara said, lifting her hands into the air and shaking her head.

Andrea caught Laurie's eye, mouthing 'Ignore her'.

Another heartbreak, Laurie thought. All her life she'd strived to be different from her mum – more independent, successful, resilient. She would never rely on men for her happiness. But now, single at thirty-five, heartbroken and struggling to hang on to her job, Laurie wondered if the two of them had more in common than she'd been willing to admit.

CHAPTER 2

Tuesday 21st November

Rachel stirred awake as the front door of the cottage clicked shut. Her bedroom was in pitch darkness, only a slim shaft of moonlight on the carpet breaking the gloom. Her mobile phone was beside her on the pillow, the space next to her in bed empty, as it had been when she'd nodded off. She checked her phone for messages – none – then the time, half-past twelve. She got up and pulled on her dressing gown, opened the bedroom door and listened out for sounds – she heard the hum of the fridge downstairs, the clatter of crockery as someone got a plate out.

Her teenage daughter Milly's bedroom was next to hers. She gently pushed the door to look inside, then put her hand to her heart, relieved. Milly was asleep there, dark-red hair splayed out on her pillow, her breathing heavy enough to hear. Milly was home. Milly was safe. How silly to have worried, Rachel thought.

She stepped down the winding, uneven wooden steps of the seventeenth-century cottage, ducking under the beam at the bottom. In the kitchen, with a plate of food in his hand, was her husband Aiden, in jeans and a checked shirt, his usual outfit when he was managing one of his barn conversions. Her heart warmed at the sight of him.

'Caught you,' she whispered, with a smile.

'Rumbled,' he said, raising one hand with a wry smile. 'I was trying to be quiet. Just got back. Having a midnight feast. Again.'

He put his plate down on the counter and gave her a hug. 'It's good to see you,' he said, pulling her close and stroking back her dark-blonde hair. She stood on tiptoe to kiss him on the mouth, running a hand gently over his stubbled jaw.

'You too,' Rachel said, pressing her cheek against his chest.

She led him over to the living room, and made space on the sofa. 'So, how did it go today?' she asked, keeping her voice low so that they wouldn't wake Milly or her little brother Zak.

'Busy. But you know how it is, every day's busy at the moment,' Aiden said, the strain evident on his face. 'Who knows when we're going to get the Westley barn finished – the twentieth of December is what we promised, but that's only a few weeks away and there's a lot still to do. There was that rain in the autumn that set us back, and this week we've had some issues with the interiors too ... I should never have sourced so much from abroad, all the deliveries are running late. But enough about work,' he said, waving his hand, and his face relaxing a little. 'I get so little time with you at the moment I don't want to waste it talking about that. How was your day, how are the kids doing?'

Rachel curled up on the sofa and tucked her pyjama-clad legs under her. 'Oh, fine,' she said. 'Your mum was over earlier, she's helping with a Christmas charity collection this year, she said.'

Aiden raised an eyebrow. 'More volunteering? I thought people were supposed to do less when they retired?'

'Bea's not other people,' Rachel smiled. 'She's unstoppable. But we always knew that. She picked Zak up from football practice too, while I was getting dinner ready. Godsend.'

'And Milly?'

'She's fine. She's been over at Kate's, studying.' Rachel went quiet for a moment.

'What is it?' Aiden asked.

'Nothing. It's just – when you came home just now, I thought it was her.'

'At past midnight?'

'Yes. She wasn't home by eleven, which is when we agreed she'd be back. I called her twice, but her phone was off. I was waiting up for her, but . . . I don't know how, I must have fallen asleep.'

'And now . . . ?' Aiden asked, concerned.

'Oh, she's fine,' Rachel said, hurriedly, with a smile. 'She's upstairs, asleep.'

'Well, that's OK then, isn't it?' Aiden said, finishing off his sandwich.

'Yes. Of course.'

'But . . . ?'

'It's not like her, is it? Coming home late,' Rachel said. 'It's not like her not to call.'

'Kate's is only round the corner, they probably just lost track of time. You know what those two are like when they get together. And Milly's been saying that she doesn't get to see Kate as much now she's changed school.'

'You're right,' Rachel said, dismissing her doubts. 'I'm sure you are.'

'Milly's home now. Don't worry,' Aiden said, putting his arm around Rachel and kissing her on the cheek. 'Now let's go to bed.'

'I brought *The Book* with me,' Bea said, taking a seat in the kitchen of Hawthorne Cottage the following afternoon. 'I thought we could give ourselves a reminder before we do the school run.'

Bea's Countdown to Christmas, or *The Book* for short, was famous in the Murray household. In there, hand-written by Bea, was everything from turkey-cooking timings to Yule-log recipes, mini chocolate wreaths to marzipan holly leaves. It was an essential part of the festive season at the Murray family home.

'Sure. Is it nearly December already?' Rachel said, glancing over at the wall calendar to check the date: 22 November. 'I guess it is. Time to make the whisky cake, at least. Let's have a look, then.' Rachel let the washing-up water drain away, dried her wet hands roughly with a teatowel and joined Bea at the table. In a striped navy and cream sweater, her cropped ash-blonde hair neatly blow-dried, Bea looked particularly young today, Rachel thought, as she reached out for the book.

'Actually I made the whisky cake last night,' Bea said. 'I was at a loose end. I'll just keep feeding it from now. I had a glass or two for myself last night,' she confessed. 'Probably shouldn't do that every time.'

'Perk of the job, I reckon,' Rachel said, with a wink.

Rachel tucked her hair behind her ear and leafed through the book, settling on her favourite page: Bea's gingerbread cottage.

As she looked at the familiar illustration, the smells of Christmas baking came back to her – ginger, cinnamon, cloves – and she recalled the very first time she'd made it. It was the year she and Aiden had moved out of Bromley, where they'd grown up, to make a new start together in the Yorkshire village that was now their home.

'Are you sure you should be . . . ?' Aiden had said, as he walked into the cottage kitchen and spotted

Rachel surrounded by cooking ingredients, laying out pieces of gingerbread on a baking sheet.

'. . . cooking, Aiden?' Rachel had replied, looking up from the cookbook and turning around to face him. 'I'm pregnant,' she smiled, 'not made of crystal. And anyway, with the due date so close, I want to keep busy.' He had leaned in to kiss her, Rachel's large bump keeping them apart.

He rested his hand gently on what was, within a month, to be their first baby. 'Next Christmas is going to be a bit different, isn't it?' he smiled. His hazel eyes danced with a mixture of excitement and nerves, the energy they'd both been running on since they found out she was pregnant.

'Yes, but starting a family can't possibly be tougher than moving to Yorkshire, can it?' she had said, with a gentle laugh.

'Not really where either of us expected to be at twenty, is it?' he had replied. His expression turned serious for a moment. 'Rach, I know it's not been easy, but thank you. For moving here, for trusting me.' He smoothed back her hair with his hand. 'I've got a really good feeling about this. From the moment we arrived I knew Skipley was the right place to start up the business, and the response so far has been brilliant. I'm hoping that within a couple of years we'll have enough money to live comfortably up here, give the baby everything she needs. Everyone says the first year or two is the hardest part. And things for you are better now, aren't they – now you've found the NCT group and everything?'

'Oh, yeah,' Rachel had said. 'I mean, I still miss everyone. Friends, Laurie mainly. But things were changing, anyway. Laurie moving to London, starting fashion college, most of our other friends going to university – I wouldn't have wanted to be the only one stuck at home. God, can you imagine that? And my family . . . well, after the way my parents reacted to the pregnancy . . . it feels better to be starting somewhere new.'

A lump had come to Rachel's throat when she thought of her mum and dad. Aiden noticed and drew her towards him for a hug.

'The thing is,' she said, after a moment, pulling back, 'even before all this, I had my doubts. You know I never really wanted to go to Bristol. I wasn't ever that set on going to uni, full stop. I just didn't want to be a disappointment to my parents. Well, now I am –' she had said, putting her hands on her bump. A smile had broken out on her face – 'and I really couldn't care less. I'm sure they'll change their minds, but if Mum and Dad decide they don't want to be part of our baby's life, then that's their loss. There's nowhere I'd rather be than here with you, starting a family together.'

*

'Do you want to do the gingerbread house this year?' Bea asked.

Rachel looked up at her mother-in-law, taking in the cottage kitchen as it was today. Fifteen years, and two children on from those early days, with Aiden's mum living nearby, Rachel was happier than ever.

'Zak and Milly love doing that with you,' Rachel said. 'You keep that. But give us a bit more to do this year. You know Aiden worries about you doing too much.'

'OK,' Bea said reluctantly, peering over at the book. 'Well, you two can do the cinnamon stars ... and the Stollen this year. And the bread sauce and sprouts, never liked them.'

Rachel raised an eyebrow, waiting for more.

'That's your lot, Rachel. I've always done Christmas round here and I'm not going to put my feet up just because I'm picking up my pension. However much my son might moan about it.'

Rachel looked at the hand-drawn cinnamon stars. Once Aiden's project was completed, they might even have time to bake them together. Christmas in Hawthorne Cottage would be chaos, it always was – with six-year-old Zak there was never a quiet moment – but with everyone together, and Aiden taking a break from work, it would be their own kind of perfect.

*

Milly got into the back seat of Bea's Mini Cooper, next to her younger brother, and strapped her seatbelt on.

'Are you allowed to wear jewellery at school, Mills?' Rachel asked suspiciously, looking over her shoulder at her daughter in the back seat. Large, star-shaped silver earrings shone out from under Milly's dyed-red hair, and it looked like she'd rolled her skirt up at the waist.

'Yes,' Milly replied. 'Well, no one said anything, anyway. It's way more relaxed than my old school.'

Rachel decided to let it go for the moment. She and Milly had already had one confrontation over breakfast that day, about why she'd got back so late the night before, and she and Aiden had to choose their battles. Once Rachel had wondered if, as a young mum, she and Milly might be like friends during her teenage years – but it seemed that with each passing month, Millie was growing more distant.

'Hi, Mills,' Zak said, turning to his big sister, a smile on his lightly freckled face. 'Tom's going to EuroDisney for Christmas, you know.'

'Really?' Milly replied, flatly.

'Yes. And Mark's getting a Wii.'

Bea turned to Rachel from the passenger seat and silently lifted her eyes to heaven, bringing a smile to Rachel's lips. It wasn't the first time Zak had brought up the extravagant Christmas presents his classmates were going to be getting. Rachel glanced back at her two children in the rear-view mirror as she pulled out of the car park.

'Well, good for them,' Milly said. Rachel caught a glimpse of her in the mirror, brushing her dark-red sweeping fringe out of her eyes. 'Their parents must be really rich.'

Rachel thought briefly of the Christmas they'd had last year, when Aiden's business had been weathering the storm and they had bought Milly and Zak everything on their Christmas lists. Before they'd had to move Milly from her private school to the local comprehensive, and stop her riding lessons. Rachel turned left on to the high street and joined a queue of traffic at the lights. 'You know that things are a little bit different for us this year, right?' she ventured.

'I knowwww,' Zak said, 'It's the astronomic downturn.'

'*Ec*onomic, dumbo,' Milly said, giving him a playful jab in the ribs. 'Santa's petrol prices have gone up. No cash for carrots for Rudolph. It's OK, Mum. We get it, don't we, Zak? About Dad's business and the mortgage and stuff.'

'Ok, good.' Rachel said, thinking anxiously of the latest stack of bills. The lights turned green and she drove on.

Milly and Zak were downstairs playing Monopoly with Bea, their contented shrieks and giggles rising up the stairwell, and Rachel took the opportunity to get the Christmas-decoration boxes down from the cupboard by her bedroom. The first one was full of the red and green baubles and white lights they used each year.

As she opened the flaps on the next box, she realised right away that it hadn't been opened for ages. The first thing she pulled out was a small tinsel Christmas tree. She smiled – she and Aiden had bought it when Zak was a newborn and they'd been too caught up in midnight feeds to organise getting a real one. She looked at the frayed and balding branches. It was time for that one to go, she decided, putting it fondly to one side. Underneath it was a tangle of fairy lights, Christmas candles and other decorations. As she took out the lights to untangle them, she saw a sleeve with some loose photos in it, out of place among the other things. Rachel flicked through the pictures – the kids as babies, Aiden standing proudly in front of one of his first completed barns. And one of Rachel as a teenager, with her best friend, Laurie. Standing outside the school gates on the last day of Sixth Form. They'd taken the photo themselves, so it was blurry and too close up. Nineteen ninety-five, it must have been, the day they finished their A-Level exams. Rachel lit up at the memory. Her unruly, dark-blonde hair was loose and she had bright red lipstick on, while Laurie's hair was dyed pale pink, chunks of dark showing through at the roots. They were hugging, faces pressed together, big smiles on their faces. The feeling of elation – Rachel could still recall it. To celebrate their first day of freedom, she and Laurie had driven to the coast in Rachel's car, blasting Pearl Jam and Alanis Morrisette out of the stereo and singing their hearts out.

Rachel glanced back at the photo. She and Laurie had been inseparable in those days. But things had changed, for both of them. She propped the photo up on the dresser, tidied the boxes away, putting the best decorations to one side, and went back downstairs.

Zak and Milly were watching TV, and relative calm had returned to the ground floor of the cottage. Rachel quietly beckoned Bea over to join her in the kitchen.

'Got time for some tea and a gossip?' Rachel asked.

'Always.'

'Sorry, I kind of left you to it,' Rachel said as she flicked the kettle on. 'Hope that's OK. You're so good at board games, and you know I'm rubbish at Monopoly.'

'I enjoyed it. I don't think I'm even letting Zak win any more. Since he turned six he's just better than his grandma, plain and simple.'

Rachel laughed, getting the milk out of the fridge. Bea moved to get some cups.

'You sit down,' Rachel insisted, 'you've done more than enough today.'

Bea went over to the kitchen table and pulled out a chair. As she went to sit down, she lost her balance, and in a split-second, as if in slow motion, fell to the floor. Rachel dashed over to help her mother-in-law, and saw a flicker of confusion and distress pass across her face.

'Are you OK?' Rachel asked gently. Bea had gone pale.

'Fine, thanks,' Bea said. 'Glad the kids didn't see that. Felt a bit dizzy. Don't you worry,' she said. Rachel noticed her hands were shaking slightly as she helped her to her feet again. Steadying herself against the table, Bea took her seat.

'Are you sure you're all right?' Rachel said.

'Absolutely. Now, I thought we were going to have a nice gossip? Let's not spoil it, Rachel.'

CHAPTER 3

Wednesday 22nd November

As Laurie walked towards the Victorian mansion block where she lived, the winter sun setting hazily over Brixton, she saw that the girl was there again. Pressing the buzzer and leaning in towards the intercom, her pale-blonde-streaked hair partially covering her face, kohl-dark eyes just visible through it.

'Jay, it's me,' the girl said huskily. Laurie felt a tug at her heart as she heard his name. The blonde must be in her twenties, Laurie guessed, not older than twenty-five. It was close to freezing out that night and she was dressed in a mini-skirt, black tights and brown-leather biker boots and a denim jacket. Barely clothed, really.

That tone, Laurie thought, taking her keys out of her bag, her Tiffany keyring jangling. What was that? Intimacy?

Laurie held her key fob up to open the front door. She and Jay were over. It was none of her business who came to the flats – and as of Monday she had much bigger stuff to think about. She held the front door open for the girl to walk through. Laurie walked across the chessboard tiles and up the winding staircase, her hand gliding over the timber rail of the wrought-iron balustrade, leaving the girl behind her in the hallway reapplying lip gloss in the mirror.

Laurie continued up the stairs, passing Jay's doorway with a quick glance. That could have been me, she thought, as she imagined Jay drawing the girl into his arms, kissing her. But she'd messed that up. Just like she seemed to be messing everything up.

She continued up to the third floor, her floor. The penthouse flat, she joked to friends – it wasn't as glamorous as all that, this was Brixton after all, but it was true that her place had the best view – on a clear day sunshine would spill in through the bay window in the living room, and she could see over the other buildings towards the city, the skyline taking in the Gherkin, St Paul's, the Shard. She also had a roof terrace that made her the envy of the block during the summer months. Initially she'd seen the flat as a first step on the property ladder, on her way to a more desirable postcode – in Primrose Hill or Maida Vale maybe, when her career really took flight – but after only a couple of months in Brixton, after meeting her neighbours, she was sold. The area, and the block itself, had worked its charm on her and now it was home – colourful, chaotic and vibrant. She never wanted to live anywhere else.

Laurie wasn't headed straight home. She stopped at the flat next door to her own and leaned down to open the letterbox. 'Hey,' she called through it. 'Siobhan. Are you in?'

She heard a shuffling of feet and a moment later was greeted at the door by her neighbour Siobhan, in checked pyjamas, her hair bundled into a towel turban, bright-green eyes shining out from her pretty, freckled face. A streak of tabby curled round her legs and purred. Mr Ripley – tabby with white paws – was Jay's cat, officially. He fed him, but Mr Ripley spent as much time ducking in and out of all the other rooms in the block, finding his way in through doors and windows left ajar, making each flat his home.

'If it isn't the style police,' Siobhan said, greeting Laurie with a smile, undoing the towel around her hair and beginning to scrub it dry roughly. 'You've caught me unawares.'

'I'm strictly off duty this evening,' Laurie said, raising a weary smile. Siobhan took a step back and motioned for Laurie to come in.

In architectural terms, Siobhan's flat was a mirror image of Laurie's – but that was as far as it went. While in Laurie's flat sparse, Japanese-style furniture and white carpets set the minimalist tone, here in Siobhan's there were decorative gilt mirrors, crocheted blankets and ethnic ornaments Laurie would never have let anywhere near her own front door.

Laurie walked through into Siobhan's kitchen, briefly turning to make sure her friend was behind her. 'Can I?' she asked, opening the fridge without waiting for an answer and taking out an open bottle of wine. 'Thanks.' She got jewel-coloured glasses from the wooden shelf and started to pour.

As the wine hit the sides of the glasses, Laurie recalled the day she'd moved into the block, four years ago.

'Imelda Marcos has nothing on you,' Siobhan had said, surveying the shoeboxes that covered almost every inch of the entrance hall. She was only a fraction taller than five feet, but with long fiery-red hair and a loud, Irish-accented voice, she was hard to miss.

'Regretting it now,' Laurie had laughed wryly. She didn't have much furniture to speak of – during her twenties she'd moved from one furnished rental to another, upgrading with each pay rise – but her accessories collection was unrivalled. The removal men she'd hired had unceremoniously dumped her boxes of shoes and clothes in the hall and then left her.

'Come on,' Siobhan had said. 'If you give me a pair I'll help you out. Got any spare size threes?'

Together they'd lugged all the boxes upstairs, and when they'd brought the last one up Laurie opened a bottle of red wine, filling mugs – the only things she could find – for them both.

'Here's to your new flat – welcome to Goldhawk Mansions,' Siobhan said, chinking her mug of wine with Laurie's. And there – in her new place, the first four walls she'd ever owned, with a new ally and drinking buddy, Laurie had felt truly at home.

'Whoa, there,' Siobhan said now, stepping in to put her hand over one of the glasses to stop Laurie filling it right to the top. 'It's a school night for some of us.' Back then, Siobhan had been a newly qualified teacher at the local comp, now she was Head of the Art Department, her evenings more often filled with parents' evenings and marking than nights at the pub. She had a few fine lines around her bright green eyes these days – one for each OFSTED inspection, she liked to say.

'She can't be more than twenty-five,' Laurie said, still fixated on the girl downstairs. 'Can she?' She took a large sip of wine and walked through into Siobhan's living room, taking a seat on her antique, green-velvet sofa.

'I haven't seen her up close,' Siobhan said, shrugging and taking a seat on the fifties armchair opposite, raking her hands through her wet hair to pull out the tangles.

'She was going up to Jay's flat, you know. Again.'

Siobhan sank back into her seat. 'Look, I hate to say it, Laurie, but Jay's a free agent.'

Laurie glumly took off her boots and brought her knees towards her, hugging them.

'I know. To be honest, it's not just that,' she said, memories of her humiliating exit from the office returning. 'God, it's just been a really crappy couple of days, Siobhan.'

'What do you mean?' she asked.

'Work,' Laurie said, biting her lip. 'It's bad.'

'Go on,' Siobhan prompted her, 'elaborate.'

'Big mistake,' Laurie said, tears springing to her eyes. 'A really stupid one.'

'Yes?'

'I messed up the design on our most important new bag. The Navajo – you know the one I've been talking about since the summer?'

Siobhan's eyebrows shot up. 'Oh no! I mean, sorry – God, that's awful. You've been working so hard on that.'

'I know. So now Danny wants me to have some time off. Two months, he said, "To get my focus back". He texted me to confirm it this morning – I'm off on full pay, but he doesn't want me back until the first of February. I'm lucky he didn't sack me. I mean, I deserve it, Siobhan. I've really let him down.' She tried to stop the tears that were building. 'Out in China – I don't know. I wasn't myself. My head was all over the place.'

Laurie had been thrown off course, and there was only one reason. She thought back to the summer only a few months before – but with the November wind whistling outside Siobhan's window, and her life in tatters, being with Jay felt like a lifetime ago.

Jay had been sitting in the striped hammock on

Laurie's roof terrace, rocking gently in it as he opened a beer for her. Seventies rare groove drifted out of Laurie's iPod dock, a lilting soundtrack to the hot summer night. They'd all been out together that night, to an outdoor film screening in the park – but before midnight Siobhan had fallen asleep downstairs on Laurie's bed.

Laurie sat down beside him, and he passed her the open bottle of Corona – she noticed how his white and grey striped T-shirt, worn with faded jeans, set off his tanned skin. He'd discarded his flip-flops alongside hers. There was plenty of space in the hammock, it was a double one Laurie's mum had sent over from Spain, but gravity had brought the two of them together awkwardly in the middle. Laurie glanced over at him. With a day's stubble on his jaw, and his dark hair a little longer now, he looked just like he had the first day they'd met, when he was carrying his guitar case up to his new flat. Jay turned to her and smiled. As if he'd hardly noticed the fact that one side of her body, clad in a strapless turquoise jumpsuit, was now pressed inappropriately closely against his.

'Siobhan's missing an amazing night sky,' Jay said, tilting his head to look back. Laurie leaned into the hammock and looked up. Even with all the artificial light from south London's bars, offices and shops, the stars shone out brightly.

'She is,' Laurie said, conscious again of Jay's body

against hers. The warmth of his arms, the faint, clean smell of him, a hint of cinnamon. Stop being weird, she told herself. She must be drunker than she thought. She took a sip of her beer, then rested it on the small wooden bench he'd made her that spring when he'd started renting his carpentry workshop.

'Maybe it's not such a bad thing,' Jay said, his warm brown eyes resting on hers, 'that Siobhan fell asleep.'

Jay's voice sounded different, softer than usual. It wasn't that usual tone, the one he used when he did neighbourly stuff, like lending her milk, or asking to borrow her *Mad Men* box set.

'What do you mean?'

'I mean, I like being alone with you,' he said, his gaze unwavering.

OK, Laurie thought. Now this was definitely getting weird. She looked away, hurriedly thinking of escape plans. 'Do you think the music's a bit loud?' she said, moving to get up.

'It's fine,' he reassured her. 'Really.' He took her hand before she could get to her feet. It felt sort of nice, her slim hand in his larger one. Her heart thudded in her chest.

And then – Jay moved towards her and they were kissing. His hands were on the bare skin of her arms, and she was kissing him, kissing Jay. Jay from downstairs. And it felt good.

She pulled away, and he smoothed her dark hair back

behind her ear. They looked at each other and then finally he laughed, breaking the tension. 'This is strange, isn't it?' he said, toying with her hand, running a finger over her palm. She nodded. A year of being friends – and now this. Yes, she'd felt something when she first met him – she'd realised right away that her new downstairs neighbour was hot. But then they'd become friends, got to know each other and the chemistry had seemed to soften to something easier to live with. Now that rush of desire was back, and it was all the stronger for knowing him better. He kissed her again, bringing her into his arms so they were lying down in the hammock together. They stayed up there, kissing, chatting and laughing for the whole warm night.

As the sun rose over the city, they crept back downstairs and Jay walked Laurie over to her flat's front door. They talked in hushed tones as Siobhan slept on in Laurie's bed.

'I had a really good night,' Jay said, smiling. 'A really, really good night.'

Laurie gasped as Mr Ripley jumped on to her lap, bringing her back to reality with a bump. 'What is with this cat?' she said, stroking his back. 'Is there anywhere he isn't?'

'He's just being friendly,' Siobhan said. 'I don't think he means to creep up.'

'Anyway,' Siobhan went on, 'Danny might be right,

Laurie. You have been stressed out lately – work, then all this stuff with Jay. Maybe a break isn't such a bad idea. I can think of worse things, can't you?' Siobhan let the question linger. Slowly, she took a Nina Simone record out of its sleeve and put it on her vintage record player.

Laurie raised an eyebrow. 'Do you know me?'

'OK, I see what you mean.'

'I hate relaxing, love my work – Siobhan, that's who I am. Simple as that.'

'I've a short memory, you're right. After all, you must be the only person ever to stay at a spa and spend the weekend scanning her iPhone and pacing around, insisting there must be something better to do than have massages and let piranhas nibble at your feet.'

Laurie smiled. That particular spa break hadn't been a friendship high point.

'What about an activity holiday, though?' Siobhan said, her eyes drifting to the window as she thought, 'you know – maybe not a yoga retreat, but painting in Cornwall, bird-watching in—'

'OK, stop right there,' Laurie said, raising a hand. 'You know you are planning your own holiday, don't you? Those all sound like my idea of hell. Bird-watching. Are you kidding me?'

'I've always thought those trips sounded fun.'

'My point exactly,' Laurie said. 'Maybe you're right about making the most of this break though. I'm gutted about what's happened, but I really don't want to be sitting around in my flat watching *Judge Judy*.

'Argh . . . this is so frustrating,' Laurie said, covering her face with her hands. 'I've slogged my guts out this year proving I'm good enough for this new role and now I've messed up and Danny's lost all faith in me.'

'It doesn't sound like that to me,' Siobhan said, draping her towel around her shoulders to catch any final drips from her hair. 'Danny's supporting you by letting you take time off – don't knock it. He clearly believes in you, Laurie, he just wants you back to your best.'

'Oh I don't know,' she said glumly. Perhaps it wasn't Danny, but Laurie herself who had lost faith in her abilities – she just couldn't picture returning to Seamless and doing her job well. 'Let's talk about something else. Distract me,' she said. 'How was your day?'

'Not bad actually.' Siobhan said, looking up at Laurie with a cheeky glint in her eye. 'Went for a drink after work with Mr Ferguson. Ed.'

'P.E. teacher Ed?' Laurie said. She watched her friend's face light up as she nodded. 'Are you interested?'

Siobhan settled her small glass of wine on an art deco side table. 'I might be,' she said. 'I didn't want to date anyone at work, but I have to say I'm tempted. I've been in the desert so long though, I might need a private P.E. class to remind me how it all works.' She let out a little snort as she laughed.

Laurie laughed too, in spite of herself – their parallel love droughts had gone on for over a year, and they'd shared every step. They'd both kissed enough frogs in their twenties – and in their mid-thirties were looking for something more – but the quality and quantity of available men seemed to have dropped through the floor. While the hot city summer had been full of good times, free festivals and Notting Hill Carnival, it had been resolutely flingless. Laurie had thought things were changing, when she got together with Jay … but by the end of September, as the leaves turned to orange and brown and conkers fell on the Windermere Road pavement, she was single again.

The record got caught in a groove, Nina Simone's rich vocals warped on a loop. 'Are you never getting an iPod dock?' she asked Siobhan, as her friend adjusted the needle. 'I mean, there's cute-retro, and then there's living in a time warp. How about I help you get this place ready to bring a man—' Laurie was cut short by an embroidered cushion flying at her face.

CHAPTER 4

Thursday 23rd November

From: Carter@yahoo.com
To: Millypede@gmail.com

Milly,

Hi! It was great to hang out with you at the pub the other night – I'm glad we managed to persuade you and Kate to stay till closing.

I have this scrap of paper with your name and email scrawled on it – so I thought I'd drop you a line. It's not every day I get to chat to a girl like you. I've seen you around before and have always thought you were gorgeous.

I'd love to get to see you again. What are you up to this weekend? There's a party on this Saturday, if you and Kate are free?

Carter x

From: Millypede@gmail.com
To: Carter@yahoo.com

Hi there,

It was fun to meet up with you guys too. Thanks for the

drinks. Way more fun than we usually have on a Monday night . . .

The party sounds great, but I have to babysit my little brother on Saturday. LAME.
How about the weekend after, maybe Friday?

Mills x

From: Carter@yahoo.com
To: Millypede@gmail.com

That's cool. Friday it is – it's a date! I'll be back in touch next week.
Cx

• ❀ •

'OK, you're right,' Bea said. 'I've not been feeling myself lately.'

Rachel took a deep breath – so she'd been right to ask. Since she'd seen Bea fall over on Wednesday afternoon, she hadn't been able to shift the feeling that something was wrong.

'I've been feeling quite dizzy and have lost my balance a couple of times,' Bea continued. 'Not just when I stand up quickly. And my hearing's been a bit off.'

For Bea to admit that she was unwell was significant: she never gave in lightly to illness. Aiden once joked that it would take pneumonia for her to get out the paracetamol, and Milly and Zak definitely knew better than to complain about colds or grazed knees around their grandma.

'Maybe it's that viral thing –' Rachel said, searching for the word – 'Laber ...'

Bea shrugged. 'It'll be something like that, yes. Whatever it is, it's an awful nuisance. Not nice at all. I had a bad spell on the high street the other day. Thankfully John from the hardware shop found me a chair to sit down on until I felt better.'

'Oh dear, poor you,' Rachel said, concerned. 'That doesn't sound good at all. Have you been to see anyone about it?'

'I went to see Dr Garrett yesterday, and she gave me a look over. Said it could be a number of things, but I shouldn't ignore the symptoms.' Bea fiddled with the buttons on her navy cardigan as she spoke. 'I'm sure it's nothing serious,' she said, on seeing the worry in Rachel's face, 'and you know how I hate a fuss over nothing. But she wants me to see a specialist.'

'OK,' Rachel said.

'It's to rule certain things out,' Bea said, 'that's all. And no doubt by the time they've done the tests this viral thing, or whatever it is, will have fixed itself.

'But here's the bore,' Bea added, turning her wedding ring on her finger, 'the specialist Dr Garrett wants me to see is in London. It's an Ear, Nose and Throat unit. She said she could refer me to Leeds, if we wanted ...'

Rachel touched Bea's hand as she fell silent. Leeds Hospital was where Bea's husband David had been taken after his riding accident, and where he had died three years ago. While much nearer by, the hospital held difficult memories for all of them. Rachel thought of Aiden and knew what he'd say; Bea should get the best care possible, in somewhere she felt comfortable.

'Well, if Dr Garrett says London, then London it is,' Rachel said, resolutely. 'And of course you're not going on your own, you know that.'

Bea opened her mouth as if to protest, but for once she seemed to give in, no words came.

'When would it be?' Rachel asked.

'She's going to make me an appointment as soon as possible, next week if she can.'

Aiden was sitting down on the edge of the bed, trying to stay calm, but concern was etched into his brow. 'I'll find a way to go down with her,' he said, pushing a hand back through his short brown hair.

Rachel had called Aiden at work in the morning and asked if he could get home in the early evening that night. She'd heard the sounds of banging and hammering in the background, and Aiden was hesitant to cut short his hours on the project, but Rachel had insisted it was important – she couldn't tell him about Bea when he was tiptoeing in last thing at night.

'So Dr Garrett has no idea what this could be?'

'No,' Rachel said, sitting beside him and putting an arm around his waist. 'They need to do some tests. It might only take a couple of days – but the doctor says we should allow two weeks, just in case. Your mum seemed quite relaxed, so that's something.'

'Have you ever seen Mum worried?' Aiden said, raising an eyebrow and forcing a smile.

Even during the hard times, like when David had died, Bea would somehow be the one calmly holding them all together. Rachel remembered what Bea had said to her at his funeral: 'I've had more love in the last thirty-five years than most people have in a lifetime. We made each other very happy while we could. That's what matters to me.'

'I'll speak to Simon tonight and see if I can ...' Aiden reached for his iPad and flicked to his schedule. 'Right, let's see.' Rachel looked over at the screen and saw day after day of meetings and tasks, blocked right up until the evenings.

'Aiden,' Rachel said, putting her hand over his as he flicked to the next week in search of space. 'Stop.'

He turned to look at her, creases at the corners of his hazel eyes. 'I'm sure if I just—'

'Look, we both know you can't afford to take the time off at the moment,' Rachel said. She had seen the accounts herself – the business's finances weren't looking good. Just one project falling through could be enough to push the company under.

'It's OK,' Rachel said, giving his arm a squeeze. 'I'll go with her.' She'd already thought through the other options and dismissed them – Bea's friends had their own commitments and most of them wouldn't be physically strong enough to cope if Bea were to faint on the journey.

Aiden's eyes met hers and she knew they were both thinking the same thing. 'But Milly and Zak . . .' he said. Aiden's current project was two hours' drive away. The school run would be an impossibility. 'We're going to have to take them out of school, aren't we?'

'Yes, I think so,' Rachel said, with a heavy heart, after weighing up the options. Zak had been so excited about his role as a Wise Man in the nativity play, and Milly was only just settling in to her new school. 'I'll talk to their teachers tomorrow and get some extra work to take with us.'

'I'll speak to Simon and delegate what I can to him,' Aiden said, glancing back at his calendar, 'if you can get Mum down in time for her appointment next Wednesday, I should be able to get to you by the weekend.'

Rachel stroked the rough stubble on Aiden's cheek and kissed it softly. 'We'll work it out, Aid,' she said. He draped his arm around her shoulder and pulled her close.

Aiden had gone to bed early for the first time in weeks. Rachel watched him for a moment, his breathing deep. In sleep, the worries of his day seemed to disappear and he looked completely relaxed.

She wandered through to their en suite in her checked pyjamas, tying her thick blonde hair up in a loose top knot. She thought about the trip to London and started to add up how much it would cost.

In recent months they'd downscaled on a lot of things, and as they had always been fairly careful with money, they still had a small cushion. But – Rachel tried to count on her fingers, holding her toothbrush in one hand: two adult and two children's train tickets, all bought last minute, then two weeks' accommodation in a London hotel for her and the kids, food and travel . . . It would come to hundreds of pounds. Aiden wouldn't be paid the final tranche for his current project until next year. His was their sole income and their bank balance was low. Even if they chose a cheap hotel, accommodation would put a major dent in the modest amount she and Aiden had put aside for Christmas. There had to be a better way of doing this.

A thought popped into her mind – of course. Laurie. It was a big favour to ask, Rachel knew that. But what were old friends for, if not for helping you out at times like these? And Laurie was Milly's godmother after all – even if that was pretty much in name only. Perhaps now was the time for a bit of bonding. Rachel's mind buzzed with the idea – this just might work.

Rinsing her mouth out and pulling on her dressing gown, Rachel crept past her sleeping husband and headed back downstairs. She took a seat at the kitchen table, lifted the lid of her laptop and, when it sprang to life, clicked to open the browser. She tapped in the address for Facebook. She'd joined a while back and uploaded photos of the kids, in response to requests from her friends and family. She hadn't checked much since then, though, and only had a handful of friends on there. But Laurie was one of them. With a sleek dark bob and smoky eyes, she looked almost like a model in her profile photo.

Laurie had a glamorous life, a successful career, stunning clothes. Rachel knew that from the photos – glossy shots taken next to catwalks and at parties during London and Paris fashion weeks. Rachel wasn't envious, she was proud of her friend. Laurie's life? Rachel reached up a hand to touch her uncontrollable blonde mop and smiled – for starters, she'd never, ever, have the hair for it.

Rachel clicked the box to send her friend a new message.

Hi Laurie,

How are you doing? It's been a hundred years, I know. ☺

I hope everything is good with you, hon. Sorry this is out of the blue, but I'm actually writing to ask you a favour – a big one. Am bit desperate!

My mother-in-law Bea is sick and has been referred to a

specialist clinic in London. Any chance me and the kids
could come and stay with you for two weeks from next week,
the 29th of November?

Rachel recalled fondly the gift that Laurie sent her
for her last birthday – a black leather belt with a
bronze, swallow-shaped clasp. It was Milly who had
spotted the brand – Seamless – and pointed out that
Laurie must have designed it herself. Rachel didn't
have many things that it went with, but it had pride
of place in her wardrobe.

Rachel got the impression her old school friend was
doing pretty well for herself these days, and while she
hadn't seen Laurie's London flat yet, Rachel imagined
it to be elegant and spacious, located in one of the
chic neighbourhoods Laurie had always aspired to:
Primrose Hill maybe.

The last time Rachel had seen Laurie was at their
mutual friend Jane's wedding the previous year. Before
coming to the wedding Rachel had grabbed the only
smart dress that still fitted her – a flowery empire-
line maxi. It was tight, she knew, in all the wrong
places – after Zak had come along she had given her
slim waist up for good. Laurie had been wearing a
one-shouldered scarlet dress set off with old-gold
chunky bracelets glinting on her olive skin, her dark
hair perfectly styled. When they'd kissed hello, Laurie
had smelled nice, sort of expensive.

Laurie would have a couple of spare rooms, wouldn't she? Living alone, she might even appreciate some company. Taking a deep breath, Rachel sent the email off into cyberspace. She got up and went to make herself a mug of cocoa to take up to bed with her – it would help her to doze off more easily.

The milk boiled, the gentle bubbling the only sound in the otherwise silent cottage. She stirred it into the cocoa powder in her mug and returned to her laptop to shut it down.

As she went to close the page, a little red box showed that she had a new message waiting. She clicked on it – she shouldn't be surprised, Laurie had always done things quickly.

Rach, hey!

It's good to hear from you. I thought you might have been kidnapped by the W.I.

Rachel shifted uncomfortably in her seat. She liked being part of the W.I., and actually some of her best friends in Skipley were members. It wasn't half as stuffy as people thought.

Well, if they force you to pose nude, I hope they give you some big cupcakes, you'd need them (you lucky thing).

Rachel's defences instinctively dropped and she smiled. Laurie was model-thin, but she had always been envious of Rachel's bust – in their early teens

Laurie's body had settled at a 34A, while Rachel had just kept going, right up to a DD. Her boobs weren't quite where they used to be, but they were the part of her body she liked best.

> So, anyway, nice surprise and you know what, your timing is spot on. You'd be welcome to stay at the flat.

Excellent, Rachel thought. She read on.

> But listen, Rach, I've had an idea that might work even better.

> You guys need to be in London, and I could really do with a change of scene. Why don't you come and stay here – and maybe I could have a break in your cottage?

Rachel took in the proposal. A house swap – she knew a couple of friends who'd arranged holidays that way and swore by it. It wasn't a bad idea – she and the kids would be able to come and go as they wanted, visiting the hospital, without being in anyone's way. For the few days Aiden was in Skipley he could stay at Bea's, leaving the cottage free for Laurie.

She took a sip of cocoa then smiled and tapped back her reply.

'Great idea,' she wrote. 'You're on.'

CHAPTER 5

Friday 24th November

'I think I might have just suggested something ridiculous,' Laurie said, scooping bubbly milk off the top of her mocha with an antique silver spoon.

It was 4 p.m. on Friday, five long days since the disaster at Seamless. Laurie had persuaded Siobhan to come for coffee at Lacey's. It was their favourite café, up a short flight of steps, hidden away in the converted arcade of boutiques and restaurants known as Brixton village market. Chunks of handmade bread overflowed from baskets on the counter, and muffins, scones and cakes filled a heavy wooden table to the side. A white pug in a knitted jumper was snuffling around Laurie's feet for crumbs, soon joined by its black companion, with complementary knitwear. The two dogs squabbled over a bit of organic cornmeal.

Laurie had spent the last couple of days at the gym trying to channel her nervous energy, filling the empty hours with spin classes, aerobics and Zumba. But the conversation with Danny, the image of the ruined Navajo handbags, were still running through her mind on loop.

The waiter brought their muffins over to them, on pretty flowered plates, and Siobhan dived on hers enthusiastically. Laurie had completely lost her appetite.

Lacey's was special, not for what it did have, but for what it didn't – babies. Somehow, perhaps because of the flight of steps leading up to it, it had dodged the buggy track. There was nothing wrong with babies, or new mums, of course – just as long as they didn't endlessly analyse their baby's sleep patterns, or give you – you know – that pitying look. But so often they did.

Siobhan seemed to be focused on removing the paper case from her muffin. So Laurie raised her voice a bit. 'I'm doing a house swap.'

'What?' Siobhan said, her eyes darting up to give Laurie her full attention now. 'Like on TV?'

'A bit,' Laurie said. 'It's sort of turned out that way. No cameras, though. Helping an old friend out,' Laurie said, raising her cup to her lips.

'Really?' Siobhan said. 'Who?'

'Rachel. I must have told you about her. From school – we used to be really close. But then she went all ... I don't know. Mum-ish. Moved to a little village in Yorkshire. Off-radar. You know how it is.'

'Oh yeah,' Siobhan said. 'The girl you went to Greece with, when you were teenagers?'

Laurie nodded. 'Yep,' she said. 'We went just before she got pregnant, at nineteen.' Laurie paused, then shook her head, remembering the moment they'd stood in her bathroom staring at Rachel's pregnancy test together, in disbelief. Neither of them had said a word for five minutes. Rachel was the smart one, she had a place at university – it should have been Laurie who'd messed up. That would have made sense.

'Are she and the dad still together?' Siobhan asked.

'Oh yes, two beautiful kids now, Milly and Zak. Aiden Murray, he was in our form group at school.'

'Wow,' Siobhan said, green eyes wide. 'That's pretty romantic, isn't it?' she said, her gaze drifting over to a smiling couple at the table by the door, taking off their hats and scarves and sitting down.

'Romantic? Do you really think so?' Laurie laughed wryly, shaking her head. 'I don't.' Laurie sipped her mocha and a picture of Aiden came back to her from their school days – tall and good-looking. Kind to her, even when his friends bullied her. She pushed it from her mind. 'Pregnant before she was twenty? Sentenced to a lifetime's worth of catalogue clothes, snotty tissues and worry? If that's romance, you can keep it.'

Siobhan narrowed her eyes, giving her that 'Now, come on, you're being a bit mean' look.

'Rachel says she's happy. But really, who wants that?

I would never swap my life with hers – not for a second.'

Back when they'd met – at twelve years old – well, maybe. In fact then she would have done anything to trade lives. Rachel, with her nice clothes, big house and expensive holidays, had made friends and got A grades with equal ease. In contrast, Laurie, with her skinny frame and dayglo shellsuits, one of the few kids at their school from an estate, had been an easy target for the bullies. Laurie hadn't been anybody, really, until she was Rachel's friend.

'Well, that's lucky,' Siobhan said. 'Because I hate to break it to you, but *Freaky Friday* wasn't a documentary, Laurie. It's pretty tough to arrange that stuff in real life.'

Laurie rolled her eyes. 'Look, I'm telling you because you're going to have new neighbours for a couple of weeks, including my goddaughter, Milly.'

'You've got a goddaughter?' Siobhan raised an eyebrow. 'Someone put you in charge of the—'

'Yes I do, OK? Rachel's daughter,' Laurie said, short-temperedly. 'She's a lovely girl. I don't see much of her – actually I've never even been up to visit, which is pretty bad really, I suppose. But I have caught up with them halfway, in Oxford, and I send her post-cards from time to time – from fashion weeks, trips abroad. She's really into fashion. Anyway, what I'm saying is that I'm off. Going to Rachel's little village – Skipley, it's called – in Yorkshire, for a bit of R&R.'

Siobhan almost spat out her mouthful of drink. 'A village in Yorkshire? I mean, the Dales are beautiful, but can I refer you to our earlier conversation about how stir crazy you got at that spa? What are you going to do up there?'

Laurie hadn't really thought that part through. 'Well, the cottage looks lovely. You know, roses around the door, the works.'

'There won't be any roses, Laurie, it's nearly December. And good luck finding sushi up there.'

Laurie realised that even sushi – one of her favourite foods – wouldn't tempt her right now. She'd hardly eaten a thing since Monday.

'On the plus side, a few Yorkshire puddings should fill you out a bit,' Siobhan said. 'But seriously, Laurie, on your own in the Dales? Are you sure you know what you're letting yourself in for?'

'I'll be absolutely fine,' Laurie insisted, with a wave of her hand. 'You know what, you and Danny are right. I do need to clear my head a bit.'

On Sunday morning, three days before she was due to leave, Laurie knocked at the blue door on the ground floor of her building. After a moment, her knock was answered by a curvy woman in her seventies with neat afro hair, her yellow and red patterned dress set off by simple gold hoop earrings and a red necklace.

'Hi, Lily,' Laurie said.

'Well, if it isn't my favourite neighbour,' Lily replied, a smile spreading across her face. 'Come in, dear. I've just put the kettle on.'

'So how've you been?' Laurie asked, walking through into the kitchen and pulling out a wooden chair at the kitchen table.

'Not too bad, thanks, sweetheart,' Lily said, getting a tray and some cups out of the cupboard. 'Fairly quiet, apart from the choir. November's never too busy. It's at Christmas that the fun really gets started.'

Ska music played out quietly from the radio, and Laurie noticed a pot bubbling away on the stove. As she glanced around the kitchen she saw that a lot of the sunflower-print wallpaper on the wall nearest the door was peeling away, and that a set of wooden shelves and quite a few of the lino tiles were badly damaged. 'Is all this from the electrics work?' she said, pointing to the wall and furniture.

'Yes,' Lily replied, bringing over the tea tray and placing it on the table between them. 'I'm grateful, of course, that they fixed things, but those men from the council certainly left an awful mess.'

Laurie ran a hand over the ripped wallpaper. 'Shame,' she said. 'You always keep it so nice in here.'

'Oh this is nothing.' Lily laughed warmly. 'You should see the living room, hardly any paper left there. They said they'd be back to decorate, but that was weeks ago.'

'But your electricity's OK now?'

'Oh, yes, the lights and plugs are all working, so that's the main thing. Can't have a party in the dark, can you?'

Laurie smiled. Each year Lily hosted her Caribbean Christmas dinner for all the residents in the block. She never turned anyone away, and her flat was always overflowing with friends and neighbours, the air heavy with the tempting aromas of jerk chicken and plantain, rum cocktails fuelling the dancing, and the rooms transformed with red and gold Christmas decorations. Siobhan and Laurie were regulars there, as were: Sean, the single dad in the basement flat, Nikki, the teenage daughter who was giving him grey hairs, and – of course – Jay.

Friends from Lily's gospel choir usually joined them, dropping in between midday and midnight, and kids from the neighbouring blocks. Last year Siobhan had brought a reindeer-shaped piñata that had been a huge hit – the kids thwacked it with sticks until sweets and chocolates spilled out all over the floor.

Christmas dinner at Lily's was one of the highlights of Laurie's year, but this time felt different. Would Jay's girlfriend be there? Did she really want to spend Christmas looking across the fruit cake at the two of them whispering sweet nothings? It hurt even to think about it.

'Your party will be great,' Laurie said. 'It always is.'

Lily poured tea out for the two of them. 'Oh, I know.

It's the people that matter. But you know how I like things to look pretty.'

Laurie nodded sympathetically, then thought back to the reason she'd come. 'Anyway, I dropped by because I wanted to let you know that I'm going away for a little while, to stay at a friend's house. She's coming here at the same time. Her name's Rachel, and she's going to be staying here with her family – two kids, a little boy and a teenage girl. So if you see some strangers in the block that's who they'll be.'

'Sure,' Lily said, taking a sip of her tea. 'Any friends of yours are friends of mine, sweetheart. Tell them if they need anything, Lily's here. You know how I like a bit of young company.'

Laurie took her tea and warmed her hands with it. Lily's flat wasn't as well heated as her own, and with the temperature outside near zero, the kitchen was cold.

'And you?' Lily said, slowly, her eyes drifting over Laurie's face and body. 'Are you OK? I mean, you know I'm not one for meddling, but you look a little skinny. And tired.'

'I haven't been sleeping that well,' Laurie said distantly.

'Is it our friend upstairs?'

'That's part of it,' she said.

'Jay's not gone and broken your heart?'

'It's not like that, Lily,' Laurie sighed.

'So you've broken his?'

'Jay and I just didn't work out, that's all.'

She'd rerun that evening a hundred times in her mind since it happened, trying to make sense of it. After the night on her roof terrace she and Jay had gone on a few dates as summer turned to autumn, and there had been more kisses, just as addictive as the ones on that first night. On their third date, they'd gone to Capelli's, their neighbourhood pizzeria – they'd been there plenty of times before with friends, but this time, just the two of them, had been different. It had felt intimate and romantic.

'Come to mine on Friday,' Jay said, as they walked home. Laurie was playfully kicking up leaves, her hand in his. 'Let me cook for you.'

Laurie only hesitated for a second. 'Yes, sure,' she said, sounding her usual confident self. But inside she was less sure, and as they walked back to the flat she fell silent. Just a couple of weeks ago she and Jay had been friends, and now, where were they heading? Why was it all getting so serious? She knew what a cosy night in at Jay's would mean, and a voice in her head nagged at her. Things were changing too quickly. She wasn't ready yet.

Jay kissed her goodbye outside his front door. 'See you this Friday, then,' he said, smiling, and letting go of her hands reluctantly. 'Seven p.m. OK?'

'Great,' Laurie nodded, pushing her doubts aside. 'See you then.'

*

At 6.30 p.m. that Friday Laurie had put down the phone on her final call of the day. Sales for the Sinaloa boots were pleasingly high. It had been a good day all round, she had finished and sent some proposals for expanding the new Navajo range to the New York office and received instant approval. She glanced at the clock as she got up to leave – she would be a little late for dinner at Jay's, but she'd pick up some nice wine to make up for it.

Danny cornered her at the door, a flustered expression on his face. 'Laurie, sorry about this, but it's an emergency. The presentation for our shareholders' meeting is in terrible shape. You couldn't help us knock it together, could you?'

An hour and a half later, Laurie's eyes were sore. She had put together the presentation easily, but time had flown – when she saved the polished presentation on to the computer she saw it was 8 p.m., and she still had a long tube ride ahead of her.

'Nightmare at work,' she said, as Jay opened the door to her just before nine. She paused for no more than a second to take in his appearance – indigo jeans and a red and black checked shirt – nice. 'I'd just finished this phone call and . . .'

She stopped talking as she picked up on the delicate smells of herbs and spices and . . . burned food.

'Ah, I'm too late for dinner, aren't I?' she said, biting her lip.

'Kind of,' Jay said, stepping back and motioning for her to step into the hall. 'But come in.'

'We can still order take-away, right?'

'We could,' he said. Laurie detected a note of reluctance in his voice, but chose to ignore it.

'Good. I'm in the mood to celebrate,' she babbled. 'My Sinaloa boots have been selling really well and—'

'Laurie,' Jay said, putting a hand to his head, a confused expression on his face. 'Did I get the time wrong? I thought we said seven o'clock?'

'We did,' Laurie said, making light of it. 'But there was an emergency – a presentation that needed doing, Danny needed me to stay. I should have called, right? But I thought if I just got on the tube right away, I'd only be—'

'Two hours late?'

'Yes,' she said. Balls. It didn't sound great, when you put it like that. 'Danny needed me.'

'OK,' Jay said slowly.

'What?' Laurie said, feeling defensive. It sunk in that she'd let him down – he'd made an effort for her, and she hadn't even bothered to turn up on time. She strengthened her resolve. She wouldn't be weak, wouldn't admit she was in the wrong. 'I'm sorry, Jay. Is that what you want me to say? I'm sorry. But work's work.'

Jay shrugged. 'Look, Laurie – let's forget it, it's not that big a deal, come through and I'll whip something else up. It's just, like you say, a phone call would have been good.'

'I know,' Laurie said. 'But Jay, it's just – your work is different, isn't it? I mean it's not like a proper career. With your band – and with the furniture stuff – you can stop and make personal phone calls and it's no biggie ... but I ...'

Jay's eyes were wide in surprise as Laurie continued.

'... I mean, I'm not saying it's not important, but I mean it's not ...'

'It's not as important as what you do?' he said. 'Laurie, God, can you hear yourself?'

'There's not the same responsibility, is there? A boss, a salary or—'

'Right,' Jay said. 'I think I get the message here. Your work comes first, and it always will. I guess it's better that I find that out now, rather than later.'

'That's ...' Laurie started. But she couldn't deny it. As much as she wanted to make things OK between them again, she couldn't tell him he was wrong. Her work did come first.

'I've worked hard to get where I am,' Laurie said, trying to justify herself. 'I can't let it slip. We can't all be dreamers like you, letting your creative bird take flight and ...'

Jay raised his eyebrows. 'Wow.'

Laurie floundered, searching for something to say to put things right. But nothing came out. Eventually

64

she gave up. She turned around and left his flat, her cheeks burning hot, slamming the door shut hard behind her.

Weeks had passed, then months, with them hardly speaking to one another, and that's how it still was. Jay had only been hers for a fleeting moment – but after that one of her best friends was gone from her life and it hurt. Really hurt. Now, on Sunday mornings she'd listen to Jay's music coming through her bedroom floor because it made her feel like she was down there with him. She should try dating other people, Siobhan said. But Laurie didn't know what she wanted any more – maybe relationships weren't for her. Maybe, after all of this, she didn't want anyone at all.

'Well, it's a shame, if you ask me,' Lily said with a shrug. 'You seemed a good pair, you two. But you're a hard-headed woman, I know,' she said. 'But anyway, it's friends you need,' she smiled warmly, 'and you've got plenty of those.'

Laurie glanced over at the pictures of Lily's grandchildren hung in gold frames on an untouched part of her wall. The question slipped out before she could stop it. 'Were you ever in love?'

'Oh yes,' she laughed. 'Or at least I thought I was. With my babies' dad, Jimmy. I had my children, now I've got my grandbabies – and they're my sunshine, even if they're far away right now. Wouldn't take back a step. But the arguing? That wasn't for me. Me and Jimmy were too young then, or maybe –' she shrugged – 'well, maybe I'm just not the settling kind.'

CHAPTER 6

Monday 27th November

From: Millypede@gmail.com
To: Carter@yahoo.com

Hi Carter,

How are things? So it looks like I'm not going to be able to meet up with you after all. Long story, but I'm going to London for a couple of weeks with my family. Bad, because I'm missing out on stuff here – but good, because I've always wanted to see London, and I get a bit of time off school.

We can stay in touch though – if you want?
Mx

'So it's two weeks you'll be gone?' Diana asked.

Rachel was sitting in her neighbour Diana's living room, on the sofa. Diana's small dog Alfie was dozing on the window seat in a patch of winter sun. The cushions were perfectly plumped, the coffee table was polished to a shine and the air carried a whiff of vanilla air freshener. Diana herself was as neatly presented as her cottage, her blonde hair wound back into a French pleat, her slightly creased eyelids dusted with pale blue shadow, and her nails painted dusky pink. Rachel, in her jeans and woolly jumper, felt like a blot on her neighbour's pristine landscape.

'It all depends how quickly they find out what's wrong with Bea. That's how long Laurie will be up here, though.'

Diana looked unsettled by the news. 'And are the kids OK?'

'Yes. Zak's absolutely fine – disappointed about missing his nativity play, but excited about our big adventure. It's absolute packing chaos at home, though, he's campaigning to take his bike.' Rachel smiled. 'And Milly – she's come round. She was reluctant at first, said something about missing out on a party or something – but she's always wanted to go to London.'

'I'm sure she'll enjoy it.' Diana said.

'It's hard to tell sometimes,' Rachel said, contemplatively. 'I used to know exactly what Milly liked, but it seems to be changing so quickly. She's at a mixed school now, of course, and I get this feeling that boys are rapidly taking over from horses.'

'Anyone in particular?'

'I don't know,' Rachel said. 'Maybe. I've spoken to her about relationships and she's told me in no uncertain terms that she won't get "knocked up at nineteen" like I did.' Rachel laughed. 'Perhaps I should be grateful for that. She's more ambitious than I ever was, that's for sure.'

'She's a sensible girl,' Diana said. 'Well, anyway, I'll miss you all. And of course I'll be thinking of Bea.'

'Hopefully they'll get to the bottom of it soon. I've never seen her like this before, Diana. Aiden is stressed about it – and then he's got a lot on at work at the moment too. He'll be around for a couple of days still. But could you check in on Laurie? She's not really ... how can I put this ... she's not exactly much of a country girl.'

'Of course. I'll pop in. Let her know I'm only next door, if she needs anything. So you say the two of you went to school together?'

'Yes. We've known each other for years. Met at secondary school back in Kent. But then, I don't know. We drifted apart somehow – you know how it is. I moved here, had the kids, her career took off in London.' Months seemed to speed past in a blur these days. 'We've stayed in touch, the odd email here and there, though. Laurie's Milly's godmother actually.'

'I'm surprised I haven't met her before, then.'

'It's a long way to travel.' Rachel defended her old friend. 'I understand that it's hard to get here. She's really busy, works in fashion and always has these glamorous events to attend. But it sounds like she's ready for a break now.'

'Well, I look forward to meeting her,' Diana said, cutting two slices of cake and passing one to Rachel.

'You OK?' Rachel ventured.

'Oh, me and Alfie,' Diana said, reaching over to stroke the dog's tummy and switching to a baby voice. 'We're getting along just fine, aren't we, darling?'

'Good. Well, I'm glad to hear that. You know that if there's ever—'

'I'm fine, Rachel,' Diana said, her mouth tight. 'I'm really enjoying being on my own, as it happens. But thanks for asking.'

'OK,' Rachel said, wishing she'd kept quiet.

'Actually I'm still hoping you might reconsider my offer,' Diana said, her tone softening, 'to help me out with some interior design for the company.'

'Oh, I don't know, Diana. I loved doing up the kids' rooms, but I'm not sure I've got what it takes to be a professional.'

'I disagree. And you know I could train you. While you're in London, think about it, at least.'

'OK then, I will,' Rachel said.

In bed that night, Rachel rested her head on Aiden's chest. 'I'm going to miss you, you know,' she said, thinking of the days they'd have apart before he could get down to London.

'Me too,' Aiden said, tipping her chin upwards and giving her a kiss.

'And if you can get down any sooner ...' she said, looking up at him.

'I don't know,' he said, 'I thought we agreed that it was OK—'

'Of course it is,' Rachel said, pulling away. 'I didn't mean it like that. I understand about your work. I'm just going to miss you, that's all.' They hadn't spent a night apart for years. 'Once you're down, if you do have time maybe we could do some things together, as a family.'

'I don't know, Rach,' Aiden said, his voice a little strained. 'I've started the handover, but I'll be managing the Westley barn remotely while I'm down in London. I can't say how much free time I'll have.'

'OK,' Rachel said, a truer picture of the coming fortnight taking shape in her mind.

'Right now I just need some sleep,' Aiden said, turning away from her on to his side.

• ❈ •

From: Carter@yahoo.com
To: Millypede@gmail.com

Hi Milly,

Ah – I'm gutted to hear you're going away. As soon as you appear, with your red hair and smiles and lovely eyes – you're vanishing. Damn.

But, YES. Let's stay in touch. It's only a couple of weeks.
And in the meantime – London. That's exciting. I went there
last year to visit my cousin – he took me up in the London
Eye and it was incredible – you can see for miles. Maybe
you can take your little brother up on that?

So, for starters – tell me more about you . . . I mean I know
you live close to the pub, and you drink Southern Comfort
and lemonade . . . and you mentioned you like Adele and
The White Stripes. But what else? The good, the bad, the
ugly?

Cx

CHAPTER 7

Tuesday 28th November

Laurie knew what she had to do. She was going up to Skipley tomorrow, Wednesday, and she'd already packed, so all she needed to do was leave the keys with someone for Rachel to pick up.

But with Siobhan and Lily both busy, she was going to have to ask Jay. It should have been easy, it was a normal favour to ask of a neighbour. But the idea of going down there, talking to him . . . they had barely spoken in over two months. Laurie had been standing in her hallway with her hand on the front-door handle for a full five minutes.

Taking a deep breath, she opened her door and walked down the stairs to Jay's flat. As she buzzed on Jay's doorbell, butterfly wings beat against the walls of her stomach. Maybe he won't be in, she thought, half-willing it to be true.

Jay answered a moment later. His dark hair was a little mussed, and he was wearing indigo jeans, brogues and a dark-red sweater. Not just any sweater, one that

73

fitted him perfectly and set off his light-brown skin. One that Laurie had seen in a shop in Soho at the start of the year, and encouraged him to buy, because it suited him. Back when they were friends and she still did that kind of thing. The sound of a radio came from inside his flat, and distracted her for a moment.

'Hi,' she said, her voice coming out a bit husky.

'Laurie,' Jay said, with a hesitant smile. 'Hi.'

The words Laurie had planned to say vanished from her mind with Jay there in front of her. Her eyes drifted to his full mouth, remembering the way he'd kissed her. 'It's been a while, hasn't it?' she managed at last.

He nodded, his eyes drifting momentarily to the floor, no longer meeting hers.

'Busy times,' she went on. 'All go, go, go at work at the moment.' She kicked herself. Where had that come from? All go, go, gone would be more accurate.

'Oh yeah,' Jay said, then after a pause, 'Well, that's good. And today? How come you're at home?'

'Holiday,' she said – best not to mention she'd been practically banned from her workplace. She bit her lip, then quickly changed the subject. 'Anyway, I was hoping to ask a favour.'

'A favour? Sure,' he said with a warm smile. 'What can I help with?'

'A friend—'

Female laughter came from inside Jay's flat, over

the sound of the radio, and cut Laurie short. She looked towards the sound; her stomach felt tight. She just wanted to give Jay the keys and get away as soon as possible.

'My friend Rachel is going to be staying in my flat for a couple of weeks. Could you give her my keys when she arrives tomorrow?' She held up her keyring. 'She'll get in at around three o'clock with her son and daughter.'

'Sure,' Jay said, nodding. 'That's fine.' Laurie passed him the keys and their hands touched for a moment. Laurie wanted to stay right there, his skin against hers, close – but he pulled back and put the keys on his hallway table.

'So where are you—' he started, looking back at her.

'Jay,' a voice called out from inside the flat. 'Your tea's getting cold here.'

It was her. That girl. 'I should probably go,' Laurie said, a heavy feeling in her chest now. 'But thanks, I appreciate it.'

She turned and walked away up the stairs, her heart thudding. The girl's voice. That was intimacy.

'But Laurie, I'll see you at Lily's party, right?' Jay called up.

'Oh yeah, sure,' Laurie said, glancing back and forcing a smile. But she realised as soon as the words were out that with Jay, like this, was the one place she couldn't be at Christmas.

*

Laurie walked through Kings Cross Station wheeling her suitcase along behind her, feeling like a reject from *The Apprentice*. It was Wednesday morning – just over a week since her life fell apart.

The 11.45 to Leeds was her first train, and she'd link up with a smaller train out to Skipley from there. Out of commuter hours, the carriage was half empty. A man with a ruddy face and a middle that pressed against the table in front of him looked at her with a welcoming smile. Two young children, presumably his, sat in the opposite seats. With a sinking feeling, she put her handbag down.

'Hello, love,' the man said. He stood up to help her heave her lead weight of a suitcase up on to the overhead shelf. 'Where are you headed to?'

Laurie never talked to strangers on public transport, and she wasn't ready to make an exception today. In that respect, while she might not have been born there, she was every bit a Londoner. 'Skipley,' she answered, hoping he would get back to the fishing magazine he had in his hand.

'Skipley, eh – ah yes, I know it, well, I've heard of it at least. You'll be going right up to Leeds then. Now we—'

The train pulled out of the station and as the man continued to talk, Laurie sank back into her chair with a deep sigh.

*

After a few minutes of fishing talk, Laurie got out her iPhone and cranked up a playlist, and the man finally went back to his magazine. Laurie looked out of the window at the passing scenery. London's now-familiar landscape – the backs of terraced houses, the Emirates Stadium, Alexandra Palace up on the hill. Just seeing the urban skyline was enough to give her a buzz. Right then, as they picked up speed, she felt like grabbing the city with both hands and never letting go.

She flicked through to Twitter on her iPhone and posted a tweet on her account:

Leaving London and heading for the Yorkshire dales, wish me luck! #rubbishatrelaxing

She smiled at the one-line replies that flooded through almost immediately.

As she read one from her cousin Andrea, she was reminded of family. Her mum. She quickly sent her a text:

Mum, hi, how are things? Sorry I've not been in touch. How are you? I'm going out of London for a couple of weeks. Having a holiday. Love Lx

A message beeped through a moment later.

L, that's great you're going on holiday. Clara said she saw you. Everything is fine here, just the usual. Love and miss you, Mum x

An hour passed, and the Victorian terraces had been replaced by roughly ploughed fields, blue skies stretching out above. The further they'd come out of the city, the louder everyone seemed to talk – the carriage was full of shrieks and chatter. She tried to focus on her iPad edition of *Vogue*, but she was vying for space with both her seat partner and a bulky plastic dog kennel and a cuddly husky that the little girls opposite her were playing with.

'Do you want to stroke him?' One of the little girls offered up her fluffy dog. Laurie smiled and gave him an awkward pat, pulling away at the touch of a sticky, jelly cola bottle stuck in his fur.

After wiping her hand, being careful not to stain her cream silk top, Laurie went online. There was something wrong with her work account, she couldn't get access to it. She sighed – she was sure there'd be messages needing an urgent response from her – and clicked into her personal one instead. She smiled to see that she had a message from her goddaughter, Milly.

From: Millypede@gmail.com
To: LaurieGreenaway@virgin.net

Hi Laurie,

I just got your postcard from Beijing and it's really cool, thank you. I've added it to the collection on my pinboard.

Laurie wasn't a brilliant godmother, she knew that – but postcards were a habit she'd kept up. She pictured her goddaughter in the photo she'd seen on Facebook – tall for her age, with dyed dark-red hair and her dad's hazel eyes. In Milly, Laurie saw some of the spark she'd had when she was younger, a hunger to get ahead, to make a better life.

We are heading down to London and to your flat today – it's all a bit mad, isn't it? I'm really looking forward to it though, I can't wait to see a bit of the city and stay at your place. Did you tell me you have a dressmaker's dummy there? I have a textiles project I'm bringing down to finish.

I hope you find something to keep you entertained in Skipley, my God, it's boring. Anyway the parentals are worried about Granny Bea, but she seems OK to me and is being all cheerful and Granny-like about having to go to hospital.

Have a good journey,
Lots of love

Milly xxx

P.S. I found an old photo of you and Mum. You are about my age and Mum has this trashy red lipstick on. The photo's nice, though. I have one of me and my friend Kate that is almost the same.

She tapped back a quick reply.

From: LaurieGreenaway@virgin.net
To: Millypede@gmail.com

Millypede! Hello.

Great to hear from you. I hope you enjoy the flat. There's a stack of fabrics in my spare room, where you'll be sleeping, I think, so help yourself to anything you like for your project. And do use Matilda (my resident dummy). She gets very lonely without a bit of attention. Zak might like her as a dance partner.

I hope Bea gets much better soon.
Sending you all hugs,

Laurie xxx

P.S. Wow, I bet I had dreadful hair in the photo. They hadn't invented GHD straighteners back then. I KNOW.

Milly's reply came back in an instant – 'Your hair's pink, actually.'

'Well,' Laurie tapped back, 'I've got no excuses for that. Safe journey, Milly – Lx.'

'We will shortly be arriving in Leeds,' the announcement came. 'Our next station with this train will be Leeds. Please take all your personal belongings with you.'

Laurie got to her feet, stretching out after the two hours she had been seated, and walked out into the station with her suitcase. She found Platform 6 and transferred on to a cramped, smaller train. When it set off it rattled through the landscape, past fields of sheep, stopping at Giggleswick, Long Preston and other places Laurie had never heard of. Apart from a granny doing her crossword, the carriage was empty, so Laurie read *Vogue* in peace, checked out what Alexa Chung was going to be wearing to Christmas gigs and what Chloe Sevigny was doing her gift-shopping in. After less than an hour she heard the announcement for Skipley.

She looked out of the window as she got her bags. There was nobody – nobody – on the platform. She glanced around at the vast, empty fields and hills. Welcome to Skipley, she thought. Was it too late to swap back?

CHAPTER 8

Wednesday 29th November

'So, kids. Here we are,' Rachel said, putting on her best smile as they emerged from the tube station. 'Brixton.'

Zak and Milly looked around, eyes wide, taking in the busy high street. It was the middle of the day, on a Wednesday and the pavements were full of people. Market stalls bustled, police sirens wailed and a born-again Christian preached through a loud-hailer. Incense sticks burning on a nearby stall immersed them in a thick patchouli fog.

'It's noisier here than at home, isn't it, Mum?' Zak said, looking up and holding on to his rucksack straps tightly.

They'd come down by train that morning, and their first stop had been the central London hospital where they'd dropped Bea off. 'She'll be in safe hands here,' Dr Patel, a calm woman in her forties, told Rachel. 'I'll be looking after her and overseeing the tests.' Rachel and Milly helped Bea unpack and get settled, and Zak gave Bea one of his books, a 'Choose your own adventure' one promising dragons and fiery volcanoes. She'd politely added it to the stack of travel memoirs by her bedside. 'Thank you, Zak,' she said, 'I'll look forward to that one.' Milly leaned in to give her grandma a gentle hug. 'I hope you feel much better soon, Granny.'

'Oh, I'll be just fine,' Bea said, shrugging off the concern, 'don't you worry about me.'

The tube had been bewildering – Zak had to be rescued when the ticket barriers shut on his rucksack – but finally they'd arrived in Brixton, and according to Laurie's directions they were just a short walk away from her flat. They'd left their larger bags with Aiden to bring down in the car, but each carried a small overnight bag.

'Right, kids,' Rachel said. They walked together on to the zebra crossing, but as they stepped out to cross it a cyclist whizzed across their path, forcing them back. When they stepped forward again a moment later a white van beeped at them and the driver shouted something unintelligible out of the window. Zak looked at Rachel, cowed and uncertain. Milly's face mirrored his. 'Perhaps let's cross at the lights,' Rachel said, walking towards them and hoping she'd got the right direction.

'I've got the route,' Milly said, showing Rachel her iPhone – Rachel glanced over curiously at the little blue dot moving as they did. 'Here we are in London town,' Milly said, affecting the tone of a posh tourist guide, 'and, to your left, please take note of the local highlights – TopShop, H&M and New Look.' Rachel couldn't help smiling as her daughter continued: 'And beyond the famous Brixton Academy, you'll see Windermere Road, home to the eminent fashion designer Laurie Greenaway and holiday home of the rich, famous – and the Murray family.'

'Look, a fox!' Zak called out, squeezing Rachel's hand and pointing to a mangy-looking specimen with a straggly tail who was sniffing around in a KFC wrapper just a few metres away.

The street wasn't quite what Rachel had imagined. She double-checked the address in her phone, Windermere Road – yes, this was it. But this place didn't seem very Laurie at all. It was an avenue of tall Victorian terraced houses, leafless, knobbled plane trees lined each side of the road and bin bags and recycling boxes overflowed on to the pavement. The houses were grand, but shabby, and cast in shade.

Rachel took a deep breath, then they all continued walking. Milly called out the house numbers as they went: 'thirty-three, thirty-one ... Zak, check out all those bikes,' Milly said suddenly, giving her little brother a nudge as they passed a house with a handwritten chalkboard sign propped up outside it. Reggae boomed from a speaker by the open door. 'Bill the

Bikeman. All Repairs', the sign read. A man with greying dreadlocks and a knitted rasta hat was kneeling down at the doorstep fixing a bicycle chain while customers waited on the pavement – a teenager with a battered BMX and a woman in a suit with her fold-away Brompton. Other bikes, old and rusty next to shiny and new, filled the front yard. 'Cool,' Zak said, staring over at Bill as he spun bike wheels. 'Hi, there,' Bill called out, with a nod.

Rachel smiled in reply, and checked Bill's door number, then looked over at the block next to it. Twenty-three – OK, there it was. They had arrived. The building, like all the others on the street, seemed to loom over them. She led Zak and Milly to the intercom and ran her finger over the numbers. She buzzed Laurie's neighbour in Flat 6.

'Hi.' A friendly male voice came from the speaker.

'Hi,' Rachel said back. 'Is that Jay? It's Rachel, Laurie's friend . . .'

'Rachel, hi,' the voice said, 'come up, I'm on the second floor.' Rachel waited for the buzz, then pushed open the heavy front door. Zak hopskotched across the black and white tiles of the wide hallway, quickly making his way towards the stairs, his steps echoing. They went up the first flight of stairs together and when they all reached the second floor, the door to Jay's flat was open. A tall, dark-haired man with a welcoming smile stepped forward and offered Rachel his hand to shake.

'Hi, I'm Jay,' he said, with the faintest trace of a London accent. His deep-brown eyes met Rachel's.

As she smiled and shook his hand, Rachel felt acutely aware of her crumpled clothes and wind-whipped hair. Laurie's brief description of her neighbour had missed out a few key details – tall, with warm brown skin and an easy manner, Jay was distractingly attractive. Rachel realised she was still gazing at him, and brought herself back to reality sharply. 'And this is Milly,' she said, smiling and flustered, 'and Zak.' She put a hand on each of her children's arms. They said hello dutifully. Rachel noticed that her daughter was quieter than usual.

'Hi. And these, I believe, are now yours,' Jay said, handing over a jangling set of keys. Rachel took hold of them gratefully. 'Welcome to Goldhawk Mansions,' Jay said. 'Not quite as grand as the name suggests, as you probably noticed,' he laughed.

'No,' Rachel said in a hurry, concerned that her doubts might somehow be written all over her face, 'I mean no, not at all, I don't really know London well – but this building seems nice.'

'I think it's cool,' Milly said, quietly.

'Why, thank you,' Jay said, giving Milly a wink. 'Enjoy your stay. Sorry I can't stop to chat, but I have to head out to rehearsals in a minute.' He grabbed his guitar case and bag from inside the flat. 'But if you need anything while you're here just give me a shout.'

Rachel nodded dumbly. 'Thanks,' she said. She led her children up the final flight of stairs to the top.

'Mum,' Milly said as they reached the top floor. 'Could you be any more embarrassing?'

Rachel peeked over the banister to check that Jay was out of earshot.

'Well,' Rachel said, nudging Milly, 'he is quite handsome, isn't he? Not many men like that in Skipley. Your dad aside, of course.'

'Bit old,' Milly said. 'But not bad, no.'

Rachel looked at her daughter for a moment – a flush in her smooth teenage cheeks. It definitely wasn't all about horses any more, that was for sure.

'What are you two whispering about?' Zak said, tugging at Rachel's wool coat. 'Can you hurry up and open the door? I need a wee. Really bad. Which one is it?'

Directly in front of them were two doors: on the left side, a green door with a tarnished bronze letterbox and two panels of what looked like original stained glass. To the right, a bright white one, with a single frosted glass panel and chrome door fittings. 'That one,' she said instinctively, pointing to the white door, then saw a stylish chrome 8 at the top that confirmed it. Rachel put the key in the lock and turned it.

Zak bombed past her into the flat. Rachel spotted the white carpets everywhere and thought of the mucky state of Zak's trainers. 'Zak! Come back and take your shoes off,' she called out, removing her own sheepskin-lined brown boots.

Zak came back and Rachel put her bag down to help him with his shoelaces. She quickly located the bathroom and directed her sock-clad son into it.

Rachel and Milly wandered through into the living room. A large bay window with slatted blinds faced out towards the road, the carpets were white and the contemporary furniture was in shades of grey, the largest piece a charcoal, L-shaped sofa in the corner. A large, thin TV screen was wall-mounted and block-colour Rothko prints hung on the wall. Above the old mantelpiece, one of the only original features, was a wide, chrome-framed mirror. Rachel made her way to the sofa and sat down. This must be the one Laurie had told her about which folded down into a bed. Rachel took the cushions off, lifted the base down and tried it out for size. She attempted a bounce, but the base was firm. Not the comfiest, but Zak would be fine on it.

'Wow, Mum, look at this,' Milly called out from another room. Rachel got up and headed towards her daughter's voice, glancing around as she walked, peeking into the bathroom – immaculate, with carefully folded, bright white towels and flannels. Aside from the expensive hair products and the rows and racks of shoes in the hallway, it was as if no one lived here at all.

In the spare bedroom at the back of the house, Milly

had her arm slung around a dressmaker's dummy. 'This is Matilda,' Milly said, with a smile. They were about the same height; Matilda's torso covered in dark green linen, and Milly, wearing cut-off jean shorts and black leggings, Converse boots and a heart-printed cardigan, her dark-red sweeping fringe hovering just above her eyelashes.

'Ah, I know Matilda well, as it happens,' Rachel said, smiling as the memory flooded back. 'Laurie bought her when she was just a bit older than you. Saved up when she was doing her textiles A-Level.'

'Laurie said I could use this stuff if I wanted,' Milly said, pointing to the corner of the room. A desk near the small window held a sewing machine, with a rack of fabric to the left of it.

'Oh, did she?' Rachel said, remembering that Milly and Laurie occasionally emailed each other and sent cards. 'Well, that was kind of her.' She glanced around the rest of the room – there was a single bed there, and a window that looked over the neighbouring gardens. This would be a nice little room for Milly. 'Do you want to get settled?' she said.

'Mum, what's this?' Zak yelled from the kitchen. When Rachel got to the kitchen he was already hauling down a Breville sandwich maker from the counter. 'No, Zak. Hang on.' She took the machine off him and put it back where he'd found it. 'Leave that. I'll fix us something to eat.' Zak wandered out.

She opened the fridge, then the bread bin – both empty. Rachel knew Laurie wasn't big on cooking – but the cupboards, freezer – there was nothing in any of them. On the side there was just a half-empty bottle of Diet Pepsi and some wine. She looked through the metal tins on the counter and thought of the pie she'd made for Laurie's arrival at the cottage – then opened the last tin, marked 'Tea'. Nope, no teabags.

'Kids,' Rachel said, popping her head around Milly's door. Zak was perched on Milly's bed, his head buried in a copy of one of his Horrible Histories books, and Milly was lying on her front, legs in the air, looking at her phone, her belongings turfed out of her rucksack into a heap on the floor.

'I'm going out to get some dinner. Do you want to come too?'

Milly shook her head no, and Zak copied her.

'OK. I'll see you in twenty minutes. Milly, keep an eye on Zak. And please try not to trash the place.'

Rachel stepped out into the street, wrapping her thick red scarf around her neck. A group of teenage boys with their hoods up were crowded around BMXs at the corner, talking in lowered voices, music pumping out of a stereo.

'Hello,' she called out cheerily, smiling and waving over as she passed them. The young men looked back at her blankly and said nothing. Siren wails filled the air, drifting from the direction of the high street. She tried once again. 'Hi!' she called, and one of the smaller boys finally gave her a little wave back, his friends sniggering and digging him in the ribs.

This felt, well, a bit different from Skipley. Rachel pulled her duffel coat more tightly around her. She got out her phone and flicked to Laurie's number.

Laurie picked up almost instantly. 'Rach,' she said.

'Hello,' Rachel greeted her. 'How are you? Did you get to the cottage OK?'

'I'm on my way now,' Laurie said, 'but the train seems to have dropped me in the middle of nowhere.'

Rachel laughed. 'Yep, sounds like Skipley. The train station's on the outskirts. Don't worry, the village is a little livelier.'

'Oh, good.' Laurie sounded relieved. 'And you, are you in the flat? Did you guys get hold of the keys OK?'

'Yes, we're here, everything's fine. I've just popped out to do some shopping. How come you never mentioned what a total dish your neighbour is?'

'Who, Jay?' Laurie said.

'Yes. Wow. Gorgeous.'

'I guess,' Laurie said, nonchalantly. 'I don't know, I can't see it myself.'

As Rachel reached the high street, commuters flooded out of the station, engulfing her in a grey-pinstriped tide.

'Listen, I'd better go,' she said, raising her voice to

be heard over the noise, 'but let me know when you get there, and if you need anything at all, just give me a shout.'

'Sure, Rach. Bye!'

Rachel put her phone away and carried on walking. Sharp-suited men and glamorous, high-heeled women pushed past in the opposite direction, knocking into her with their briefcases and handbags. The first turning she reached was Electric Avenue; reggae and hiphop competed from sound systems on each side of the street, and traders called out to market their wares. The market was full of movement – locals jostled, picking out brightly coloured ingredients and haggling with the stallholders. Up and down the street, slabs were heavy with fresh meat and seafood, fruit and vegetables in every colour, pots and pans, pirated CDs and DVDs.

Rachel stepped towards the nearest fruit and vegetable stall and gawped at the fruits. Giant mangos, starfruit, ugli fruit . . . bananas hung in fat bunches above oranges and grapefruits that looked so juicy they might burst. She reached a hand out towards a pile of large dark avocados.

'No squeezing!' the middle-aged woman running the stall shouted out, making Rachel jump. 'Ha, I frightened you, didn't I?' the woman said, putting her hands on her generous hips and letting out a hearty laugh. Rachel smiled back, relieved. 'Look, darling,' the woman continued, sorting through the avocados. 'I'll pick out the good ones for you. But if I let everyone have a squeeze there'd be nothing left but mush at the end of the day. Now, how many are you after?'

'Four, please.' As she looked at the array of exotic fresh fruits a smile crept on to her lips. 'And I'll have a pineapple, four bananas, two mangos and a yam too, please.'

'My, what a pretty lady,' said a man walking past, with a cheeky wink. Rachel looked around her to see who he was talking to.

The woman running the stall laughed again as she passed Rachel the bagged-up fruit. 'How's that – a pretty woman and she doesn't even know it.'

From: Millypede@gmail.com
To: Carter@yahoo.com

Carter,

Hello from the Big Smoke! I've only seen a bit of London so far, but it's definitely different from Skipley. In a good way (is there any other?). There are some great shops near the flat.

So, me! (Well, you did ask – the good, the bad and the ugly, right?).

I love everything to do with Paris – the style, the fashion, the films. Everything, basically. It's my dream to go there.

I used to like horses, I still sort of do, even though I don't ride much any more. I hate the Kardashians, who are famous for what? But then I never miss an episode. I like sixties girl groups like The Supremes and The Ronettes. I have a little brother called Zak, the one I had to babysit for. He's only six, loads younger than me – blatant accident, even though Mum and Dad swear he was planned. He makes me laugh 80 per cent of the time.

But you asked for the bad and ugly stuff too (?!) Let's see. The bad is that the other 20 per cent of the time I want to kill Zak. The ugly is that I smoke out of my window some nights at home, and then spray perfume all around in case my mum or dad walk in. Mum acts like we're friends, I know she's always wanted us to be, but the truth is I don't tell her half the things I do. Oh, also – I borrowed Kate's top the night you met me and I've brought it down to London with me, by 'mistake' . . .

Anyway, this is a bit weird isn't it? Talking to you when I don't really know you. But there's no one else to talk to around here (no offence), so it's nice to write.
]
Zak's poking me in the side right now, it's really annoying. I'm going to go so that I can tickle him and show him who's boss.

Is Carter your real name, or a nickname? What should I call you?

Milly x

CHAPTER 9

Wednesday 29th November

Laurie paid the driver, got out of the taxi and got her suitcase from the boot. As they'd turned off the high street on to Snowdrop Lane, she'd recognised the seventeenth-century thatched cottage right away, from the photos. She smiled – from the carefully tended garden to the Christmas wreath hanging on the front door, it was Rachel all over.

As she strode on to the rustic paving stones of Rachel's front path, one of her stiletto heels got stuck in a crack, denting her newly positive attitude. Resting on her suitcase with one hand, she battled to wiggle the heel free, an icy wind coming straight through her blazer jacket to her delicate silk top. It was pitch black outside and she could barely see what she was doing. She swore loudly into the cold night air, then finally managed to pull her heel free.

Stepping carefully in the centre of the paving stones, pulling her suitcase after her, she reached the large wooden front door of Hawthorne Cottage. Remembering

Rachel's instructions and using the light of her iPhone, she found the key under a terracotta flowerpot near to the doorstep. She eased it into the lock and pushed the heavy door open.

Laurie flicked on the lights, put her bag down, closed the door and took in her new surroundings.

After her phone conversation with Rachel back at the station, Laurie had spotted a lone Ford Escort waiting in the taxi rank.

'You headed to Skipley village, love?' the driver, an older man with greying sideburns, had asked, leaning out of his window.

'Yes I am, as a matter of fact,' she said, 'Snowdrop Lane'.

'Where's it at?' the man asked, squinting against the rain that had just started to fall.

She showed him the screen on her phone with the address on it. 'Oh, Snowdrop Lane,' he said, as if she'd said something entirely different. The rain was picking up and she wanted to be inside and dry as soon as possible. 'On't other side of hill, that is. Jump in then.'

Talk radio blared from the front seat. Thankfully the driver didn't seem any more in the mood for conversation than she was. Rain on the window streaked the brown and green landscape, hills and dales, an occasional cottage or pub breaking up the nature. Laurie wound down the window and tentatively sniffed at the fresh air. Her nostrils filled with the smell of cow dung.

'Don't go letting in the rain back there,' the driver shouted grumpily over the local news. Rachel wound the window back up.

A sheep lorry they'd been caught behind finally turned off the main road and the taxi drew up to the village high street. It was getting dark, but Laurie could make out the main street sweeping uphill, with flower shops, charity shops and cafés lining each side and a clock tower at the top with a tall Christmas tree by the side of it. Little clusters of fairy lights were threaded through the trees and on the streetlamps, creating the illusion of giant snowflakes falling. Laurie smiled to herself, and felt something she hadn't expected – a shiver of excitement. Skipley was beautiful – like something out of a film.

Inside now, Laurie looked around the cottage. There were low, beamed ceilings and an open-plan kitchen, dining and living room. Oatmeal carpet, thick curtains and a large sofa warmed the living room and embroidered cushions were strewn on the sofas and across a window seat. It didn't look bad – Rachel had style, but it was so – well – cluttered. How did Rachel find anything? How did she have space to think with all these soft furnishings going on? The country kitchen was dominated by an Aga, and huge, unfamiliar copper cooking implements hung from hooks.

Laurie's eyes drifted to the winding staircase – the bedroom must be up there, she thought. As she walked over, she paused to look at the framed photos that lined the walls. Aiden and Rachel on their wedding day – outside the Bromley church they'd got married in. Rachel looked so young, in that strapless white dress Laurie had helped her to pick out in Debenhams, her blonde hair pinned up and threaded through with pink roses. Aiden stood proudly next to her, at least a foot taller, broad-shouldered and dressed in an off-the-shelf suit. There, in another photo, was Rachel, a little older now, and a young Milly in the garden, then one of Aiden and Rachel on the beach with both the kids. The perfect family.

At the top of the stairs Laurie found the large, oak-beamed bedroom. Against the far wall was a king-sized bed with a pretty, handmade quilt draped across it.

She peeked into the room on the opposite side of the landing. As she flicked on the lights she saw a mural on the wall of waves and a distant desert island, then caught sight of the centrepiece – the bed – decorated as an elaborate pirate ship, with a toy parrot hanging from the rigging and a pirate captain painted on to the wall behind it. Laurie smiled to herself – so this must be Zak's room. A quick look at the jigsaws and toys overflowing from the shelves and boxes confirmed her suspicions.

The last room on this floor must be Milly's, she deduced, crossing the landing towards it. She put on the light, casting the room in a pale purple glow and looked around. The mural on the left-hand wall was a painting of the Champs Elysée, with Parisian cafés and boutiques painted on in simple black detailing, leading to a painting of the Eiffel Tower by the window. Framed French film posters covered the wall to Laurie's right. Translucent fabric was draped from the ceiling, veiling Milly's bed, and French wooden wine crates stored her school books and shoes.

Laurie raised a hand to her mouth – the room was stunning.

She walked downstairs, tapping out a text to Rachel:

Arrived at the cottage, everything OK. Love Milly and Zak's rooms! Lx

Rachel's reply came back a couple of minutes later:

Great. Glad you like! Room cheaper than a trip to Paris for M. Ha. P.S. Aiden might pop around later. Love Rx

Laurie set a bath to run, put on Rachel's fluffy pink dressing gown and then went downstairs. She put an M&S chicken dish in the Aga to heat up and then put the radio on while she relaxed in the bubbles.

An hour and a half later, Laurie awoke to the sound of the smoke alarm's eardrum-piercing screech. Jumping out of the bath, she dashed downstairs, opened the Aga's door and the kitchen filled with thick smoke, blackening the walls around it.

Laurie searched for the alarm, desperate to stop it – the smoke wasn't helping at all. Waving her arms out in front of her to clear a path in the fog, she followed the sharp screeches. The ding-dong of the doorbell chimed. Pulling Rachel's dressing gown more tightly around her, her wet hair still dripping, she went to answer it.

'I'm guessing there isn't an actual fire,' said the neatly turned-out blonde at the door. Dressed in a lilac blazer and matching skirt, she marched straight past Laurie, giving her no more than a cursory glance. 'The alarm's over here,' she said, grabbing a wooden chair, climbing up on it and detaching the battery. 'There,' she said, rubbing her hands together smugly. 'That's better. Peace at last.'

She stepped down from the chair and turned towards Laurie. 'Rachel mentioned she was having a friend come and stay,' her tone was measured and cool. 'You must be Laurie.' Laurie nodded. 'I'm Diana. Now, what on earth have you been doing to their kitchen? Don't you know how to work an Aga?'

No, Laurie thought, she didn't. In her block they had ovens, and central heating, and she'd really never found either of those lacking. Siobhan thought Agas were cool, of course, along with every other near-extinct household item, but Laurie couldn't understand why anyone would want a hulking great mass of metal in their kitchen.

'I thought I'd be able to smell it when the food was cooked,' Laurie said, in her own defence. Diana took out the embers in disgust. 'Is this a ready meal?' she said contemptuously, pulling apart the more recognisable pieces of meat and holding them up to get a closer look.

'Yes,' Laurie said, reaching over the sink to open the kitchen window to clear a bit of the smoke, 'but it had the oven option on it.' She shrugged her shoulders as nonchalantly as she could manage. Diana widened her eyes in disbelief and put a hand up to her necklace of delicate pearls.

'Oh dear, no,' Diana said, bringing her thin, plucked eyebrows together and causing tiny creases to appear around her cat's-bum mouth. 'That's not the way.'

'Yes, thanks,' Laurie said, snatching the charred packaging from Diana and putting it on the hob to cool off. 'I can see that now. It doesn't help much, though. Do you happen to know if there's a good takeaway round here?'

'Takeaway?' Diana repeated, spitting out the word

as if Laurie had just asked her where she could go to meet some fellow swingers. 'I don't really know. I prefer to cook from scratch, myself.' A look of profound distaste was fixed on her face, as if she feared that some of Laurie's culinary incompetence might rub off on her if she didn't keep her distance. Laurie wouldn't have even asked if she wasn't bordering on desperate – she'd only picked up the one M&S meal from the station, which was now in blackened pieces, and after the long journey she was starving.

'There's a farmers' market on in town on Saturday,' Diana said. 'You'll be able to get some healthy supplies in then.' She gave Laurie, in the pink dressing gown she'd borrowed from Rachel's bathroom, a look up and down.

Laurie returned Diana's stare. She longed to give the stuck-up woman a piece of her mind – but bit her tongue. She owed it to Rachel not to ruin her neighbourly relations on her very first day.

'OK. Well, thanks, Diana, for your help,' Laurie forced herself to say as she ushered her visitor towards the door. Diana didn't need much encouragement, striding out the front door without a backward glance.

Laurie closed the door after her and leaned against it for a moment. She looked around Rachel's cottage, at the smoke-filled kitchen, freezing air now coming in through the open window, and let out a long sigh.

*

It was only later, once she'd got dressed, that she saw the bottle of wine on the table. Rachel had left a bottle of Oyster Bay, her favourite, out for her, and next to it was a typed, laminated house manual. She looked at the handwritten note that was clipped to the front of the manual.

Welcome to our home, Laurie. I hope you have a really happy stay! Here are some details to help you get settled.
Rach x
P.S. There's some food for you in the pantry.

Laurie located the little room that led off from the kitchen and found the home-made pie that Rachel had left her. Typical Rachel, Laurie thought, with a smile. But as much as she longed for a proper hot meal, Laurie couldn't face the Aga again. Instead she found a cupboard full of snacks, presumably for the kids, and opted for a feast of Mini Cheddars, Quavers and dry-roasted nuts, grabbing the packets and filling bowls. She picked up the house manual and took a seat in the armchair near the fire – or where the fire would be when she'd worked out how to light it – and poured herself a large glass of white wine. She popped a Mini Cheddar in her mouth and opened the manual, flicking past the carefully word-processed details about the heating, searching for the wireless password. She brought her iPad out of her handbag and tapped it in, clicking on the page that allowed her to remotely access her Seamless work emails.

Danny had told her before she left that Jacques would be in charge of handling her work emails, but she was sure he'd have a hundred queries. Poor Jacques would probably be desperate to hear from her by now. She watched the tiny buffering circle creak around on her screen, anticipating design queries and requests, and then an error page came up. The same one she'd seen on the train: access denied. She refreshed the page and tried again.

Laurie drained the rest of her glass of wine, refreshing the page repeatedly until what had happened finally became clear. Danny had locked her out.

Laurie was startled by a knock at the front door: after polishing off a couple of glasses of wine trying to soften the blow of her total work ban, she was still struggling to take it all in. She made her way to the front door, bracing herself for the gust of cold air.

'Hi, Laurie.' Aiden was standing on the doorstep, wearing jeans and a dark coat.

'Hello,' she replied, running a hand over her hair to tidy it. 'Wow. It's been a long time since I saw you last.'

He leaned forward to kiss her hello. 'Yes. Years.'

Aiden hadn't really changed – the same broad shoulders, hazel eyes and strong jaw. There were patches of grey hair at his temples now, and perhaps he was a little fuller in the face, but other than that, he looked the same. At school there was something about Aiden, a vibe, that made you want to be around him – and even in that brief moment when they said hello, Laurie noted that he still had it. She wondered for a moment if he was assessing her in the same way.

'I just thought I'd pop by and check you were settling in OK.'

'Thanks,' Laurie said, smiling. Then she remembered the blackened mess of the kitchen walls. You could faintly smell the smoke from the doorway.

'Could you just wait here for a second?' she said, her heart racing. She ducked back into the kitchen, leaving Aiden open-mouthed in surprise on the front step of his own home as she closed the door on him.

She dashed into the kitchen and scanned the shelves, then flung open the kitchen cupboards – eventually she located some air freshener under the sink and sprayed it liberally around the kitchen and into the living room. The blackened walls glared at her accusingly and the smell lingered. In the open-plan living area they were impossible to hide. Shit. She'd have to fix that, but there was no time now.

Laurie returned to the front door. 'Sorry about that,' she said. 'I thought I heard the phone, but I must have imagined it.' She stood blocking the doorway so that Aiden couldn't see past her.

'So I spoke to Rachel this morning,' Laurie said, trying to divert attention. 'Sounds like they are settling in well.'

'Yes, she's finding her feet, I think.' Aiden was peeking behind her, presumably looking for an invite in and away from the freezing temperature outside.

'Can I . . . ?' Aiden said. Laurie's mind raced.

'Give me a tour of the neighbourhood, and show me Bea's cottage? I'd love that!' Laurie said, grabbing her coat. 'No time like the present, eh?'

CHAPTER 10

Thursday 30th November

'Slow down, Zak,' Rachel called out, as her son hurtled through Green Park on his bike, towards a group of elderly Japanese tourists. A delicate-looking lady with a white parasol clung on to her husband in fear as Zak whizzed past. 'So sorry,' Rachel called out. They smiled politely, but looked a little traumatised.

'Zak!' Milly called out, picking up pace on her own bike and catching up with him, holding the back of his bike to slow him down.

Rachel had had the idea for their outing on her way home from an early visit to Bea at the hospital. It had been a difficult morning – Bea looked tired and drawn, and the white, sterile ward was quieter than usual. The first batch of tests had proved inconclusive, so the doctors had booked Bea in for an MRI scan later that morning. As she approached the block Rachel thought of Zak and Milly cooped up in the flat. They'd perked up when she'd given them their Advent calendars to open the following day – but they were due an outing, they'd hardly seen London beyond the hospital and flat yet.

'Morning,' Bill called out as she passed. He was in his front yard, putting a bike chain back on.

'Morning,' she'd replied.

'Are you staying next door?' he asked, readjusting the striped woolly hat on his head slightly. 'In Lily's block?'

'This one here,' she pointed at it. 'Yes. Yes we are.'

'Tell her Bill says hello,' he smiled. 'It's been a while.'

'Sure – when I meet her,' Rachel said. Laurie had mentioned a Lily, hadn't she? 'Actually, Bill, could I ask you a question?'

'Of course you can,' he said, getting to his feet slowly. 'What can I help with?'

'You look like the local expert. Is there anywhere I could rent bikes around here, so the kids can see a bit of the city?'

'You can borrow those blue ones in town, pretty handy. But they're just for grown-ups. You've got a little one, haven't you?'

'Yes, Zak. He's six.'

'Borrow this one for him.' Bill hauled over a small BMX from a stack of bikes behind him. 'It's my grandson's, but he's at school today, won't be needing it.'

'That's really kind,' Rachel said, imagining how Zak's face would light up on seeing it.

*

As Zak bombed down in the direction of Buckingham Palace, out of his sister's reach, Rachel hoped she'd be delivering the BMX back to Bill in one piece. An Airedale terrier leapt towards his wheels and Zak just managed to swerve to avoid it.

'How about some hot chocolate?' Rachel called out with what little breath she had left, pedalling hard to keep up. She pointed to a small café in the middle of the park – sitting down for a while would at least keep Zak out of the way of tourists.

'OK,' Zak said, screeching to a halt.

Milly and Zak rested their bikes up against the wall and Rachel bought hot chocolates for all three of them. They sat down at a small metal table, bringing their cups towards them for warmth; their breath was visible in the cold air that morning.

'Buckingham Palace is huge, isn't it?' Zak said, looking over. 'Do you think we'll see the Queen?'

'I'm not sure about that,' Rachel said, 'she probably heard you coming. What do you think, Mills? Would—'

Rachel looked over to Milly, but her head was bent over her phone, texting, oblivious.

'Millllly,' Zak said, jabbing his sister in the side.

'What?' she said.

'Nothing important,' Rachel said. There was a distance in Milly's expression, as if she were partly somewhere else. 'Are you OK, Millypede?'

'I'm fine, Mum,' Milly snapped.

Rachel flinched, then tried to get things back to normal.

'OK, well, while we have your attention, where do you fancy cycling to next?' Rachel asked. 'Shall we go down to the river? We've still got a bit of time before your dad's train gets in.'

'Yes, the river! Let's go and see the boats!' Zak gulped down his hot chocolate and bounced to his feet.

• ❀ •

From: Carter@yahoo.com
To: Millypede@gmail.com

Hi Milly,

It's good to hear from you. And damn, you are even cooler than I thought . . . I've always wanted to see Paris too. When did you say you were coming home again?

You mentioned Kate, actually I bumped into her on the high street yesterday. We chatted for a while, mainly about you. She told me you want to be a fashion designer, is that right? She also said she's having a house party this weekend as her parents are going away, and she wishes you could be there.

Carter x

P.S. You asked about my name. Carter's my surname, but it's what most of my friends call me. And talking of nicknames, where's yours from? It's cute.

From: Millypede@gmail.com
To: Carter@yahoo.com

Hi Carter,

If your friends call you Carter, then Carter it is. You asked about my nickname, well my dad started calling me Millypede first, and it stuck. It's silly, but I kind of like it.

What Kate said is right, I've always liked designing clothes, so my dream is to do it for a living. I WISH I could go to her party this weekend. But my grandma's still not well and we're going to be in London for a while.

London is fine, my Dad's getting down today so hopefully that'll chill Mum out a bit. I brought a copy of *The Hunger Games* down with me so I'm reading that at the moment. It's amazing – I really want to see the film.

What are you up to this weekend?

Milly x

From: Carter@yahoo.com
To: Millypede@gmail.com

Hi Milly,

This weekend is all about chilling out for me. Seeing friends on Friday. Lying in. Playing some Playstation probably.

Enjoy your book. I've not read that, but I've heard it's good – I prefer films generally (hope that doesn't make me sound dumb?!). Anyway, we can watch it together when you're back?

I wish you were here now. I can picture you now – cool red hair, awesome clothes, great smile. So that I can remember, can you send me some pictures of you?

Carter x

• ❋ •

'I missed you, Rach,' Aiden said, hugging her as they stood in the hallway. 'I know it's only been a couple of days, but still.' Rachel pulled back to look at him: his skin was chapped from the cold December wind, and the lines around his eyes looked deeper than usual.

'Well, I'm glad to hear it,' Rachel said, smiling, 'because this isn't going to be a regular thing.' It felt right to be back in his arms again.

'The kids are upstairs,' Rachel said, 'they can't wait to see you either.'

'Great,' he said. 'Could you give me a hand with the bags?' Aiden asked. 'Milly's weighs a ton.' Rachel picked up a suitcase and shoulder bag and made her way to the stairs.

'So how's Mum?' Aiden asked. 'Any more news? I mean, I've talked to her on the phone, but she didn't give much away. You know what Mum's like.' Rachel gave him what she hoped was a reassuring smile and touched his arm.

'I saw her this morning,' Rachel said. 'They're still doing tests, and a ...' She'd tell him about the MRI scan later. 'Come upstairs and we'll get you warmed up. Milly made a cake last night. Lemon drizzle.'

A glow started to return to Aiden's cheeks. 'Now you're talking,' he said, looking almost carefree for a moment.

'How's work been?' Rachel asked, as they neared the front door. The lightness disappeared from his face.

'Not great,' he said. 'All the structural stuff is done, but the interiors are a nightmare. Some of the built-in cabinets and shelves finally arrived from Italy, but a lot of the pieces were water-damaged in transit.' He shook his head, an anxious expression on his face. 'They've offered us a refund, but we're running so close to the deadline on this. I haven't let the client know yet. I'm just hoping we can sort out a replacement.'

Rachel stopped on the landing and put her hand on Aiden's arm, giving him a gentle squeeze. 'You'll do it,' she said. 'You always find a way.'

'I hope so,' he said. 'Anyway, what's the place like?' he asked. 'Laurie never really struck me as the domestic type.'

'It's nice,' Rachel replied. It was nice – just not really how she would have decorated. With the white walls and monochrome furniture, lack of cushions and curtains and no photos of friends and family up on the walls, the flat was a little bare. Aiden caught the

113

hesitation in her voice. 'It's very stylish but not much like the cottage,' Rachel said, tucking back a stray strand of her hair.

'You've always been so different,' Aiden said, with a gentle laugh. 'Funny how you ended up being friends. Mind you, she's changed a bit, hasn't she? I stopped by at the cottage and we went back to Mum's house and had a glass of wine there, had a chat, talked about old times and all that.' A faint smile came back to Aiden's face. 'She's really glamorous now, isn't she? She looked like she was going to a club, walking along in her high heels ... If those blokes who picked on her at school could see her now, they'd be sorry, wouldn't they?'

Rachel suppressed a pang of jealousy. It was true – Laurie was the archetypal swan. Back at Hawley Comprehensive, she was the half-Spanish girl who'd turned up in a baggy pink tracksuit with a gold scrunchie holding her hair back. Nowadays, poised and elegant, it was as if she were cut from a different cloth. Rachel concentrated now on turning the key in the lock.

'Skipley won't know what's hit it,' Aiden added.

Rachel pushed open the door and could already hear Zak dashing over. 'Dad!' Zak called out, rushing into the hallway, his hands and apron colourful with paint. Milly followed, stepping into her father's welcoming arms and hugging him. Zak joined in the hug, grabbing hold of his dad and leaving colourful handprints all over his white shirt.

As they got ready to go to the hospital, Rachel grabbed some bananas from the fruit bowl for them to eat on the way.

'We'll have a proper family dinner when we get back,' she said to Aiden. 'I made some shepherd's pie.'

'Great,' Aiden said, zipping up Zak's anorak.

As she glanced back at the fruit bowl, Rachel spotted a beige fruit with an uneven surface.

'What's this?' she asked, picking it up and running a finger over the dimpled skin. It wasn't one she'd picked up from the market. She'd never seen one like it before.

Aiden peered at it over her shoulder, and Zak slipped away into the hallway. 'A breadfruit, I think.'

'Oh,' Rachel put it back down, 'did you bring it from home?'

'No,' Aiden said, with a shrug. 'It's pretty exotic. You don't get many of those in Skipley.'

Zak's shouts echoed off the walls as they walked down the bare white hospital corridors. It was 5 p.m., and Rachel was at the hospital for the second time that day. Milly caught up with her brother, her bronze ballerina pumps skidding a little on the white lino, and whispered to him to be quieter. To Zak, visiting Bea was all just a game, but Rachel could sense Aiden's anxiety building. As they neared Bea's ward Rachel took Aiden's hand and held it in hers. He accepted her touch gratefully.

As they pulled back the green curtain around Bea's bed, for a moment no one, not even Zak, made a sound.

'Well, hello,' Bea said, breaking the silence, sitting up with a bright, cheery smile on her face. She registered Aiden's reaction. 'What were you expecting, me to be half-dead over here?' She laughed, and put her Sudoku down on the side table. 'Take more than a bit of wobbliness to beat me, you know.' Rachel was relieved to see that Bea looked better than she had that morning.

Aiden's face relaxed. He leaned in towards his mother and landed a gentle kiss on her cheek. 'Good to see you.'

'And about time too,' she teased, accepting with a smile the bright yellow roses he'd brought for her.

Milly and Zak kissed their grandma hello and Aiden took a seat by the side of the bed. 'So what's the gossip, Mum?'

Bea smiled. 'Wish I had more to entertain you with,' she said, with a shrug. 'Only so much fun you can get up to in this place,' she said, leaning forward. 'Although there was a nice young girl who arrived yesterday. Chatty thing.'

'And how are you feeling?' Aiden asked.

'Oh, still dreadful,' Bea said, toying with her necklace. 'I mean some days are better than others, but this morning I stood up and it was as if the floor came to meet me. Vertigo.'

'Does Dr Patel know?'

'Oh yes, I've told her. They're all doing their best. They've done all sorts of tests on me, but no answers yet.'

'Rachel said you had an MRI scan this morning?' Aiden asked, concerned.

'Oh, yes, but it was no bother at all,' Bea said, with a wave of her hand. 'You just lie down, don't you? And they pop you in the tube.'

'I've seen that on the TV,' Milly said nonchalantly, fiddling with the plait in the front of her hair.

'Well, there you go,' Bea said to her son. 'They do it all the time, Aiden, it doesn't mean anything. So now we're just waiting for the results – at my age you get awfully impatient, you know. I've told the doctor that my bridge club's having Christmas drinks in a fortnight and there's no way on earth I'll be missing those.'

Rachel and Aiden exchanged a knowing look and Aiden stifled a smile. Bea's social life was absolutely non-negotiable.

'So,' Bea asked chattily, bringing her hands together and turning to her grandchildren, 'what do you make of London so far?'

'Amazing,' Zak said, pushing his Lego spacecraft up and down the edges of her hospital bed. 'We went out on bikes this morning, saw the Queen's house.'

'Buckingham Palace? Oh, that's nice,' Bea said, nodding. 'Well, of course there's no end of things to do here. There are the museums,' Bea suggested. 'The Science Museum, or the dinosaur one? The Natural History Museum? You'd like that, wouldn't you, Zak?' she said, ruffling his hair.

'Yes. Tom in my class brought me back a Stegosaurus hologram ruler when he went there.'

Milly stayed quiet, scuffing the toe of her ballerina pump on the lino floor. Rachel went to put her arm around her, but Milly moved away.

'They'll go out to see things,' Aiden said, taking off his jacket, his cheeks a little flushed from the dry warmth of the hospital-ward heating. 'But, Mum, we're here for you, not to have a holiday.'

'Oh pff,' Bea said. 'You should be making the most of it. We'll be back and busy with Christmas before you know it. There's going to be so much to catch up on – we've only done the very first recipe in the book, haven't we, Rachel?'

Rachel held Bea's hand gently in her own. 'Now, about Christmas, Bea. You can put your feet up. Aiden and I have talked, and with you being ill and everything, we'd like to put it on this year.'

'Oh no, I won't have that,' Bea said, sitting up in bed

and shaking her head. Then she lifted a hand to her forehead, as if the sudden movement had caused her pain. For a moment she looked exposed, vulnerable.

'No arguments,' Aiden said firmly. He must have seen it too.

Bea leaned back on her pillows. 'Well, let's see,' she said. Her smile had faded away.

Rachel turned at the sound of the curtain being pulled back, and saw Dr Patel stepping through. She gave a polite smile to Rachel and Aiden.

'Mrs Murray,' Dr Patel said, clutching her clipboard to her chest and turning to Bea. 'I have the results of your MRI scan through. Would you like your family to stay with you while we discuss them?'

'Milly,' Bea said, sitting up straighter in bed. 'Would you be a love and go down to the shop with Zak? I could really do with a new Sudoku book. Your mum and dad will meet you down there when we're finished talking to the doctor.' A flicker of worry passed over Milly's face as she took a handful of change from Rachel and led her brother away.

Dr Patel closed the curtain and opened Bea's file. 'As you know, we fast-tracked the results of your MRI scans and we now have more information.'

Aiden shuffled uncomfortably in his seat. 'And what – what have you found?'

'The scans revealed a mass in the inner ear, close to the brain.'

Bea's usually calm brow was creased in worry. Rachel's stomach felt tight – she wanted to rewind the last few minutes and start the conversation again.

'A mass?' Aiden said. 'What does that mean? What kind of mass?' His face had paled to near-white.

The doctor continued.

'The pressure of the mass on your brain has almost certainly been causing the symptoms you've been experiencing,' Dr Patel said, glancing down at the paper on her clipboard and putting her reading glasses on to read it. 'Dizziness, vertigo – it's the reason you fainted on the ward the other day.' Aiden looked alarmed, and Rachel felt the same way – it was the first they'd heard of it.

'It's also behind the slight tinnitus – the ringing sound.'

Bea's face was blank, and she remained silent.

'Now, as you say, Mr Murray, it's important to find out what the mass is,' Dr Patel said, putting the papers down. 'So that we can decide how to treat it.'

Dr Patel took her reading glasses off. 'The next step is to do a biopsy. Your case is a priority for us, and I've scheduled the test in for tomorrow.'

'A biopsy?' Aiden said, haltingly. Rachel put her hand on his leg, to reassure him. 'Do you mean to say she might have . . . ?' The unspoken word hung between them.

Rachel instinctively covered Bea's hand with her own. Bea responded by holding it tightly.

'I'm sorry,' Dr Patel said. 'I know it's not the news any of you will have been hoping to hear. Issues of this kind can be difficult to diagnose, so it's good that you came here when you did.'

'Thank you, Dr Patel,' Rachel said, operating on autopilot. 'You'll keep us up to date, won't you?'

'Of course,' the doctor said. 'I'll be in touch as soon as we have the biopsy results.'

'So, who's for seconds?' Rachel asked, lifting the serving spoon, ready to dish up more shepherd's pie.

Aiden stayed quiet, even though it was his favourite meal.

'Me, please,' Zak said, putting out his plate. Rachel spooned him out a fresh portion.

'Milly?' Rachel asked, then spotted that her daughter was texting under the table. 'You know the rule about phones at the table,' she said, firmly. Milly looked up from under heavily mascaraed lashes, and gave her mum a despairing look. 'Seriously, Mum, just one text?'

Rachel raised an eyebrow disapprovingly and Milly put her phone on the kitchen counter behind her with a sigh.

'You and Kate have only been apart for a few days,' Rachel said, trying to lighten the atmosphere. 'What can there be to catch up on?'

'Everything.' Milly replied, brushing her dark-red fringe out of her eyes and slumping back in her seat.

Milly's answer reminded her of her own teenage days. When Rachel was Milly's age, she and Laurie used to spend all evening on the phone to each other, even though they'd spent most of the day at the same desk at school. And Milly was right – back then it had seemed like there was everything to catch up on. In those phone conversations, with Rachel stretching the cord of her hamburger phone between her fingers, they'd had so much to talk about. Which posters from *Just Seventeen* they'd Blu-tacked on to their walls, which boys they'd spoken to at school. And when it came to boys, for Rachel it had always been Aiden. Every time he'd looked over at her, asked to borrow her calculator, each word he spoke to her in the lunch queue – she'd dissected every single detail with Laurie.

Getting through to Milly when she was in a mood was near-impossible. The girl sitting opposite Rachel at the dinner table now, chin jutting out and a sulky expression on her face, was like a stranger to her.

'Come on, Milly,' Aiden said, stepping in. 'You know that the rules are the same here as they are at home.'

'Can I get down from the table then?' Milly asked, putting her cutlery together on her plate.

Zak wriggled in his seat, picking up on the tense atmosphere. 'If Milly's getting down, can I play my DS now?' Zak asked, ignoring the food on his plate and moving his chair back with a screech.

'Oh, go on then,' Rachel said, giving in. With Aiden near-silent and the kids itching to get away, this wasn't quite the reunion dinner she'd been hoping for.

Milly left the kitchen and Rachel heard the door to her room close.

Aiden cleared the plates and put them in the dishwasher, distractedly.

'Aiden,' Rachel said. 'Do you think Milly's OK? She's still acting strange, more so since we got here, distant. Don't you think?'

'She seems fine to me, Rach. She's just being a teenager – don't worry about it.'

'No,' Rachel said, getting up and taking the glasses over to the dishwasher. 'I'm sure there's something up. I think maybe it's hard for her being away from her friends? Or she's worried about Bea? Can you try and talk to her? She's shutting me out.'

'Rachel,' Aiden said, closing the dishwasher and fiddling with the knob to find the correct setting. 'Can you try and relax? I'm sorry, but I've got other things on my mind right now.'

'You're right, sorry. But maybe we could take them out somewhere special. I was reading in *Time Out* about a Reindeer Wonderland event in Hyde Park. There's an ice rink, reindeers, that sort of stuff. We could have a family trip—'

'Rachel,' Aiden said, frowning. 'You know I have to finish the Westley barn, overseeing that from here is going to be a full-time job – and then there's Mum. I mean, who knows what's going on there.'

'Yes,' Rachel said, going into survival mode. 'Well, let's try to stay positive. I'm sure Bea will be fine, and we'll still find a way to do Christmas.' She touched Aiden's arm lightly. 'Even if—'

'Rachel,' Aiden shook his head, exasperated, and raised his voice slightly. 'Don't you get it?'

Rachel's words hung in the air, sounding ridiculous to her now. She'd just been trying to make things better, but somehow she'd managed to make them worse.

'Didn't you hear what the doctor was saying? Mum could have cancer, Rachel. This isn't about whether we get home for Christmas any more.'

Rachel's eyes filled with tears at the shock of Aiden's words. His usually gentle voice was brittle with stress and frustration.

He sat down at the table, his head in his hands. 'I'm sorry, Rachel. It's not your fault, of course it's not. It's just – I'm scared. I'm really scared that we might lose Mum.'

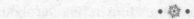

From: Millypede@gmail.com
To: LaurieGreenaway@virgin.net

Hi Laurie,
Is it OK if I ask you something? I don't know who else to

talk to, Kate doesn't know any more about boys than I do, and I'm definitely not going to ask Mum, she's on my back all the time at the moment.

There's a guy I've been chatting to. I haven't known him long, but we've been messaging each other. He's sent me a couple of playlists to listen to, and I've sent him some photos of me, a video of us messing about on bikes in London. He liked that. When we talk he makes me feel good, like I haven't really since I moved school. It's weird because before I met him, I thought I liked someone else, a boy in the year above at my new school. But I don't know if he was ever interested, probably not.

Anyway, I've only met this guy once, but we really clicked, we talked all evening. I can't stop thinking about him. He wants to see me again when I get back to Skipley, but I don't know how Mum and Dad will feel about it – I've never had a boyfriend before.

Anyway, do you think I should go for it? Hope you can give me some advice!

Love

Milly xxx

CHAPTER 11

Friday 1st December

'Mocca-cin-o,' Laurie said to the teenage boy serving her in the café on Skipley High Street. He raised an eyebrow and glanced behind him at what they had on the shelves. At a gangly six foot, his eyes were nearly level with the highest one.

'We've got instant,' he said, pointing at a jar of Nescafé on the shelf that was mostly laden with boxes of Yorkshire Tea. His hair was short and mousy, and Laurie noticed the beginnings of some sideburns. 'Or, hang on, mocha, that's got chocolate in it, right?' He tilted his head, thinking, 'I could do you a hot chocolate too, mix them up – would that do you?'

'You're serious . . .' Laurie said, despairing, putting her leather handbag down on the counter and looking the guy behind the counter in the eye to make sure. 'Oh, God help me,' she said under her breath, wondering what she'd done wrong in a former life to end up here. 'An instant coffee if that's what you've got.'

It was Saturday morning, 9.30 a.m. Laurie hadn't been able to sleep, a thunderstorm rattling at the windows all night, and she'd decided to get up rather than trying to nod off again. She'd been in Skipley two full days now, but with the nonstop rain she'd hardly left the cottage, holing up on the sofa with magazines and books. She'd been going out of her mind with boredom, but with the help of Rachel's manual had worked out how to use the Aga and light a fire. Today the storm clouds had finally cleared, and while it was still mostly grey, the rain had stopped.

Walking out of the cottage bleary-eyed that morning, she'd quickly realised just how unsuitable all the clothes she'd brought with her were – Skipley was bitterly cold. She had her fitted scarlet wool coat, but nothing else warm at all. Before she even reached the end of the path, she'd turned around, ducked back inside the house and raided Rachel and Aiden's coat cupboard. She found some Hunter wellies in her size which she had slipped on gratefully, and a thick white scarf. Nearly there – then she spotted some fake fur earmuffs, they were actually quite cool, probably Milly's, she thought. She donned them and checked the overall effect in the living-room mirror. For one day only, style would come second to comfort.

Dunn's Café was the first place on the high street she'd found open. It was the kind of café she would never have dreamed of going into back in London –

formica tables with tea stains on, a frying-heavy breakfast menu, and not a whiff of vintage furniture or any cupcakes. But it looked warm, she thought. It would do.

Now, as she waited for whatever drink of questionable quality was being prepared, she wondered if it had been a mistake to compromise her usual standards. She took out her mobile and checked it, but she didn't have any reception. Slowly, slowly, she tilted her chair back until her head was nearly touching the window. She held her phone up towards the window until she thought she glimpsed a bar of reception appear. 'YES,' she hissed.

'You all right there?' the boy said, putting her mug of coffee down on the table. His words brought her crashing back to the ground with a jolt. As her chair legs made contact with the floor again her coffee splashed out across the table.

'Absolutely fine,' Laurie said, putting her phone down on a dry patch. She could see him struggling to hide a smile.

'You're new around here, aren't you?' he asked. Laurie didn't respond. She hoped it would be perfectly obvious she wasn't a local – if Diana was anything to go by, she certainly didn't want to be mistaken for one. 'Well, I'm Ben.'

'Laurie,' she replied coolly.

Ben was still standing by the table. Oh no. Did he

want a chat? She took a copy of the *Skipley Post* from the rack to her left to make it clear that she had no wish for any further conversation. As he lingered, she pretended to look very focused on the front page. She scanned the headlines – a local rescue racehorse had won a charity race.

'We don't get that many visitors, you see,' he said.

Still on the front page – some old pots had been found in a recent visit by *Time Team*. She rifled through the rest. Didn't they have any proper news around here?

'I mean in Skipley, we do – tourists in the summer. Americans and that. But not here, in the café.' Laurie tried to shut out Ben's voice.

There must be a local celebrity or two, Laurie thought, keeping her head down and tucking a chunk of her thick dark hair behind one ear. Hadn't Kate Moss got married in a little village like this one? Celebrities were always hanging out in remote places, weren't they? Where the paparazzi couldn't find them?

After what felt like hours, but must have been about ten minutes, Ben finally gave up and walked back to the counter. Laurie took a sip of the coffee – it was watery.

Her second thoughts about having come to Skipley were shouting so loudly in her head right now that there was hardly room for anything else. She allowed herself to daydream for a moment about where she could have been if she hadn't maxed out her credit card last month – browsing racks of clothes in Bloomingdales, eating in a restaurant in Rome. Instead here she was – in the rain-sodden English countryside, with instant coffee and a teenage boy for company.

Laurie's gaze drifted out of the window, and she saw that the promise of her arrival, with its glittery, snowflake-light welcome, hadn't completely faded. The high street, with an old-fashioned sweet shop and a pie shop, did look quite picturesque. There was another shop selling fabric and wool, a bakery and what looked like a boutique – a granny-type of boutique, but some clothes, nonetheless. Laurie held the hot mug closer to her. At that moment a familiar face caught her eye – heavily styled blonde hair sweeping into view from the side of the window. Diana.

Laurie panicked, then grabbed her newspaper and held it up high so that her face would be obscured from the street side.

'Know Mrs Humphries, do you?' Ben called over, obviously still at a loose end with no other customers to serve.

'Diana? Yes,' Laurie said. A reminder of the run-in with her new neighbour on Tuesday night immediately made Ben seem more appealing company. 'I mean, I've met her once.'

He laughed as Laurie shifted the newspaper so that she remained blocked from Diana's view. 'You won't be able to hide for long round here, you know,' Ben said.

'Just watch me,' Laurie retorted.

'She's all right really,' Ben said. 'Her bark's worse and all that. Actually she used to be really nice. She does interior-design stuff. My mum loves her style – she helped my parents out with the living room for mates' rates. If you pay full whack, it's really expensive.'

'Oh, right,' Laurie said, warming a little to Ben's friendly company.

'Then her husband Richard ran off,' Ben continued, 'with her Puerto Rican tennis coach – a guy.' Laurie looked up from the classifieds she'd been pretending to scour. 'Really?'

'Yes,' he said, 'but good riddance, my mum said. Richard was a prat, everyone knew that. She's much better off without him.'

OK, Laurie couldn't lie, she was just a teensy bit interested. 'And now?'

'Now she's on her own, she gets on with her work and all that, she's just a bit grumpier.'

Well, that explained some things, Laurie thought. She drained her cup of coffee, wincing just a little – it really was terrible. As she got up and put the paper back she caught sight of a classified ad right at the bottom of the page:

Interested in Fashion? VOLUNTEERS NEEDED.
Skipley Community Centre, Weekdays 1–4 p.m.

Laurie's eyes lingered on it for a moment, then she folded the paper and put it back. She pulled her coat back on and buttoned it up. 'Right, well, thank you,' she said. 'It was nice meeting you, Ben.' He gave Laurie a wink. She closed the café door behind her and stepped out into the street.

While she'd been drinking the awful coffee in Dunn's the village had woken up; a farmers' market was being set up over the road, in the square by a church. Stallholders were cheerfully putting out cheeses, vegetables and pastries on their stands. It was only a stone's throw away, she thought. She might as well take a look.

Putting her earmuffs back on to protect her from the biting cold, Laurie crossed the high street and made her way over to the stalls. Mums with pushchairs chatted in a huddle and an elderly lady passed a sample of locally made preserve to her partner for him to taste. From a grey start, it had turned into a crisp, bright, winter's morning in the Yorkshire village, and blue sky stretched out overhead, lighting up the surrounding hills.

Laurie had been to farmers' markets in London, but this was different, knowing that the produce had been made within walking distance. Laurie picked up a cinnamon whirl from the pastry stall. 'Not seen you around here before,' the woman said, unashamedly scanning Laurie's face as she handed over the change.

'I'm visiting,' Laurie replied.

'Well, welcome to Skipley, in that case,' the woman said, with a bright smile. Laurie nodded and attempted a smile in response, then walked into the square in the centre of the market where a brass band was starting up. As they tuned up their trombones and trumpets, a small crowd of locals gathered in front of them. Laurie stood by the steps of the church, bathed in winter sunshine, eating her pastry and listening as the band struck up a tune.

When they stopped for a break ten minutes later, Laurie wandered back to the stalls. She stopped at one selling chutneys and tried a bite-size sample on a cracker. The flavours – apricot, allspice, dates – danced in her mouth.

'This is delicious,' she said, her words slipping out and drawing a smile from the chubby-cheeked lady running the stall. 'My ma's recipe,' she said proudly. 'Christmas chutney. Great for gifts.'

'I'll take two jars, please,' she said. They'd make nice presents for Siobhan and her Aunt Clara. She bought some hot apple and ginger to drink from the same woman, and drifted from one stand to another, trying tasters. Soft cheeses dissolved deliciously in her mouth and she nibbled on bits of local sausages and hams, buying the ones she liked best.

The final stall she reached was full of fresh herbs. She looked at all the green – it was like an impenetrable jungle to her. Salt and pepper was as far as she ever got in her cooking.

'What's ...' she asked the tall man in a flat cap behind the table. He must have seen the puzzled look she was trying so hard to hide. She didn't even know what questions to ask.

'... good with what?' he asked kindly, his blue eyes shining. 'Rosemary with lamb,' he started, then here's coriander for ...' Laurie listened as he talked her through each herb. He made it all seem easy. 'Thank you,' she said, as she paid him for four bunches of herbs and tucked them away in her bag.

Her arms were laden with full shopping bags when she looked up at the clock tower and saw that it was nearly midday.

Laurie walked back up the high street towards Rachel's cottage. Perhaps there were worse places to be than Skipley, after all. Most people seemed friendly, and best of all they didn't know a thing about her – they knew nothing about Seamless, or Jay, or the fact she would be single at Christmas, again.

A couple of friends or neighbours paused on the pavement to chat, smiling at Laurie as she passed them. In the grocery store, villagers were already stocking up on Christmas supplies – bottles of wine, mince pies and packs of charity Christmas cards. Here, in the middle of nowhere, she felt different, more relaxed. Her usually frantic pace slowed right down as she walked in Rachel's borrowed wellies.

Perhaps here in the Yorkshire Dales, without work to think about, and far away from Jay, she could be the person she wanted to be – or at least find out who that was. She might not be in Skipley for long, but maybe, just maybe – it could be the gap year she'd never had.

She had gone away after A-Levels – when she and Rachel had just turned eighteen – but she hadn't been volunteering in an orphanage or anything. She'd spent the summer on the beach in Greece with Rachel.

It had been dark when their ferry had pulled into the port of the island of Paros, but an elderly Greek lady had quickly zeroed in on Laurie and Rachel, escorting them to a rental apartment. 'Cheap and good,' she'd insisted, waving laminated photos. She'd led Laurie and Rachel along the beachfront and down a dark lane.

They'd spent the flight to Athens poring over their Lonely Planet *Greek Islands* guide and finally settled on Paros – plenty of bars for Laurie, and white-sand beaches for Rachel. They'd been daydreaming about the trip for ages, during the long weeks of exam revision – now they were finally here. With rucksacks packed full of bikinis, sarongs and suncream, their plan was to find bar jobs and stay out the whole summer; two, three months, maybe.

The apartment the woman let them into was plain,

but functional. The window shutters were down so they couldn't see the view, but they could hear the waves crashing outside.

'It's fine for us,' Laurie said, 'we'll take it.' She handed over their deposit and they put their bags down. Laurie saw the landlady out, and as she closed the door, heard a yelp come from the bathroom.

'Cockroaches!' Rachel called out, running into the bedroom, her pretty face pale. OK, Laurie thought, as she poked her head around the bathroom door. So there were a couple of cockroaches in the bathroom, scuttling around by the shower plughole.

'As soon as we get jobs we'll find somewhere better,' Laurie reassured Rachel.

Standing on their balcony the next morning as the sun rose over the sea, it was as if they'd landed in paradise. White sand stretched out in front of them and the beach bars were starting to open up; all around they could hear the chatter of locals and tourists as the island gradually came to life.

'So – today the job hunt begins,' Laurie said.

'Today?' Rachel said, laughing. 'C'mon, Laurie. Look at that beach! Anything but sunbathing today would be a crime.'

'OK, I've done it,' Laurie announced a fortnight later, coming home to the apartment with bags of food shopping. 'I've found us work.' After a couple of weeks sunbathing and touring the island on mopeds, drinking in the bars at night, Laurie was itching to start earning some money.

'What?' Rachel asked, looking up from the spot where she was stretched out, cat-like on the balcony, her usually pale legs tanned golden.

'Yes, jobs, lazypants,' Laurie said. 'No need to thank me. I know it's been a dream living with our cockroach friends, but I'm getting a little bit bored now of you moping around missing Aiden. And we're skint.'

Rachel put her paperback down on the table. 'I know, I know. Where is it?'

'O'Reilly's. The Irish bar in town.' She dumped the bags on the kitchen counter and began to unpack. 'I know it's not quite the dream we had – you know, little taverna with Greek salads and all that – but the guy who runs the place seems nice enough.'

'What's his name?'

'Barry.'

'Barry?'

'Look, Rachel. Beggars can't be choosers. Our next month's rent is going to be due soon, and we're getting seriously low on the old drachmas.'

Unfortunately, with Barry holding on to their tips, it turned out that serving tequila to sunburned tourists didn't pay enough for them to move to a better place – or even keep them in their own apartment. A month after they'd set out, Rachel and Laurie were back at Heathrow Airport, with Aiden waiting in Arrivals to meet them.

At home in Bromley, with a rapidly fading tan and a plan that had come unstuck, Laurie was faced with a long summer stretching out in front of her and an empty wallet. Six weeks later Rachel found out she was pregnant, and slowly, the two of them started to drift apart.

Laurie reluctantly agreed to help her mum out at the salon, applying fake nails, making appointments and getting to grips with rollers. In the evenings she worked on her portfolio of fashion designs for the course she was signed up to at Central St Martins in London. That summer Laurie had managed to get together some cash to take to college, but she certainly hadn't found herself.

But now here she was in Yorkshire. She took in the lively babble of voices around her. What was it you were supposed to experience on your gap year?

Unintelligible dialect – she had that here.

Challenges – she thought of Diana's hostility the other night. Tick.

Culinary differences – she glanced over at the pie shop. Oh yes.

There was one more thing, wasn't there?

She glanced at the people who surrounded her: the bobbly scarves and checked trousers, gaudy flower-prints and overstyled hair. Yes – the potential to *help people*.

She thought back to the ad she'd glanced at in the paper – 'Interested in Fashion? Volunteers Wanted'.

She had a week and a half left in Skipley before she and Rachel swapped back: a gap week. She wouldn't be coming back with beach-tied braids or flip-flops, but maybe she could do something character-building. Laurie had always done things quickly – surely that could apply to finding herself too?

CHAPTER 12

Monday 4th December

Rachel was standing at the kitchen table, dismantling the sculpture Zak had made over breakfast out of tins, cereal packets and a plantain. It wasn't just the bread-fruit, Rachel thought. Various things had started appearing in the flat. There was the plantain, too – and the plectrums she'd found on the coffee table, the new copy of *Guitar Weekly*.

'Minor disaster,' Aiden said, putting his head around the kitchen doorway. 'Sorry, Rach, the shower's broken. It just came off the wall, the attachment thing. There's water flooding out.'

Aiden was acting as if this week were just like any other but his face betrayed him – it was pale with stress, and his frown lines had deepened. The news about Bea's biopsy would be coming in the next couple of days, and they both knew it could change everything. In the middle of the night Rachel had woken up to find an empty space where Aiden normally lay, and heard the low hum of the TV in the front room. She'd touched the sheets next to her, still warm. He must be having trouble sleeping too. Dr Patel's words had been going round and round in Rachel's head all night.

'Flooding?' she said.

'A bit, yes. I'm really sorry, Rach, I'm going to have to run.' Aiden was hurriedly scrubbing his hair dry with a towel. 'I've got to get to this meeting,' Aiden explained. 'It's with a furniture design company – I'm hoping they might be able to knock us up a few things for Westley.'

'Don't worry,' Rachel said. 'Honestly, go, get ready.'

Aiden ducked out of the kitchen and Rachel peeked into Laurie's pristine bathroom. 'Thanks. I'll make it up to you,' he shouted from the bedroom.

Rachel took in the scene – water was gushing from a hole in the wall into the freestanding bath and trickling down the wall onto a stack of clean white towels. Zak dashed in off the sofa and stood watching, transfixed. 'It's like a waterfall,' he said, as Rachel draped an arm around his shoulder. 'Isn't it, Mum?'

Rachel rolled up the sleeves of her checked shirt and leaned in to take a closer look. Her plumbing skills were pretty rudimentary, but if she could fix it herself, she would. But as she tried to stem the flow with a towel held in one hand, and lifted the towels off the floor with the other to inspect the damage, she saw that they'd hardly soaked up any of the enormous puddle underneath.

'Oh no, Aiden,' she called out, 'do you think it'll go through into the downstairs flat?'

'Er, I guess it might,' Aiden replied. He was standing in the bathroom doorway, pulling suit trousers on over his white Calvin Kleins and biting his lip. 'It's not good, is it?' He took another look in at the water cascading out. 'Seriously, Rach, all I did was hold it, I promise.'

She dialled Laurie's mobile. 'Look, it's OK,' said Rachel, with the phone still at her ear. 'You get on your way. We'll get it sorted. See you back here later?' The call was going through to Laurie's answerphone.

Aiden grabbed his briefcase and gave her a kiss. 'Yes. I'm going to go and see Mum before coming home,' he said, squeezing her hand. 'And thank you. I *will* make it up to you, I promise.'

He leaned down to give Zak a hug before heading out of the front door and closing it behind him with a slam.

A moment later, Milly emerged from her bedroom and peered into the room, mascara smears under her eyes. She seemed to be sleeping in later each day. 'What's going on?'

'It's a minor disaster,' Zak parroted.

'That's about right,' Rachel said. She was standing next to the wall, pressing a towel against the tiles to stop the flow. It was then that Milly stepped forward into the doorway, in her purple pyjamas, to reveal that she was holding a white-pawed tabby cat in her arms. She stroked its ears gently.

'Oh, right. Well, look what I found in my room,' she said, swivelling her body around slightly so that the cat in her arms was facing Rachel. It mewed gently.

'A cat!' Zak called out, stepping nearer and reaching out to stroke its back.

'A cat,' Rachel sighed, and smiled. 'Right, just what we need. Listen, guys, I've got to pop downstairs and let them know they might have Niagara coming through their ceiling in a minute. Can you keep an eye on things, Mills?'

Milly nodded yes, and then swiftly batted Zak's hand away from the cat. 'Gently, Zak. And not backwards, he doesn't like it.'

'Don't worry, Mum, we will all watch the waterfall while you're gone,' Zak said.

From: LaurieGreenaway@virgin.net
To: Millypede@gmail.com

Hi Milly,

Great to hear from you – and wow, this sounds like exciting news. I think you must be the first person ever to come to ME for romantic advice, I'm not sure I'm the expert there, but I'll do my best! I'd say carry on getting to know each other, and go with your gut feeling. He sounds really nice

– and very into you (who can blame him). I'm sure whatever you decide, your parents will come around to the idea, it might be weird for them at first, but they love you and will want you to be happy. Plus, they're pretty reasonable, as parents go.

Good luck and keep me posted. And enjoy London – it's the best city in the world!

Laurie xx

Rachel kept on pressing the bell as music was playing in Jay's flat and she reasoned he must not have heard it when she rang the first time. The door opened on her third ring.

'Rachel, hi,' Jay said with a smile. 'Sorry – have you been waiting? It's a bit loud in here.' She was almost too flustered to notice how his white T-shirt set off his golden skin. Almost.

A man passed behind Jay through into the kitchen, followed by a young blonde woman. 'Harley, our drummer,' Jay said, gesturing backwards – 'and Amber – Harley, can you turn it down a bit?' Jay asked, looking over his shoulder.

'Sorry to bother you,' Rachel said. 'But it's a bit of an emergency, I'm afraid. There's a problem with our shower. The attachment came away from the wall and all watery hell has broken loose. So there's a chance you'll have a leak coming through your ceiling – I guess –' she said, peeking into the flat to check the layout was the same – 'it would be your bathroom ceiling.'

'Oh that shower,' Jay said calmly, 'I know it well.' He smiled. 'Don't worry, it's happened before and for some reason the water's never come through.' Jay's laidback manner was contagious, and Rachel found herself relaxing a little. The shower really didn't seem like such a big deal all of a sudden. 'Laurie had some issues with it when she first installed it. I can come up now and sort it out for you now, if you like?'

'No . . . I mean,' Rachel floundered, 'I didn't mean that.'

'It's really not a problem,' Jay said. 'Seriously, it didn't take long at all last time.'

'It was this part here,' he said, pointing to where the shower tap attached to the wall as he dried his hands. 'I've fixed it, but you'll just have to be gentle when you're using it.' He swept up the wet towels and chucked them into the laundry basket in the corner of the room. 'Laurie was totally set on getting this freestanding bath,' he said, smiling and shaking his head. 'It was in *Elle Decor* or something.'

Rachel smiled. 'Well, thank you. So much – we really appreciate it. I think you've earned a cup of tea. Will you stay for one?'

'Sure,' Jay said, putting his tools to one side and following her through into the living room.

Rachel took some chocolate-chip biscuits out of a packet and put them on a plate, then brought them with the tea into the living room.

'You're a lifesaver,' Rachel said.

'Honestly, it's fine,' Jay said. 'Actually it's given me a break from Harley's nagging,' he smiled. 'We've got a gig tonight and I think he's nervous, he thinks we haven't rehearsed enough.' He laughed. 'Band politics. Worse than families.'

Rachel poured the tea and offered Jay the plate of biscuits.

'You're a musician?' Rachel asked.

'Yes,' Jay said. 'Harley and I started a band in our twenties and we play gigs every so often, tour a bit.'

'Is it full-time?' Rachel asked.

'It used to be, but recently I've been busy starting up a small business. I trained as a cabinet-maker a while back and recently I've had a few commissions. Just got a workshop around the corner so I can expand.'

'Sounds interesting,' Rachel said.

'I enjoy it,' he said. 'Anyway, how are you guys settling in up here?' he asked, looking around.

'Good, thanks,' Rachel said. 'Zak and Milly found a cat this morning, they're playing with it in her room, that's what's keeping them quiet.'

'Don't tell me,' Jay said, narrowing his brown eyes. 'Tabby, white paws, bags of cunning?'

'Is he a regular at yours too?' Rachel asked.

'He should be,' Jay joked. 'He's mine – his name's Mr Ripley. So-called for his talents at finding his way into other people's flats. I do feed him, I promise,' he laughed. 'He's just got an adventurous spirit. Anyway, if Zak and Milly are playing with him I'll just grab him when I go back down. So, feline visitors and disobedient showers aside, are you enjoying your stay?'

'Yes,' Rachel said. 'Although it's not a holiday. My husband Aiden's mum is sick in hospital and she needed to see a specialist here.' Rachel glanced down and took a sip of her tea.

'Oh,' Jay said, sitting forward on the sofa. 'I didn't realise. I'm really sorry to hear that.'

'Thanks,' Rachel said. 'We're just grateful to Laurie for letting us stay here, for suggesting the house swap. I don't know how we would have managed otherwise.'

'A house swap?' Jay said.

'Yes, she's staying at our place. A cottage in a tiny Yorkshire village probably isn't her usual scene.'

Jay smiled in surprise. 'Yorkshire? Wow. I knew she was going on holiday – but that's not quite what I pictured. I don't think she's been further north than Hampstead before. How is she coping?'

'She said something about wanting a change of scene. And Skipley really is beautiful.'

'I'm sure it is,' Jay said, sitting back into the sofa. 'Laurie in the countryside,' he said, as if he was picturing it. He went quiet for a moment, then a smile crept back on to his face. 'In those heels she wears?'

Rachel smiled. 'I left her some wellies.'

'Now there's an image. And what, then you'll switch back before Christmas?' Jay said, and Rachel nodded.

'Shame, in a way, that you won't be staying longer, I mean. Christmas here is great. Lily puts on an amazing spread. A lot of kids there too, Zak and Milly would enjoy it.'

'Oh yes, Laurie told me about that,' Rachel said. 'But Christmas for us is just family. We're a bit boring like that.'

'Nothing boring about it,' Jay said, finishing his cup of tea. 'Listen, I should go. But thank you for the tea.'

'No, thank you,' Rachel said, 'you really saved the day fixing that leak.'

'No worries,' he said. 'See you again soon. Now, if you don't mind I'm just going to try and persuade my cat to come home with me.'

From: Carter@yahoo.com
To: Millypede@gmail.com

Hi Milly,

I like the photos you sent, thanks. I'm sitting in the Lion and the Unicorn, where the four of us were the other night.

Wondering what songs you'd be putting on the jukebox if you were here now. I wish you were. They've got loads of Motown stuff, like the Supremes. You said you liked them, right? I'm going to put a song on for you now.

Carter x

From: Carter@yahoo.com
To: Millypede@gmail.com

Hi Milly,
Me again. What's your phone number? Can I call you? I saw Kate again and asked for it, but she wouldn't give it to me for some reason. I don't know, she was being weird. Listen, Milly, I want to talk to you properly, hear your voice.

Carter x

• ❄ •

When the doorbell rang at just after seven that evening, Rachel assumed it was Aiden.

As she walked past the chrome-framed mirror above the mantelpiece, she caught sight of her reflection and frowned. She looked older, tired, and she had new lines around her eyes. She was worried about Bea, about Aiden, about Milly – and it all showed.

She opened the door to find Jay, with a pretty, auburn-haired woman by his side.

'Rachel, hi,' Jay said, smiling. 'Just wondered if you fancied coming to our Christmas gig tonight. It's only up the road. Siobhan is going –' he seemed to twig then that the two women hadn't met – 'sorry,' he said, gesturing from the auburn-haired woman to her and back again, 'Siobhan, Rachel, Rachel, Siobhan.'

'Oh, hi,' Rachel said, feeling conscious of how she looked, still in her tracksuit bottoms and an old T-shirt of Aiden's. 'I've heard a lot about you from Laurie.'

'Don't believe a word of it,' Siobhan said, a wide and genuine smile on her face. 'Sorry I've not come by earlier. I've been swept off my feet in a romantic whirlwind,' she said, with a glint in her eye. 'Out of the desert after years in it, Rachel. Fabulous.' Her smile was contagious and Rachel found herself instinctively returning it.

'Thanks for the invite, but sorry,' Rachel said, shaking her head. 'I can't really, I mean Aiden is at the hospital and Zak's—'

The buzzer interrupted Rachel, and she held her hand up to excuse herself as she answered the intercom. 'Hi, love, it's me –' Aiden's voice came through – 'forgot my keys, sorry. Can you buzz me in?' She pressed the button and heard the distant sound of the front door opening and closing. When Aiden emerged from the stairwell, Rachel introduced him to Siobhan and Jay.

'I'm not normally such a drowned rat,' Aiden said, smiling and running his fingers through his soaking hair and trying to shake off some of the moisture. 'It's bucketing down out there.'

'Any news?' Rachel asked. Aiden shook his head: 'Tomorrow, they said.'

'We were trying to convince your wife,' Siobhan said, 'and of course you too,' she added, 'to come out with us, to Jay's gig.'

'A gig?' Aiden said. 'I'm shattered unfortunately – but, Rach, why don't you go?' he said, putting his laptop bag down in the hallway behind Rachel and starting to take off his rain-drenched coat. 'I can keep an eye on things here.'

He turned back to Jay and Siobhan, and said, behind his hand, 'By which I mean I will collapse in front of the TV, but if there's a fire or a burglary I might still be some use.'

'Go on, Rach,' he said, 'Seriously. You should go.'

'Are you sure?' Rachel asked. 'But with everything that's going on ...'

'Do you really think Mum would want us moping around? There's nothing we can do until we know more. Go on, go out. You could do with a break.'

'OK,' Rachel said, hesitantly. 'Siobhan, would you mind hanging on for ten minutes while I find something to wear?'

'Siobhan and Rachel,' Siobhan said to the guy at the door of the pub, 'we're on Jay's list.' He checked his clipboard, then pressed stamps against their wrists. Rachel looked curiously at the black smudge on the inside of her wrist. 'Does this stuff come off?' she asked. Siobhan just smiled and took her by the hand down the stairs to the music venue.

Before they'd left the flat, Siobhan had seen Rachel pull out a bobbly grey vest top and a cream cardigan from her suitcase at the flat, and waved her hand in horror. She'd gone straight for Laurie's wardrobe, rifling through it.

'Here,' she said, passing her a long-sleeved black-lace dress with gold lining. 'And take these . . . size 5 OK?' Siobhan asked, flinging a pair of black leather boots towards Rachel. The heels were higher than she was used to wearing. Rachel slipped on the clothes, then turned to look at her reflection in the mirror. 'Not bad,' Siobhan said, passing her a tiny, old-gold vintage handbag with a slim strap to complete the look.

As Rachel walked into the basement venue, she felt suddenly conscious of how dressed up she was.

'Now, what's your poison?' Siobhan asked, a wicked smile on her face. 'And no, I'm not getting you a shandy.'

'I don't know,' Rachel said, 'surprise me.'

Siobhan got them both JDs on the rocks and Rachel winced at her first taste of the whisky. She glanced around the unfamiliar setting and reasoned that the quicker she knocked the drink back the sooner she could go home. A mixture of teenagers and older men lined the bar, shouting at each other over the music. Were they looking at her? She shifted uncomfortably. 'Don't worry about the crowd,' Siobhan said, squeezing her arm and reading her mind. 'You're going to love Jay's band.'

By the time the support act had wound up Rachel had all but downed two drinks – Siobhan had replaced her empty JD with another before she could protest. The crowd were warming up and Rachel was surprised to find she was starting to relax into things.

After a break Jay came on stage, and Siobhan clutched her arm. Harley sat down at the drums, the bass player tuned up and Amber adjusted the microphone to her height. As Jay strummed the opening chords to their first tune, Amber's bittersweet vocals kicked into a raw, sultry version of 'Santa Baby'. The gritty music gave an edge to what could have been a honey-sweet song, and the hairs on Rachel's arms pricked up. Siobhan turned to her and gave her a nudge. 'Told you,' she mouthed.

The tempo picked up after that. Jay's band launched into tune after tune of soul-fuelled rock – to a crowd that was hungry for more. Siobhan grabbed Rachel's hand and the two of them started to dance on the crowded floor. Rachel, in her knee-high boots and Laurie's gorgeous dress, looking into Siobhan's smiling face, felt something she hadn't felt in years – free. And when the bass player caught her eye through the crowd, she couldn't help but smile.

After the second encore, the band finally left the stage, and Siobhan led Rachel to a room around the back. Bathed in a post-gig glow, the band were sitting around on plastic chairs, drinking from bottles of beer. Jay was beaming. 'Nice one,' Siobhan said, slapping her friend on the back. 'Your best yet.'

Amber offered Rachel a beer and she took the bottle gratefully. 'I really enjoyed that,' Rachel said. The bassist turned towards her, 'It helps when you have such an attractive audience.' His eyes ran, fleetingly, over her body.

'Enough of that, Alex,' Jay said to him, with a playful warning look. 'She's a married woman.'

Harley suggested they go on to a club, but Jay looked at Siobhan and Rachel and said he was ready to call it a night. He was booed by the rest of the band, but insisted he was wiped out. The three of them headed home, laughing and joking on the way, Siobhan jumping in puddles as they went. Rachel had the sensation she'd known the two of them for years. They didn't know the ins and outs of her life – no – she hadn't wanted to go into any of that. That evening, even though it had felt selfish, all she'd wanted was to forget about being a wife, a mum, a daughter-in-law, and that's what they had helped her to do. They went into the block and came to a stop outside Jay's door.

'Jay, are you going to fix us both a nightcap then?' Siobhan asked, leaning against the wall with a cheeky grin.

'Of course,' Jay said, 'come right in.' He held his door open for them to walk through.

Rachel checked her watch – it was past midnight, she should really head back upstairs. But, she reasoned, another twenty minutes was hardly going to make a difference. Aiden and the kids would already be asleep – and she didn't feel like going to bed yet.

She smiled and walked into Jay's flat, noting how different it was from Laurie's. Instead of white carpets, here there were floorboards, exposed and varnished, and simple, colourful Scandinavian-style furniture that warmed up the room. On the walls were framed prints of film posters and record sleeves, and plants weaved and draped their way over the shelves and mantelpiece, bringing hints of green to each corner of the room. Siobhan lay down on the dark-red sofa and put her feet up on the end. Out of nowhere a tabby cat with white paws appeared and jumped up on to her stomach. 'This is Mr Rippple ...' she said, stroking him lazily. Her sentence tailed off and her eyelids started to droop.

'She always does that,' Jay said with a shrug, 'she's famous for passing out in the middle of parties.' Jay motioned for Rachel to follow him into the kitchen. 'Excuse the chaos,' he said, stepping over a large khaki rucksack as he went through into the kitchen to pour their drinks. 'Harley is staying at the moment, between flats, and he brought loads of stuff with him.'

'Oh, I see,' Rachel said, as she stepped over the rucksack carefully and took a seat on a wooden stool next to the brunch bar in the kitchen.

Jay pulled a bottle of rum from a wooden drinks cabinet in his kitchen and got out three small glasses.

'Does your girlfriend not mind him staying?' Rachel asked. 'I mean,' she corrected herself, shaking her head, 'sorry, I didn't mean to pry.'

Jay passed her a shot and brought his over to the brunch bar, sitting down with her. Rachel glanced across at the windowsill, the carefully tended chilli plants, shelves heavy with recipe books and spices, framed photos of family.

'I don't have a girlfriend,' he said, 'I live here on my own usually.'

'Oh, sorry, I thought ...' Rachel said, embarrassed that she'd misunderstood.

'Amber?' Jay asked, with a smile, and Rachel nodded. 'Our diva vocalist? She's been totally smitten with Harley since the day she joined the band – three long months of unrequited love.'

'Tonight is the night, she told me when we left just now. Who knows, maybe it will be.' He held his hands up. 'I think Harley's pretty terrified of her, though, to be honest. Anyway, thankfully she's not my type.'

Rachel sipped at her rum. Here, in Jay's flat, after a night out, she felt like a new person, younger. Her responsibilities had floated away during the evening, leaving space for someone she'd forgotten she could be. 'And what exactly is your type?' Rachel asked, emboldened by Jay's frankness, and the rum. She leaned forward and put her elbows on the table, resting her chin on her hands.

'Well,' he said, looking directly at Rachel with the hint of a smile on his lips. 'That's easy. Fun, sparky, playful, pretty. Smart enough to keep me on my toes.'

'So this woman,' Rachel tilted her head, considering what he'd said. 'Where are you going to find her?'

'Where?' Jay said, leaning back in his wooden chair and toying with the glass in front of him. 'I've already found her, Rachel. I didn't have to look very far at all.'

His dark gaze lingered on her and silence hung between them.

Rachel looked away, picked up her glass and downed the last of her rum in one. But as she swallowed the alcohol, she choked, and as she struggled to get her breath back she broke into a full-blown coughing fit. Oh God, she thought, remembering Aiden and her children asleep upstairs. I should never have come here tonight. Her face was burning. As she continued to splutter, Jay got up and moved towards her, putting his hand gently on her shoulder. 'Are you all right?' he asked. 'Do you want some water?' Her coughing gradually subsided.

'Yes. Sorry,' she said, filling her lungs with air and regaining her composure, waving a hand by her face to cool her red-hot cheeks. 'Really not used to rum,' she said, laughing nervously. Jay's face was just inches away from hers and she could feel the heat of his body. He gave her another concerned glance to check she'd really recovered.

I've been out of the game far too long, she thought, as Jay returned to his seat. I'm so naïve.

Jay was the one who finally broke the silence. 'Powerful stuff, this,' he said, raising the bottle with a smile. 'Anyway,' he said, as if he wanted to draw a line under their previous conversation. 'Finding her was the easy part, as it turns out. It was difficult to make things work. It's not going to happen, I know that. I've known that for weeks.'

Weeks. Rachel let the word sink in. Weeks – that definitely ruled her out. And – breathe. Her smile slowly returned.

'What makes you think that?'

'The way she acted when we were together – we had a few dates in the summer. But it didn't work out.'

'What happened?'

'I didn't want to be second on her list.'

'Second? What was first?'

'Her work. Which I respect ... I mean, I've always liked that she's so passionate about what she does. But what I realised is I want a relationship with her – the whole deal, nights out, nights in, good moods, bad moods, holidays together. I don't just want a date here and there, when she's got a free evening and things are quiet at work.'

'Fair enough. Maybe with time ...'

'Maybe,' Jay said, 'but she made her feelings pretty clear, and I need to move on. We'd probably drive each other nuts anyway. She's not exactly the easiest of women,' he smiled. 'But she's also pretty hard to forget. She makes me laugh, she's got this drive ... and I don't know. She's addictive.' He shook his head with a wry smile. 'The thing is we're friends too, or at least we used to be. More than anything, I really miss her.'

Rachel smiled sympathetically.

'I know.' He laughed, brushing his hair out of his eyes. 'It's maddening. But we used to hang out. Talk to each other about stuff. No one else even comes close.'

'If I'm guessing right here, there aren't many women like her,' Rachel said, thinking of her oldest friend.

The kitchen door swung open and hit the wall with a thud.

'Hey,' Siobhan called out, stumbling tipsily into the room, Mr Ripley clutched to her chest so tightly he was emitting sharp miaows of protest. 'What's going on with the bar, eh?' she smiled. 'Mr Ripley's come looking for his rum.'

'Thanks,' Rachel said to Jay as they said their good-byes at the end of the night. She'd finally convinced Siobhan that they should go upstairs to their beds, rather than polishing off the rest of the bottle. She had one arm around her now, and Siobhan was singing 'Santa Baby' softly into her shoulder. 'Tonight was just what I needed. To let loose for once. I really enjoyed it.'

'Any time,' Jay said, leaning in to give her a friendly good-night kiss on the cheek. It felt really good to click with people she'd only just met. 'And now,' Rachel said, with a nod to Siobhan, 'it really is time for bed.'

CHAPTER 13

Tuesday 5th December

Laurie's gap-week project wasn't getting off to a very promising start.

'Hello,' she said, her voice echoing off the bare floorboards of Skipley Community Centre and up to the rafters, hung with gold tinsel and decorations. In front of her about a dozen women, aged between forty and seventy, were sitting down around tables heaped high with clothing. The hum of conversation had stopped and they all stared back at Laurie in silence. In a red dress and high heels, Laurie realised instantly that she was seriously overdressed.

After what felt like an eternity, a dark-haired woman in a fuchsia poloneck and a tweed skirt put down the coat she was holding and took a step towards Laurie.

'Can we help you?' she asked, her voice strained. I want to disappear, Laurie thought, her heart sinking to the soles of her shoes. Why had she thought it was a good idea to come?

She gathered her strength. 'I saw the advert in the

paper,' she said, her voice booming out again a bit more than she'd intended it to. 'For volunteers?' She floundered around for something else to say. 'I think I can help you,' she said. 'I'm a fashion designer.'

'Oh, are you?' a lady with a steel-grey bob asked icily, looking Laurie up and down. The woman had a too-big navy body warmer on over her yellow sweater.

Laurie was rapidly developing a new respect for Rachel, surviving in Skipley. The locals at the farmers' market had seemed friendly, but this lot – well, they were less like the Calendar Girls – more like military boot camp.

'Yes,' Laurie said, then, in a last, desperate bid to give herself some kind of authority, 'in London.'

That was when she spotted Diana at the back of the room. The icing on the cake. Laurie sighed. Diana stood up and Laurie locked eyes with her.

'Well, come and sit down then,' Diana said, brusquely. 'And let's get you to work. One of the ladies will show you the ropes. Joyce?'

Ten minutes later, Laurie was sitting down bagging up old clothes, surrounded by black plastic sacks. When she was attempting to paint the kitchen that morning, with some spray paint she'd found out in the shed, she'd thought the day couldn't get any worse. Instead of covering the burn marks, like she'd hoped it would, she'd only dulled the black to grey, and created even more of a mess in the process. But as she stuffed old clothes into bin bags she realised she'd reached a whole new low.

Joyce, the eldest lady there, with cropped, grey hair and pink cheeks, turned to talk to Laurie. 'We've been collecting clothes donations since September, and now we're sending all the good quality coats to Winter Warmers, a local charity,' Joyce explained, holding up a red puffa jacket. 'They then distribute the warm clothing through the homeless shelters in Leeds.'

'Anything that's torn, stained or unsuitable gets put aside. You can help sort that out today. We store those clothes out in the back cupboard,' she'd said, 'and then when we have enough we sell them off to the rag man.' Laurie's spirits sank lower. Diana had made sure she'd have the worst job, out of spite, she was certain.

Interested in fashion, the ad had said, hadn't it? If this wasn't a charity, Laurie would have been tempted to sue them for false advertising.

As she bagged up old sweatshirts and ripped jeans that weren't good enough to send on, she listened as the women gossiped about a Christmas barn dance. (A barn dance? Laurie thought to herself, just when she'd thought Skipley couldn't get any further from a decent cultural scene.)

When Laurie had filled three bags a yawn slipped out. 'Who's for a cuppa?' she asked.

She'd half-expected a frosty response, but instead

quite a few of the women looked as if she'd just made their day.

'Café's open,' Laurie announced from the kitchen and one by one the ladies got up off their chairs and walked over. She'd made a big red teapot of tea, and laid out slices of the carrot cake that she'd bought at the bakery. She poured out the tea, then passed the mugs round into the ladies' grateful hands. As she picked up her own, she spotted a little radio in the corner of the kitchen. She reached over and fiddled with the knob, trying to make sense of the non-digital settings.

'I Wanna Dance with Somebody' crackled into life, and she noticed Joyce start to tap her feet as she sipped from her tea. 'I always rather liked this one,' she said, ignoring Diana's disapproving glare. Pam, the lady in fuchsia, started to hum along through a mouthful of cake.

They left the radio on as they worked. A couple of hours in, Laurie got what she could only assume was a promotion: sorting the decent coats and woolly jumpers into men's and women's.

'Have you just moved here, then?' Joyce asked her, quite softly, while the others were engaged in a chat about *Strictly Come Dancing*. Laurie shook her head. 'I'm just here for a break. I'm staying at my friend Rachel's house.'

'Rachel . . .' Joyce looked like she was searching for the face to put to the name. 'Oh yes, Bea's daughter-in-law. Sweet girl. Nice kids.' Joyce smiled. 'Now Bea, there's a woman for you. Heart of gold, Bea's got. She'd be here now, if she hadn't been taken ill. Awful worry, that, we've all been thinking about her.'

'Rachel and her family are staying in my place in London, so they can look in on her,' Laurie said. She felt a pang of homesickness as she thought of Gold-hawk Mansions, her flat, Siobhan.

'Oh that's good, isn't it?' Joyce said, then added, 'It's nearly four. He'll be here in a minute, the charity fella, to pick up the clothes. You put those black rag bags out the back, Laurie, and we'll get this lot ready.' Laurie got to her feet and picked up the black sacks, taking them out to a dusty storeroom.

When she got back a car horn was tooting outside and the women were hurrying to do up the bags of winter woollies they'd been sorting.

'Oh, don't you worry,' Laurie said, with a smile, grabbing an armload of bags from Joyce and Pam, ignoring their protests. All in the spirit of Gap Week.

Diana opened the heavy main door with her bags in one hand, and Laurie just managed to catch it before it slammed in her face. Diana walked ahead down the path to the waiting van, about ten metres away.

The van's back doors were open and Diana was bundling the bags in, laughing and joking with the male driver. Laurie walked towards them, but tripped and dropped one of the bags she was carrying, splitting it. The contents spilled out across the path. Laurie sighed, then put the remaining bags down and began to gather up the loose clothes. A woolly hat with a snowflake pattern and a navy coat lay on the path. As she reached down to pick up the coat, she spotted the van driver crouched in front of her, the snowflake hat perched on top of his – disarmingly attractive – head.

'Can I have this one?' he asked, a smile lighting up his face. He had dark-blond hair and stubble lined his jaw – in the winter sunshine his bright blue eyes shone out. There was no doubt about it. He was . . . totally, totally hot. A countryside Ryan Gosling. In a moment it dawned on Laurie – no wonder the ladies had been falling over each other to get to the door.

'Sure, it's yours,' Laurie said. 'But stealing from charity? That can't be good for your karma, can it?'

'Oh, I dunno,' he said, taking the hat in one hand and scooping up Laurie's bags in the other. 'It's not stealing, as such. I've given them quite a lot of my time – I reckon we could negotiate something.' She walked with him over to the van. Diana was standing there, glaring at Laurie, the man chucked the clothes into the back. He turned back to face Laurie, and then glanced over at Diana, looking for an introduction.

'Patrick,' Diana said hesitantly, then waved her hand

over to Laurie, 'meet Laurie.' It was as if it pained her to say it.

'Nice to meet you,' Patrick said, shaking Laurie's hand. She felt a shiver of excitement as his warm skin touched hers. Was that a sort of fizzle she was feeling? How ridiculous, Laurie reprimanded herself, pulling her hand away. This guy wasn't her type at all. He looked younger than her, and she never, ever went for younger men. She preferred dark hair too. And tall guys, like – she stopped herself. She couldn't compare every man she met to Jay.

Her eyes drifted down – even under a wool jumper she could see that his body was taut and toned, and his jeans hung really quite well on him.

Diana had slunk off back to the church hall, leaving Patrick and Laurie staring in mute silence at one another.

'Good to meet you too,' Laurie said, dragging her eyes back up to meet his.

'I hope it won't be the last time,' he said, with a captivating smile. 'Are you going to be volunteering here regularly? The run-up to Christmas is our busiest time.'

If someone had told Laurie three hours ago that she'd be contemplating spending any more of her precious time with the women in the community centre, she'd never have believed it. And yet, over the last couple of hours the women had seemed to soften, at least a little. Joyce even seemed quite, well, nice. And no one ever said Gap Week was going to be easy.

'I'll be here, yes,' Laurie said, feeling the wintry chill and pulling down the sleeves on her cardigan so her hands were covered. She hadn't thought to grab her coat before stepping out.

'Well,' Patrick said, 'I'll see you again then.' He reached into the back of the van and took another hat from a bag in there. 'And I think you should have this one, to keep you warm in the meantime.' He put a fluffy koala hat, with a big woolly black nose and grey flaps that covered her ears, on her head.

Laurie frowned. She was not – absolutely not – an animal hat kind of girl. Faux-mink, maybe. But Primark-knitted koala? Never. Wearing a hat like this was something Laurie wouldn't abide. Yet she didn't take if off.

She stood dumbly, hat in place, as Patrick got back into the van and started the engine. With just a brief backward glance and a smile, he drove away down the country lane.

When she got back inside the community centre, koala hat in hand, the women were huddled around the doorway. They had clearly been watching every second through the window.

'So, Patrick,' Pam said, giving Laurie a nudge. 'Pretty easy on the eye, isn't he?'

'Nothing special,' Laurie shrugged, tossing the hat into a pile of unsorted items. She swung around to see everyone smiling at her. 'So you can all stop looking at me like that.'

CHAPTER 14

Wednesday 6th December

'I've just heard from the hospital,' Aiden said.

'OK,' Rachel said, taking a breath. 'Let's sit down.'

They went together into the living room and Rachel closed the door behind them. They sat on the sofa in silence.

Slowly, Aiden put his phone down on the coffee table and took Rachel's hand in his. 'Right,' he said, taking a deep breath.

'Right . . . ?' Rachel said.

'Sorry, it's just sinking in,' Aiden said, shaking his head. 'What Dr Patel said. I'm not sure I understand everything, but here goes. The mass she talked about is a tumour, in Mum's inner ear, near her brain.'

The word tumour hung in the air. Rachel willed him to continue.

'But the biopsy showed it's benign – it's not cancerous. It's something called acoustic neu . . . something. Neuroma. Like she predicted, it's what's been causing all of Mum's symptoms.'

'So it's definitely not cancer?' Rachel asked nervously.

'Yes,' Aiden said, taking her hand. 'So obviously that's good news. But it's not the end of the story,' he went on. 'They've explained the situation to Mum. As she's older, and the tumour is likely to grow slowly, they could leave it, wait and see what happens. But then she'd be stuck with the symptoms, they won't get better on their own. The only way to get rid of the dizziness she's been feeling is to operate. Dr Patel says the tumour is in an accessible place, and they should be able to get it all out in one operation. That's what Mum wants to do.'

'OK,' Rachel said, biting her lip. 'Surgery? God. Poor Bea.'

'I know,' Aiden said. 'It's a big operation, six hours, and there would be a period of around two months when Mum'd have to rest. But apparently the outlook is good, and there's no reason for the problem to come back.'

'Right,' Rachel said, as the facts sank in. Their worst fears hadn't been realised. And if everything went well, Rachel thought, unconsciously crossing her fingers and wishing – they'd be able to go home and be there for Christmas. The kids would have their grandma back.

The handle on the living-room door twisted and opened, and Milly appeared in the gap, peering through. 'What's going on?' she asked. 'Why are you two hiding in here?'

'We're not hiding, darling. Come in,' Rachel said. 'Actually, can you get Zak too? We've just had some news about your grandma.'

'The operation's today,' Rachel said to Diana, pacing the living room, phone in her hand. 'I wasn't sure if Bea had already told you herself.'

'No,' Diana replied, sounding concerned. 'Actually I haven't heard from her at all since you left for London, so it's been on my mind. I'd convinced myself it was going to be something minor, though.'

'I know,' Rachel said, 'me too. I don't think any of us had bargained on it being as serious as this. But there's a lot to be thankful for – it's not cancer. The doctors are optimistic about Bea's recovery, so hopefully we'll be back up in time to get things ready for Christmas.'

'I'm glad to hear it. Do give her my love, won't you? I'll send some flowers – something to cheer her up after the operation.'

'That's kind of you, Diana. She'll appreciate that.' Rachel perched on the end of the L-shaped sofa. 'So, how is everything going up there? Have you had a chance to meet Laurie yet?'

'Everything's fine, work has been really busy in the last couple of weeks. I have met Laurie, yes.' Diana hesitated for a moment before carrying on. 'From the look on her face I'd say it's been a bit of a shock to the system, coming here. But I'm sure she'll settle in.

She even came down to the community centre today, to help out with the charity collection, so she's certainly making an effort.'

Rachel's eyebrows went up in surprise. She tried to picture city-smart Laurie sitting with Diana and Bea's friend Joyce, in the slightly shabby, basic community centre. The image brought a smile to her face.

'She's a bit of a funny one, though, isn't she, Rachel? Turned up at the centre in a red dress that wouldn't have been out of place on a catwalk, and stiletto heels. I mean there's no need for that kind of attire in Skipley really, is there? And she's . . . well. Not much of a dab hand in the kitchen by the looks of things, either. That's all I'll say. Very different from you, Rachel. I can't see how you two came to be friends.'

'Opposites attract, I suppose,' Rachel said, with a shrug. 'And old friends, well, even when your lives go in different directions, you have all that history together, don't you?'

'I suppose,' Diana said, sounding unconvinced. 'Listen, Alfie's whining for a walk, I'd better take him out. I'll be thinking of Bea today. All fingers crossed. You'll let me know how she gets on, won't you?'

'Of course, Diana. Speak to you soon.'

Aiden poured their morning coffee into two mugs. 'What about that Reindeer Wonderland event you mentioned?' he said. He and Rachel had decided it was better to keep Zak and Milly busy, take their minds off their grandmother's operation.

'That's what I was thinking,' Rachel said. 'I suggested it to them. I just need to convince Milly it's going to be more fun than a trip to Oxford Street.' Rachel could hear her daughter talking on her phone in the bedroom. She hadn't been out of her room all morning.

'Reindeer Wonderland sounds brilliant,' Zak said, overhearing them and bounding into the kitchen. 'Ice skating outside, real, live reindeers, are we going, Mum? Please can we go?'

'Let's talk to your sister again in a minute,' Rachel said. 'But I'm fairly sure it can be arranged, yes, Zak.'

Aiden put an arm around his son and planted a kiss on the top of his head. 'You be good for your mum today, Zak. And if you see Santa, could you tell him that I've been a really good boy this year?' He paused. 'And for the record I'd love a yacht. And if he has space on his sleigh, then a Porsche too.' Zak giggled and leaned in to his dad for a hug.

'Are you sure you won't join us later?' Rachel asked Aiden.

Aiden looked at his son briefly and then back at Rachel. He dropped his voice to a lower, more serious, tone. 'I thought you understood,' he said quietly.

'I do,' Rachel said. 'It's just, it would be so nice if—'

Aiden breathed out slowly. 'You know I'd love to,

Rach. But my head's still spinning from the quote that last furniture company gave me – I've got to find someone else who can install the shelving and units more cheaply. And then with Mum's operation—'

Zak jumped in right away, 'Is Granny Bea going to be OK?'

'Don't worry, honey,' Rachel said, ruffling Zak's brown hair and trying to push aside her own fears. 'After her operation, Granny Bea is going to be ready for anything.'

Rachel, Milly and Zak's first stop was the outdoor ice rink, close to the entrance. Rachel queued up at the boot-hire stand, and Zak and Milly sat down on a bench to watch couples and families sweeping around the ice with varying degrees of elegance.

'A pair of size 5s, size 4s and size 13s please,' she asked the surly female stall attendant, handing over her Uggs, Milly's DMs and Zak's trainers.

'Here,' the woman said, dumping three pairs of skates unceremoniously on the counter. Rachel started to wonder if this had been the best place to bring Milly and Zak. It had been years since she'd been ice skating and she was sure she'd be spending half the time on her bum.

Rachel walked back to the bench and knelt in front of Zak, helping him get his small feet into the ice skates as Milly put on her own. There was a faraway look in Milly's eyes.

After a shaky start, all three of them were soon gliding around the rink – Milly had a real talent for it. Rachel slowly started to remember the ice skating she'd done when she was younger and was able to lead Zak around. As Milly spun in the centre of the fairy-lit rink, a wide smile on her face, for a moment all of Rachel's worries disappeared.

'But he definitely liked it, didn't he, Mum?' Zak said cheekily. He had smuggled Rudolph Junior a mini mince pie while Rachel was distracted.

'You really mustn't do that again, Zak. Like the reindeer keeper said,' Rachel said, trying to keep a straight face, while out of the corner of her eye she could see Milly failing to stifle her giggles. 'I mean, imagine,' Rachel continued, 'if he ate mince pies from everyone who came in here he'd soon be far too fat to take off.'

'And then,' Milly chipped in, 'how would Santa deliver all of our presents?'

Rachel took a bite from her own mince pie, then shook off a small lump of mincemeat that had fallen down on to her snowflake scarf.

She put her arms around her daughter and son and they walked towards the elaborate enchanted lake in the middle of the park, with Santa's grotto in the centre of it. A few metres in front of them was the jetty, where green and white-clad elves rowed visitors out in sleigh-shaped boats.

'Now, who's up for rowing out to the grotto?' she said, pointing to the lake ahead of them. Families and couples wrapped up in duffel coats and bobble hats were piling into the little boats captained by elves. Zak and Milly didn't waste a minute, they raced each other across the park, towards the water, their laughter ringing out.

· ❉ ·

From: Carter@yahoo.com
To: Millypede@gmail.com

Hi Milly,

I'm not being funny, but it's been a couple of days and I haven't heard anything from you. Have I done something wrong? What's going on?

C x

From: Millypede@gmail.com
To: LaurieGreenaway@virgin.net

Hi Laurie,

Me again. Can I ask your advice? About this guy. I don't know – he was so nice at first, and now he's just being well – intense. He seemed really cool when we met, but that was only once. My friend Kate called me today and said he's been asking her and some of my other friends about me. What do you think I should do?
Milly x

From: LaurieGreenaway@virgin.net

To: Millypede@gmail.com

Hi Mills,

Hmm. So he's really keen. Nice, but also a bit of a turn-off, right? Maybe give it a bit of time, play it cool, see if he chills out a bit. It's good (and of course a sign of his fantastic taste) that he obviously really likes you. As you're away from home, you have some space to make up your mind, right? Wait and see, I reckon.

Good luck,

Love,

Laurie xx

• ✲ •

Rachel had expected to find Aiden at home when they got back, but the flat was empty. She settled Milly and Zak down with their tea and left the room to call him.

'Rach,' he said, picking up almost immediately.

'Hi,' she said. 'Where are you? How did it go today?'

'I'm on my way back from the hospital,' he said. There was the trace of something in his voice that she barely recognised, it sounded like fear. 'It didn't go well.'

'What do you mean?' Rachel said, her heart starting to race. 'Didn't they remove the tumour?'

'No, It's not that …' His voice broke. 'Something happened in surgery, Rach. Something went wrong.'

Rachel's hand flew up to her chest. 'What do you mean, wrong?'

The line went silent for a moment.

'Mum didn't come around from the anaesthetic, Rach. She's in a coma.'

CHAPTER 15

Wednesday 6th December

Laurie put on a red gingham apron and cast her eye over the array of ingredients laid out in the cottage kitchen. Outside it was a dark winter evening, but inside the cottage it was bright and cosy.

She tried to ignore the muddied mess of the kitchen walls, made worse by her attempts to cover up the initial smoke damage. She really hadn't held back at the farmers' market at the weekend, and there was a lot of food left over – the only problem was that she didn't have a clue what to do with any of it.

She scanned the recipe books on the kitchen shelf, looking for something simple enough for her to manage. She pulled one out, a hand-made hardback, with gold lettering across the cover. She saw right away that it wasn't an ordinary recipe book – on the cover were the words: *Bea's Countdown to Christmas*. She thought then about Rachel's emotional phone call earlier that evening – she'd called to say Bea had fallen into a coma. Laurie had insisted that they stay in her flat as long as they needed. They needed to be there, and she'd find something to keep her busy in Skipley.

Laurie sat down and opened the book. Inside were prettily handwritten Christmas recipes with dates next to them. It was all so organised – Laurie saw that according to Bea's plans, some of the dishes, like the Christmas cake, should already have been prepared.

The recipes looked simple enough for even Laurie to follow. She found one for glazed ham and figs that looked grand and impressive in the illustration, and checked she had all the right ingredients.

She poured a glass of wine and sipped it as she went, preparing the ham and figs according to the step by step instructions. Cooking wasn't all that hard, was it? She looked at the half-drunk bottle of red wine on the counter. Perhaps that was the secret. She put the food in the Aga, being careful to set the oven timer – no way she was going to get caught out this time.

The landline phone rang.

'Laurie.' Siobhan's warm Irish tones couldn't have been more welcome. She curled up in the squishiest armchair there and poured herself another glass of red wine as they talked.

'How's it all going?' she said. 'How are you coping out there in the countryside? Are you starving?'

'No,' Laurie said. 'Actually, I'm cooking a meal right now. A proper one.'

'Crikey,' Siobhan said. 'Have you been brainwashed?'

'Nope,' Laurie replied. 'There's just not much else to do around here. Danny's cut off access to my work email, so I can't even check my messages.'

'And you're OK about that?'

'I wasn't at first,' Laurie said. 'But now – actually I don't really mind that much.'

'Well that's good to hear. And how are the locals?'

'Oh, some are nice. Not all of them welcome outsiders with open arms, but I'm working my way in.'

'How? Bake sales?'

'Noo . . .' Laurie laughed, 'actually, no . . . I'm doing some charity work.' She carried on talking over Siobhan's laughter. 'How's school going anyway?'

'Oh fine, most of my Year Tens are coming to the after-school art club now. It's chaos – but hopefully we'll get a few more passes this year.'

'Sounds good. And have you met Rachel?' Laurie asked.

'Indeed I have,' Siobhan said, 'we went to Jay's gig together the other night.'

'Oh, you did?' Laurie asked, feigning nonchalance.

'Yes – she's lovely. First time I'd been out in ages, actually. I've been, how can I say it, a bit tied up lately.'

'Tied up?' Laurie said. 'It's P.E. Man, isn't it?'

'Yep. Ed. Totally into it.'

'I knew it!' Laurie, said. 'I can't believe you're deserting me. Sorry – what I mean, of course, is good for you, you deserve it. I mean, Christ, it's been long enough coming. Right – I want the full run-down when I'm back.'

'Absolutely.'

Laurie paused for a moment, thinking of Jay, the gig they'd all been to without her. 'How's everything else in the block?'

'Do you mean how's Jay?'

'No, I don't,' Laurie snapped back, defensively.

'Well, not that you care, but he's fine, I think. I haven't seen him much lately. He's been doing more of his furniture stuff, I think. Are you wondering about that blonde girl, the singer?'

'I'm not wondering anything,' Laurie said. 'Is she a singer? What, in his band?'

'Look, do you want me to ask him about her?' Siobhan said. 'Find out what's going on, rather than us just guessing?'

'No!' Laurie said. 'Definitely not. Don't ask him anything. I don't want him to think I'm snooping around, that I can't let go.' The oven timer pinged. 'Look, Siobhan, I've got to go, my dinner's ready. But thanks for ringing.'

As she got the ham out of the oven, Laurie looked again at all the food she had – the ham alone was big enough for two people, and then she still had all the cheeses she'd picked up at the farmers' market. What was she going to do, sit here alone gorging herself on the whole lot? Then something else caught her eye – the blackened walls. She couldn't let Rachel come back to that mess.

A thought flitted into Laurie's head. She did her best to dismiss it, but, to her annoyance, it wasn't going anywhere. It was what Ben from the café had said about Diana. She was an interior designer, right? Surely, in return for a nice dinner, she'd be able to offer a bit of advice on fixing things up?

Maybe Diana had her reasons for being the way she was, Laurie reasoned. Perhaps she'd been a little hasty in writing Rachel's neighbour off so quickly. She hadn't been that bad at the community centre, she'd even introduced Laurie to the other women – and, Laurie thought idly, Patrick. Her eyes drifted back to the walls – surely Diana would be able to suggest something?

Taking a deep breath, Laurie got up, pulled on her coat and headed over in the direction of what she was pretty sure was Diana's cottage. She must be mad, she thought, as she walked towards a house that was nearly identical to Rachel's, only with an even more immaculately pruned front garden. A Christmas wreath hung on the door, just above a bronze knocker. Before she could change her mind, Laurie lifted the knocker and brought it down in a series of quick raps.

When Diana finally opened her front door, she

looked almost pleased to have a visitor, and to Laurie's relief accepted her invitation graciously. In the background the TV blared *Don't Tell the Bride* into an elegant, Laura-Ashley-inspired vision of a living room, with white sofas and flowered drapes. 'Wait a second while I grab Alfie,' she said, going up the stairs. 'He always likes going to Rachel's place.' As she waited in the hallway, wondering who or what Alfie was likely to be, she caught sight of some cardboard in the green recycling box in Diana's kitchen. She stepped forward to take a closer look. Ha! Laurie thought with a rush of satisfaction. A Domino's pizza box was poking out the side.

'Spray paint,' Diana said, tears of laughter coming to her eyes. 'You tried to paint over it with that?' She held up the can in disbelief.

'I know,' Laurie said, starting to see the funny side. Diana had been kinder than she'd expected about offering to help. 'Desperate times. I've not painted much myself before.'

'Listen,' Diana said, 'this should be easy enough to fix. It doesn't take an interior designer, you'll be able to get everything you need at the hardware store on the high street. Some emulsion will do it, a couple of layers. Take a photo in daylight and then you'll be able to match the colour better.'

*

Half an hour later Laurie and Diana were sitting at the kitchen table in the cottage, most of the way through a bottle of Malbec.

Alfie, it turned out, was a 'chiweenie' – with the body of a dachshund, the ears of a Chihuahua and – based on this evening's performance – the appetite of a Great Dane. Under the table, he darted between their feet, trying to catch scraps, every so often emitting a high-pitched yap.

'You did pretty well, here,' Diana said, loading her fork up with ham. 'An improvement on your last effort, anyway.' A sly smile crept on to the corner of her lips.

'Thank you,' Laurie said, not rising to the bait. It had been with a mixture of pride, surprise and relief that she'd realised the meal was not only edible, it was actually quite tasty.

Diana drained her third glass of wine. 'No, thank *you*,' she said, slurring her words a little. 'For inviting me. I know you must have thought I was stuck up.'

It was only because her mouth was full that Laurie managed to maintain a tactful silence.

'I know that's what most people think, nowadays,' she went on. 'But it's not that. You know what? It's just been a really, truly crap year, Laurie. And sometimes trying to be nice, on top of it all,' she said, banging the table for emphasis, 'is just too damn difficult.'

Laurie saw her neighbour in a new light. She hadn't planned on getting Diana plastered – but if she'd known it would reveal the real Diana, she might have.

'I'm over it, really I am,' Diana said, taking another sip of wine. 'But seriously –' she shook her head mournfully – 'you think you know someone . . .'

'. . . and they leave you for a man?' Laurie ventured.

'How did you . . . ?' Diana squinted tipsily and waggled her finger in Laurie's direction.

'Just a hunch,' Laurie lied.

'I mean how could I not have realised, right?' Diana said, sweeping Alfie up on to her lap and stroking his bat-like ears.

'He may not even have known, himself,' Laurie said. 'Anyway, now you can move on to better things.'

'You're right, you know,' Diana said, stroking Alfie's head so that his eyes looked even bulgier. 'Actually, since Richard left the business has been going from strength to strength, so he did me a favour on that front.'

'What kind of interiors do you specialise in?' Laurie asked.

'Oh, I do everything really – cottages, windmills, barns . . .' she said. 'Been doing it for years, but with a bit of a push behind the marketing it's really taking off at last. Aiden and I have worked together on a couple of barn projects. You know, I keep telling Rachel she should get involved.'

'Really?' Laurie asked, surprised. She'd always assumed Rachel was content being a stay-at-home mum.

'Yes – genius, she is. The way she's decorated the kids' rooms here – all her own ideas.' Laurie smiled, thinking of the pirate ship in Zak's bedroom. 'I'd like to be able to offer that kind of thing – and I'd be happy to pay for her to have a bit of training. You can teach the details, but you can't teach flair – and that's what Rachel's got. Anyway, work on her for me, will you? She keeps coming up with excuses.'

'I'll see what I can do,' Laurie said, resolving to bring it up with Rachel the next time they met. Rachel had always been the last person to realise her own talents.

'And in the meantime,' Laurie said, getting up, 'I think it's time for dessert.' Diana nodded in agreement and Laurie got a tub of caramel pecan ice cream out of the freezer. She cleared away the supper plates and then brought the tub over along with some bowls and spoons.

'So that guy today,' Laurie said, nonchalantly, as she tried to ease a spoon into the rock-hard ice cream. 'Patrick. Are you . . . er . . .'

'Am I interested?' Diana said. 'Well, I won't deny he's attractive . . .' A slight blush crept on to her face, 'but he's far too young for me. I'm in good nick, I know –' she swooshed her hair playfully and smiled – 'but I'm not deluded. I'm forty-six.' She shrugged. 'Patrick's just a bit of eye-candy, that's all.'

Diana leaned towards Laurie conspiratorially. 'I did

do a little research, though, I have to confess,' she said, in a stage whisper. 'And I happen to know he's single. So the path's clear.'

'Oh no,' Laurie said, shaking her head, 'I wasn't asking for me.' But then again, she thought, Skipley had become just a fraction more interesting.

'It's none of my business,' Laurie said, looking critically at the baggy outfit Diana was wearing. 'But have you lost weight recently?'

'Oh, yes, I did a bit. The divorce diet, after Richard left,' Diana said, looking down at her body and then back up with a shrug.

As Diana helped Laurie load the dishwasher, Laurie noticed how the white blouse and loose navy slacks she was wearing swamped her.

'It's just,' Laurie said, standing back and tilting her head, 'it strikes me that your clothes are too big for you. Come with me,' Laurie said, putting the cutlery she was holding down and leading Diana over to the hallway mirror. 'Look at this,' she said, starting to pull back the fabric so it hugged Diana's figure more closely. She peeked over Diana's shoulder so that the two of them could see the difference.

'Oh God, you're doing that Gok-thing, aren't you?' Diana said, laughing.

'I might be,' Laurie replied. 'But, seriously, Diana, look at all this extra fabric. Let me take these in for you. I'm sure I saw a sewing machine up in Milly's room.'

Diana looked at her suspiciously, and then, as she saw that Laurie wasn't going to take no for an answer, her defences gradually dropped. 'OK,' she said, with a smile. 'Do your worst.'

'Anything else back at yours?' Laurie asked.

'Ah,' Diana said. 'Are you sure you're up for the challenge?'

CHAPTER 16

Thursday 7th December

'Fionn wasn't like the other lions,' Milly read out loud, from a hardback book. 'From the moment she separated herself from the pride and approached me across the plains of the Masai Mara, I felt a connection – she wasn't aggressive, she was trusting of me, and I instinctively trusted her. I knew that I was putting my life at risk, just by standing there, but as Fionn nudged my hand gently with her head, with that first contact, I felt sure we were going to be very good friends.'

Rachel looked over at Bea as she lay in the hospital bed. For a moment you could believe that she was just sleeping. As always, she had her gold locket on around her neck, the photo of her late husband David close to her chest. As she breathed the locket gently rose and fell.

But Bea hadn't woken up since the operation yesterday. Aiden was sitting in a chair by her side, holding her hand in his. Dr Patel had told them that it might help to talk to Bea, that it was possible she'd be able to hear their voices. But she hadn't been able to tell them anything more. She said it was impossible to predict if, and when, Bea's condition would improve.

'Do you really think she can hear me?' Milly said, closing the book.

'I'm sure of it,' Rachel replied, putting her arm around her daughter's shoulders. 'And that book was a good choice, she's always liked reading about Africa.'

Silence fell around the bedside. Even Zak was quiet, staring up at his grandma with a sad look in his eyes.

'Mum,' Aiden said finally, 'we brought you a little radio. A digital one, you know how I keep saying you should have one. Well, here it is.' He reached down to get it from the floor and put it up on her side table, plugging it in but not switching it on. 'You can listen to Radio 4 now, I know you wouldn't want to miss *The Archers* just because you're not well.'

Rachel had a lump in her throat as she heard the strain in Aiden's voice. She reached over to take his hand, but he turned away.

'How about we all go over to Brockwell Park and get some fresh air,' Rachel said to Milly and Zak when they got home. 'Maybe check out the playground?'

'Yes!' Zak said, his eyes lighting up. He dashed out into the hall to put his trainers on.

'How can he be like that,' Milly said, 'with Granny so ill?'

'He cares. You know that, Milly. But we can't just sit around worrying about Granny – she wouldn't want that. We'll go and see her when we can, and the rest of the time she'll know we're thinking of her. But we need to keep ourselves strong for her.'

Milly shrugged sadly.

'Come on, Mills,' Rachel said, picking up her plate and putting it on the side. 'Jay said there's a girl your age downstairs, in the basement flat, called Nikki. What do you say, shall we call on her?'

'OK,' Milly said, a little reluctantly. 'Let's do that.'

'I'm just taking the kids out,' Rachel said, putting her head into the living room, where Aiden was sitting. 'Hopefully it'll give you a bit of space to think.'

'Thanks,' Aiden said, bent over his laptop on the sofa. 'That would be good. We're having a nightmare with the carpenters we brought in.'

'Good luck, sweetheart,' Rachel said, touching his arm reassuringly.

With winter coats, hats and scarves on, Rachel, Zak and Milly trooped down the stairs. The stairway continued on down to the basement, and Rachel started to lead the way. She bent to look down at the floor below; it was darker down there and there was a faint smell of damp.

'Mum,' Milly said, from her position in the entrance hall. 'What are you doing?'

'Flat number 1, Jay said.'

'Yes,' Milly replied. 'But what, are you going to call on her yourself? Don't be embarrassing. I'm fifteen, not Zak's age.'

'Oops,' Rachel said, coming back up. 'You're right. Sorry.' She held her hands up in surrender. 'How about Zak and I wait here and then you can just nip up and tell us what your plans are.'

'Better,' Milly said, and went downstairs. Rachel tilted her head slightly towards the stairwell. After the door opened she could hear teenage giggles. It sounded positive.

Milly came up the stairs a moment later. 'Me and Nikki are going to go to TopShop,' she said. Rachel leaned over the banister and saw a girl with cropped blonde hair with a pink streak. She gave a little wave.

'I'll see you and Zak back at the flat later,' Milly said.

Rachel tried to shrug off the feeling of rejection. 'OK. Be back in time for dinner. Have you got your—'

'Yes, I've got my mobile, and my wallet,' Milly sighed.

'Right then,' Rachel said, pulling on her mittens. 'Nice to meet you, Nikki,' she called down the stairs.

Milly gave her a glare. 'See you later.'

Rachel sat on a low wall and watched Zak scale the climbing frame. He'd made a couple of friends already, and was pointing out to them the best way to get to the top. Rachel took a sip from her take-away coffee, and then held it with both her gloved hands to warm them. Zak looked over at his mother and gave her a wide smile, and Rachel waved back. In an instant she saw that Zak, her little boy, was growing up quickly.

Would there come a day when Zak, like Milly, would be longing to get away from his family? Rachel sighed wistfully at the inevitability of it. After all, Milly had once shared everything with her mum and dad – from hopes and dreams to schoolyard jealousies and squab-bles, but these days her moody silences were becoming more and more frequent. Rachel drank her coffee slowly, looking around at the other parents and chil-dren in the busy playground – did other mothers find it this hard to let go?

As she drained the cup, she called out to Zak that it was home time.

Milly came home just before six with a new striped scarf, and some thin bronze hoop earrings.

'Wow,' Rachel said. 'I like those. Hold them up.' Milly pushed her hair back and held one up to her ear. 'They suit you,' Rachel said. 'So you got on with Nikki then?'

'Yeah,' Milly said. 'Nikki's really cool. She was telling me about this art workshop that Siobhan from next door runs – she's a teacher at Nikki's school. It's after school on Fridays, and she thinks it would be OK for me to go too. Can I?' Milly's face was bright; she looked happier than she had done in days.

'I don't see why not,' Rachel said. 'So long as Siobhan doesn't mind an extra heap of trouble turning up.'

Milly gave her a look.

'I'm teasing,' Rachel laughed. 'A very talented heap of trouble, I meant.'

'And, Mum,' Milly said, 'there was one other thing. Nikki asked me if I wanted to go to Camden with her at the weekend. Is that OK?'

Camden. There was a market, wasn't there? She didn't know much about it really.

'Let me check with your dad,' Rachel said.

'Pleeaase, Mum,' Milly whined, putting on a winning smile.

Rachel put her hands up, laughing. It was good to see a flash of the happy daughter she knew. 'OK, OK, you can go.'

From: Millypede@gmail.com
To: Carter@yahoo.com

Sorry I haven't been in touch. It's been kind of busy here, and my grandma has got really sick. Anyway, we're all trying to keep going as normal. I made a new friend, a girl who lives downstairs. She lives with her dad and he's pretty relaxed about letting her do things. I'm kind of jealous about that.

It's a bit weird being down here right now as it's getting Christmassy and we normally decorate the house around now. But my gran's really ill, so we don't know when we're coming back at the moment.

I'm going to go now, supper's ready. I hope everything is good with you.

Milly x

From: Carter@yahoo.com
To: Millypede@gmail.com

There you are! Hello.
Am I imagining it, or are you kind of hot and cold with me, Milly? Do you not want me to call you? What's going on? I mean I know you said your gran's ill, but I don't understand why you've changed so much. Can you send me your number?

Cx

CHAPTER 17

Friday 8th December

'How do I look?' Diana said, emerging from the toilets and swirling around in her newly tailored red dress. Laurie had taken in the waist and lowered the neckline a little, then brought the existing straps together, turning the dated style into an elegant halterneck.

'Wow,' Laurie said, bringing her hands together. Diana was beaming. The other women smiled appreciatively.

As Diana went to get changed again, Laurie settled down next to Joyce and began bagging up more winter coats. Joyce turned towards her.

'Lovely job you did on Diana's dress,' she said. 'You couldn't do something with this old blouse of mine, could you? I mean, if you're not too busy?' She held the fabric of the blouse away from her body and sat back slightly so that Laurie could get a proper look at it. The shape was flattering, but it had lost its colour – and something about it was stuck in a mid-80s rut. 'I hardly ever buy new things, you see,' Joyce said. 'Not on my pension.'

'Sure,' Laurie said. 'I can have a go. But don't kill me if you hate it.'

Joyce gave her a wink. 'With this old thing?' she said. 'The only way is up.'

'Dreadful news about the Christmas dinner,' Pam said, across the table. 'First time in years they've had to cancel it.'

The other women chorused their agreement. 'Such a shame,' Diana said.

Joyce turned to Laurie to explain. 'It's at one of the homeless shelters in Leeds,' she said, 'each year they put on a Christmas dinner, but this year, what with the cuts, they can't afford it.'

'Andy, the manager, is absolutely crushed,' Diana said. 'I spoke to him this week, he called to say thanks for the latest delivery – he works so hard for that place. Year on year he's put his own time into making Christmas Day at the shelter special. I don't think he's spent it with his own family since he joined. But he says seeing what a difference it makes for the homeless people there has always made it worthwhile. He's still trying to think of a way to raise money, find a way to put it on, but they've got more of their day-to-day costs to cover now, too. He can't see how they'll be able to do it.'

'All we can really contribute is the rag money,' Joyce said, 'but that's never much, is it?'

The women slowly returned to their work. The germ of an idea started to form in Laurie's mind.

'Hey,' Laurie said to Diana, 'how about this for a plan?'

Diana looked up from the linen-bound book she was logging figures in.

'Some of the clothes we send to the rag man are actually pretty good quality. They might not be warm enough for the winter, and obviously some of them are damaged, or faded, but there are some decent fabrics in there.'

Diana stayed quiet as she waited for Laurie to continue.

'What about if I had a go at customising them?'

'How would that help?' Diana asked, confused.

'With a few original outfits we could have a fashion show here – at the community centre – and auction the pieces off.' Laurie said. 'Christmas Glamour' – she waved her hand as if she were spelling it out in lights – 'Under the Hammer!'

She waited for Diana to absorb the brilliance of her idea.

'One-off designer pieces – with all the proceeds going towards Christmas lunch at the shelter.'

'Sounds like a lot of work,' Diana said, sceptically, dropping her head and going back to her note-making.

'I could handle it,' Laurie insisted, running with the idea now, excited at the prospect of having a new project to manage. 'We'd want it on a weekend, say the Saturday after next . . . the sixteenth, so that Andy would have time to get the dinner organised afterwards. It looks like I'll still be here then, and we'd have a week and a half to plan it. Tight, but I've managed worse. What do you reckon?'

'All right,' Diana said. 'If it'll keep you quiet, let's put it to the room. Ladies,' she said, her bold, brassy voice ringing out. 'Laurie's suggested a clothes auction – to raise money for the Christmas dinner. What do you think? Shall we give it a go?'

One by one, the women nodded, then chorused their approval.

'Looks like it's a yes,' Diana said.

'I was thinking of Christmas Glamour Under the Hammer as an evening event,' Laurie said as the women listened, mugs in hand, during their tea break. 'We could set up a catwalk . . .'

'There are some big wooden blocks out the back,' Diana suggested. 'I think the Am Dram people used them to make stages.'

'Great,' Laurie said, 'we can use those. Then we'd charge a small entrance fee to watch. And after the show, bidding on the pieces would start. So, we'll need some models,' Laurie smiled encouragingly. 'Go on, who's up for it?'

The women looked at each other hesitantly. For a moment no one said a word.

'I'm game,' said Joyce, raising her hand.

'I could give it a go,' Pam added. 'Although I'm not sure I'll be any good.' With her delicate bone structure and natural grace, Pam had a timeless glamour; Laurie was pleased she'd volunteered.

'I'll step in for one,' Diana said, and slowly another two women raised their hands too. 'Great,' said Laurie and made a note of all the names.

'So,' Laurie said, looking at her notes. 'I'm working on the designs, a couple of you have kindly offered to help out with the sewing, set-building's under control, the supermodels are sorted. What about publicity?'

Pam said her sister owned the local printers and could run them off some posters to put up around town. Julie, a quiet woman Laurie hadn't spoken to before, said that her son could set up the event online and put out invites that way. 'Ben's a whizz at that stuff,' she said.

'Right,' Laurie said. 'It sounds like we're well on our way, then. I guess we ought to get back to work.' She looked over at Diana for confirmation.

'Actually, while I have you all here,' Diana said, 'I wanted to invite you all to my Christmas drinks.' She pulled some invitations out of her handbag. 'None of that digital business for me,' she laughed, 'I prefer doing things the old-fashioned way.' She passed the cards around – they were hand-illustrated, with a picture of her cottage on the front and the name of each of the women written at the bottom.

'It's next Friday, the 15th, so it'll be the day before the show. We'll probably all be ready for a drink or two by then.'

Laurie smiled to herself as she took the invitation. She never thought she'd be so pleased to be invited to something at Diana's house.

She ripped the sacks open and sifted through the contents. Like a clothes moth she ignored the common cheap fabrics and went only for the best, laying them out on her table. Once she'd decided which materials to work with she found a large pair of scissors and cut out all the bits that were still usable, discarding any sections that were torn or frayed. There were some simple dresses and jackets that would make really good bases for the designs.

The other ladies gossiped at a gentle pace as they all worked. Being here reminded her of what it was she loved best, designing and making clothes, not sitting at a computer or battling with suppliers as she seemed to spend most of her time doing nowadays. Laurie chopped and sorted and filtered fabrics, starting to form pictures of how she wanted some of the finished pieces to look.

When she looked up at the wall clock it was nearly quarter to four. Laurie had been so caught up, she hadn't realised the time. Fifteen minutes. She tried to ignore her escalating nerves, but as the clock edged closer to the hour, she was acutely aware that Patrick was about to arrive. She thought of the way she'd felt talking to him earlier that week. What Diana had said last night – about him being single – meant that maybe she hadn't been imagining the chemistry between them. That morning she'd told herself that there was no harm in dressing so that she looked her best. She'd picked out one of her favourite outfits – indigo chinos and a pale yellow jumper, with chunky jewellery in jewel shades.

As the big hand on the clock hit twelve, Laurie felt a rush of anticipation. Her gaze went to the window, and she listened out for the sounds of a vehicle approaching. She pictured Patrick's warm smile and those dazzling blue eyes. What could she ask him? Or should she just play it cool and wait for him to say something first?

The minutes ticked by until at ten past four she finally heard the van pull up. Donna Summer was blasting out of the tinny radio and – miraculously, given the rush the day before – none of the other women seemed to have realised that the van had arrived. Laurie picked up a couple of the full bags on the floor and walked over towards the door, propping it with her foot so that she could bundle the bags through without ripping them. As the other women woke up to what was happening, she embraced her head start and walked towards the van, a smile creeping over her face as the driver's door opened. She instinctively started to pick up pace, her pulse racing.

A tall, grey-haired man with a thick beard stepped out of the van. Laurie's heart sank. She looked behind the man into the van's cab, but Patrick was nowhere to be seen.

'Here, let me take those off your hands, love,' the man stepped forward to offer.

Laurie stepped into the local hardware shop on Saturday morning, and cast her eye around the uncharted territory. There were two other customers in the lighting aisle. Laurie strode past them and made her way over to the household paints.

She'd been up until midnight the night before, bent over the sewing machine in Milly's room, making alterations to jackets and skirts, getting them ready for the auction. She'd sketched out some designs in the early evening. It took her mind off the disappointment she'd felt at not seeing Patrick. Making breakfast in the morning she'd been confronted by the smoke-blackened walls of the cottage kitchen again and, armed with Diana's tips, felt ready to tackle them.

She cast her eye over the emulsions and wood paints, and got up a photo of the paint colour on her iPhone. She held the phone up against the sampler sheet of shades and squinted, trying to work out which one was the closest match.

'It's Magnificent Magnolia,' came a voice over her shoulder. Male, husky, with a northern accent. She turned towards the sound and came face to face with Patrick. He was dressed in faded jeans and a black wool sweater and a smile had crept on to his lips. A wave of adrenalin coursed through her as their eyes met.

'Do you think?' she said, coyly, hoping her nerves didn't show. 'I was wondering about "Inimitable Ivory"' – she held up the shade so that he could look more closely.

'Definitely the magnolia,' he said, pointing at the tin. 'What are you painting, anyway?'

'Kitchen walls,' Laurie said, a little sheepishly. 'Had a bit of an incident. You?'

'DIY,' he said, holding up some shelf brackets.

There was a moment of silence and the air felt heavy between them.

'Can I give you a hand?' he offered. 'I'm not too bad at house painting, as it happens.'

Laurie hesitated for a moment. Having at least one person who knew what they were doing would definitely help.

'That would be good.' She picked up a roller and a couple of brushes and took them with the tin over to the counter. 'If you're sure you're not busy?'

'Oh, this shelf can wait,' he said, nodding to the

brackets in his hand with a wry smile, 'it's waited six months already. My DVD collection hasn't complained about the floor yet.'

'Nice road, this,' Patrick said, letting out a whistle as they passed the pretty cottages on Snowdrop Lane.

'Oh, it's not my cottage,' Laurie explained hurriedly. 'I'm house-sitting for a friend. I'm not from here.'

Patrick tilted his head, seemingly taking in her sharp haircut, high heels and jewel-toned accessories. 'You're not from the village?' he laughed. 'You're kidding me.'

Inside the cottage, Laurie and Patrick covered the countertop and floor in newspaper, and Laurie blasted up some tunes while they worked. Patrick had stripped down to a T-shirt to paint and Laurie couldn't help but notice his toned body. After twenty minutes they'd got the kitchen looking more or less the same as when she'd arrived, although the newly painted patches had come up brighter.

'It's looking pretty good now, isn't it?' Laurie said, standing back.

'Yes, all ready for you to burn something else,' Patrick joked.

Laurie rolled her eyes playfully in response. 'Tea?' she offered.

'I thought you'd never ask,' he teased. 'Wait,' he said and put one hand on her shoulder and with the other touched her hair, reaching to take out some paint that had dried there.

As he pulled the fleck of paint out gently, Laurie noticed the enticing fullness of his mouth. He was so close and for a moment she thought he might just –

A picture of Jay's face flashed up in Laurie's mind. She remembered the comforting, sexy smell of him. His dark eyes, the way he made her laugh, just seemed to get her. As Patrick leaned in closer, and she smelled his aftershave, something inside her resisted. She turned away abruptly to flick the kettle on. 'Yorkshire Gold?' she asked.

'Sure,' Patrick said quietly, pulling back. 'Two sugars.'

Damn it, Laurie thought as she got out the mugs. How was it that Jay could ruin things for her even when he was miles away?

'Thanks for the help,' Laurie said, her voice restrained. 'I really appreciate it.'

The moment had passed, the intimacy between them had gone – she wanted to kick herself.

'You're welcome,' Patrick said, as she got out teabags and put them in their mugs. 'Listen,' he said, touching her forearm so that she'd look back at him. She glanced up into his blue eyes, his gaze unwavering, intense. She felt a shiver of excitement run over her skin.

'I know you're not here for long,' Patrick said. 'But tell me you've got time for me to take you for a drink?'

*

As Laurie closed the door after Patrick later that evening, a smile spread across her face, and she did a little jig on the spot. She had a date. And he was really, really nice.

She put on a CD and went over to light the fire. After a little while the small flames on the logs flickered into life, and Laurie settled down at the kitchen table with a doorstep sandwich laden with Stilton. Things in Skipley were definitely looking up.

CHAPTER 18

Saturday 9th December

Rachel poured out glasses of orange juice for her and for Zak. She decided that now was as good a time as any to raise it. Yes, with Bea in a coma they had bigger things to think about, but she couldn't ignore what looked very much like stealing.

Rachel sat down with Zak at the kitchen table and put out some of the objects she'd found during the course of their stay: the plaintain, breadfruit and plectrum. Aiden and Milly had claimed to know nothing about them, so the list of suspects was down to one. 'I'm puzzled, Zak. Help me out. Do you have any idea where these things have come from?' she asked gently.

His green eyes wide in his freckled face, he was the picture of innocence – but he was wriggling in his seat. 'I haven't stolen anything.'

Rachel waited for him to go on.

'They were given to me,' Zak insisted.

'By who?'

'Lily gave me the fruit,' Zak said, picking it up, and

running a chubby finger over its rough surface. 'It's a breadfruit – a fruit, but it fills you up like bread,' he smiled. 'And she also gave me the plant-thing.'

'Plaintain,' Rachel said. 'And Lily is . . . ?' She tried to place the name, she knew she'd heard it only recently.

'. . . The nice lady downstairs,' Zak filled in the gap. Of course, Rachel remembered now.

'It's my fault,' Milly shouted from the front room. Rachel got up from her seat and went into the living room where Steve Carrell in an elf suit was frozen on the plasma screen. Milly turned around to face her mum. 'Don't blame Zak. I let him wander around a bit when you were at the hospital, run up and down the stairs and stuff. I didn't realise he'd start making all of these friends. Freak.' She rolled her eyes playfully.

'Oh, right,' Rachel said. Milly really shouldn't have let Zak run wild. But she and Milly had been getting on well so far that day, so Rachel chose not to ruin things. As Milly set the DVD to play again, Rachel turned back to Zak. 'You haven't been bothering anyone, have you?'

'No,' Zak protested. 'They invited me. It was only Lily, and Jay – and he's your friend too. So,' he asked, 'Can I not be in trouble please?'

'You're all right,' Rachel said, ruffling his mousy hair.

'Why don't you come and meet Lily yourself?' Zak asked, picking up a 3D jigsaw from the counter that

Aiden had brought down for him. 'We can show her this. She loves jigsaws, and she's really good at them.'

'OK,' Rachel said. 'Five minutes. If you're sure she's happy to have visitors?'

'Yes,' Zak said. 'She invited me the other day, and she's going to go crazy about this jigsaw. Wait till I tell her it's a 3D one.'

Rachel ducked her head into the living room. 'Milly, do you want to come downstairs with us and meet one of the neighbours?'

'No thanks,' she said, her eyes glued to the TV. 'This film is nearly at the end. It's getting to the bit where they all have to sing to make Santa's sleigh take off.'

Rachel recalled watching the film together the previous year, the whole family watching on the sofa and armchairs at the cottage. Far from home, with Bea in hospital, the happy memory was almost painful to revisit.

Zak and Rachel walked down the stairs together, and Zak chattered on merrily. 'She said the other day that she likes me visiting. She's old, you see, and her grandchildren live on an island. She showed me on her globe – it's miles away.' His steps sped up.

'Do you know where?' Rachel asked.

'Where the pirates are,' Zak said. 'The Caribbean. She's always smiling. Well, usually. The other day I surprised her, and she looked a bit sad. She said something about her wallpaper.'

They reached the ground floor and Zak pointed over to the blue door on the left-hand side of the entrance hall. He walked over, reached up and knocked on it. A moment later the door was answered by an older woman wearing a sunshine-yellow dress set off by pretty gold drop earrings with green stones. Rachel's gaze drifted to the woman's apron – red, with floury handprints on it, only slightly disrupting the elegance of the overall look. The woman smiled at Rachel, then bent down slightly to put a hand on Zak's shoulder. 'Back already? Now here's a surprise,' she said, in a warm West Indian accent. She stood back up again. 'And you must be Zak's mother,' she said, holding out a hand. 'This young gentleman has been telling me all about you. I'm Lily.'

'Hi.' Rachel held out her hand. 'Yes, Rachel. Pleased to meet you.'

'Well, come in, won't you?'

'Zak wanted to show you his new puzzle,' Rachel said, apologetically, 'I hope that's OK.'

'Isn't that lovely, dear?' She looked at Zak's new toy as he held it up for her. 'Of course it's all right.'

Rachel stepped tentatively into the flat, which was colourful and cared-for, with a bright green sofa and mustard-yellow throws and cushions. A decorative punch bowl sat on a flowery tablecloth in the kitchen, and gold-framed photos of friends and family lined the walls. As she turned, she saw that some of the prettiest wallpaper was peeling away, and sections of the flooring and walls were damaged. The mess looked out of place in such a well-kept flat. Perhaps that was what Zak had been talking about on their way downstairs.

'The puzzle's 3D, Lily,' Zak said. 'It's of Santa's grotto, with reindeers. It says ages eight and up, and I'm only just six. Mum and Milly are older, but they're no good at jigsaws.'

Lily raised an eyebrow at Rachel. 'Is that so?'

'I'm afraid that's absolutely true,' she said, holding her hands up and smiling to show she wasn't offended. 'Really, you're welcome to it.'

'It would be an honour,' Lily said. 'And your timing couldn't be better. I've just finished my baking for the day. I've been making my famous Caribbean Christmas cake.' She took in a deep breath through her nostrils. 'Just get a lungful of that smell – mmm, mmm.'

In the living room, Lily put her reading glasses on and bent down over the coffee table so that she could help Zak to find the straight pieces.

Rachel watched Zak and Lily smiling as they worked together, just as Zak usually did with Bea, playing games on Christmas Day. Rachel felt a tug at her heart – it was just like a scene from the cottage, with Lily in Bea's place. She thought of Bea lying motionless in the hospital, and as it struck her that they might never have another family Christmas with her a lump came to her throat. Could the memories she already had of

Bea be the only ones she'd ever have? Without any warning, Rachel's tears started to fall.

Lily caught sight of her crying. 'Are you OK, dear?' Lily mouthed silently, over Zak's head.

Rachel bit her lip and wiped away the tears, giving a little nod and trying to force a smile. She felt ridiculous – here she was in a stranger's flat, sobbing.

'Zak,' Lily said, gently. His eyes darted up from the jigsaw. 'Now I have your fine young self here, could I ask a favour? You know that computer thing you offered to help me with? Do you think we could look at it now?'

Zak nodded and sprang to his feet. 'Sure.'

'Your mum and I'll keep going with the jigsaw,' Lily added, 'the computer's just in the kitchen, on the counter.'

Zak dashed up from his seat and into the kitchen, then turned briefly to Rachel. She put on as normal an expression as she could manage. 'I'm setting up her Skype,' he said proudly, before dashing out of the room.

'My son got me a laptop for my birthday,' Lily explained, leaning forward. 'Said we could talk on it – I would be able to see the little ones, my grandkids, over in Trinidad.' Lily shrugged and smiled. 'Thing is, I haven't worked out how to do anything more than email on it.'

'Oh,' Rachel said, brushing away her tears, a swell of pride almost pushing away the sadness. 'Zak's great with computers, he'll sort you out.'

'He said it's easy.' Lily smiled. 'Ha! Well, I'll be the judge of that. So, dear,' she continued, her voice just above a whisper. 'Tell your Auntie Lily. What's the matter? Are you OK?'

'Oh, yes, fine,' Rachel said, sitting up straighter in her seat.

'I mean, are you really OK? Because your friend Laurie asked me to keep an eye out for you – and you don't look that OK to me.'

'Sorry,' Rachel said, accepting the monogrammed white handkerchief Lily passed her. 'I don't know why I'm telling you all this when we've only just met.' Rachel shook her head, but Lily just smiled and nodded for her to go on.

'It's just hard,' Rachel said. 'The waiting, not knowing whether or not Bea is going to wake up. The kids seeing their grandmother like that.'

'Hard times are the real test of a family, aren't they?' Lily said.

Rachel nodded, and thought of the strain on her relationship with Aiden as they both struggled to keep normal life going.

'But, if you all stick together, Rachel, you'll come

out the other side stronger. I guarantee it. And Zak – he's a smart one, isn't he?'

Rachel smiled. 'Yes he is. And you're right,' she said, taking a deep breath. 'And Bea would hate to know that we were worrying about her like this.'

'Found it,' Zak shouted, bursting back into the room with Lily's laptop in his hands.

He perched on the edge of Lily's armchair and turned the laptop to face her. 'So you've got a webcam up here,' he pointed, 'and over there they'll have one on their computer too. Mum can you set you up an account, and all we need to do is find a time when your family are online and we can call.'

Lily smiled, and raised her eyebrows in happy surprise at Rachel. 'How exciting,' she said. She checked her watch, but her face fell. 'Oh, but they'll be at the beach now.'

'That's OK,' Zak said, 'You just need to text them so they can say when they're free.'

'We might have to save that for another day, I'm afraid, Zak.' Rachel said, getting to her feet. 'You and Milly need some tea. Your sister'll be wondering what's happened to us both.'

'Come back another day, in that case,' Lily said to Zak. 'And we can finish off the jigsaw too.'

'And I'll be seeing you again too, I hope,' Lily said to Rachel, smiling, and then leaning forward to envelop her in a warm, comforting hug.

From: Millypede@gmail.com

To: Carter@yahoo.com

Hi C,

Thanks for the new playlist you made me, I like it.

Nothing's up. I'm sorry if I made you feel bad. I guess it's easier to email than speak on the phone, that's all. I feel like my parents are always listening out, and in this flat they'd be able to hear everything.

I've had a good day today. I went with Nikki to Camden – have you ever been there? We had the best day hanging out by the lock, and buying jewellery and things. I picked up a couple of presents for friends and then we walked down to where Amy Winehouse used to live. There are still some flowers and things in front of the house, and there were other people who'd come to see it. Everyone was chatting and it was cool.

We met up with some of Nikki's friends from school – I know some of them already from when I went to Art Club with her the other day. Two of the guys, Alex and Ryan, had brought some beers with them and we walked down to the canal, just drinking and talking for ages.

How are things over in Skipley?

Mx

From: Carter@yahoo.com
To: Millypede@gmail.com

Milly,

So, maybe I'm reading this wrong – but first you don't want me to call, and now you're out with this girl and a load of guys, drinking, and you're telling me about what a great time you had?

Something seems a little wrong with this picture, Milly? I know we're not going out or anything, but you know I like you. Call me a fool, but I didn't really expect you to be down there flirting with other guys and lining up alternatives. When we met you seemed like a nice enough girl, but it sounds like London has changed you.

C

From: Millypede@gmail.com
To: LaurieGreenaway@virgin.net

Hi Laurie,

OK, I hope you don't mind me emailing again. So, this guy I've been talking to has been getting really stressy. He thinks I'm down here flirting with other people – but I'm not. Of course I'm not. I've made a couple of friends here, and that's it. To be honest mostly I'm just thinking about Granny and hoping she gets better. Like all of us are. What should I say to him?

From: LaurieGreenaway@virgin.net
To: Millypede@gmail.com

Hi Mills,

First of all, I'm so sorry to hear about your Granny Bea. I'm glad you wrote, I'm thinking of you all and send you an extra-special hug. It must be such a hard time for you guys. From what I hear your grandma is a real fighter, though.

So that's weird, that this guy is getting jealous – but I suppose maybe he's at home, bored, and can't help thinking you're having far more fun without him? Perhaps if you could reassure him that you're looking forward to seeing him again when you're back?

Lxx

CHAPTER 19

Monday 11th December

'Are you kidding?' Laurie said, sipping her mulled wine and laughing. 'Are they going to give you a fat suit to wear underneath the Santa outfit?'

'Yes,' Patrick said, sheepishly. 'Although in a way I'm glad they think I need it.' He peered down at his toned stomach. 'God, the things I do for this job,' he laughed, 'out on Christmas Eve, in the middle of the village, shaking a bucket.'

It was Saturday evening, and Patrick and Laurie were sitting in the Lion and the Unicorn, a small pub that was a ten-minute walk from the cottage, across what were now some very snowy fields.

Patrick had come to pick her up at seven, just as she had finished applying her eyeliner and putting the finishing touches to her outfit: a simple black sweater dress that set off her glossy bob, accessorised with chunky silver bracelets. When she opened the front door Patrick gazed at her admiringly. 'Hi,' he said, greeting her with a kiss on the cheek. She took in the faint smell of aftershave. 'You look gorgeous. It's a shame you're going to have to pile on the layers. Have you seen it?' He looked around and Laurie saw that snow was falling in heavy flakes.

With a little slipping and sliding along the way they'd arrived at the pub and Patrick ordered them in some mulled wine, finding them a quiet, candlelit table in the corner. She'd taken a sip of the warm drink and feeling had started to return to her fingers. The pub was full, with locals crowding around the bar, fairy lights twinkling above it and Wham's 'Last Christmas' playing out over the speakers.

'I'd chuck you 50p,' Laurie said, imagining Patrick with a Santa beard. He'd probably still look pretty hot.

'Is that all?' he protested, laughing. 'I'm clearly going to have to up my game then. Maybe I could moonlight in the evenings as an elf to double the donations?'

'Too tall,' Laurie said. 'Such a shame I'll probably be back in London by then – otherwise obviously I'd be the first to offer my assistance.'

Laurie kept having to remind herself that she hardly knew Patrick. She normally felt so awkward on dates, searching around for something to say – but with Patrick it was easy. She felt really relaxed in his company.

'But seeing as you've got a bit of bulking up to do for your role,' she said, grabbing a pub menu from the side, 'shall we get some food? I'm starving.' Her appetite was starting to return – since she'd been in Skipley, she'd started enjoying food again.

'A woman after my own heart,' Patrick said.

As they got up to go to the bar to order, Laurie instinctively picked up her handbag and phone and took them with her.

'It's OK to leave your stuff, you know.' Patrick smiled.

'Oh,' Laurie said, quickly scanning the room. Admittedly the potential robbers were limited. In fact, wasn't that Ben, the teenager from the café, over by the jukebox? She was pretty sure he wasn't a criminal. He looked up and acknowledged her with a nod.

She put her things back down on the bench and went with Patrick to order. She shrugged. 'City habits die hard.'

The landlord's expression was kind and welcoming. He was in his mid-fifties, with greying hair and a slight ruddiness to his cheeks. 'I've seen you around, I think,' he said. 'What's your name?'

'This is Laurie,' Patrick said, before she could answer. 'She's staying in Hawthorne Cottage. Laurie, this is Graham.'

As Laurie reached her hand out to shake Graham's, a sheepdog dashed towards her, snuffling energetically at her feet and legs. 'Wahhhey,' she said as the dog nudged the back of her knees with his nose and nearly knocked her off balance. She clutched on to Patrick's arm to steady herself.

'And this,' Patrick said, bending down to ruffle the

dog's fur and getting covered in licks in the process, 'is Gadget.'

'Been here in the pub since he was just a puppy,' Graham said to Laurie, 'he wouldn't be without the company. Loves people, he does. He thinks he's human, really.'

Gadget let out a little bark of confirmation, then snuffled around Patrick's ear.

'Anyway,' Patrick laughed, 'where was I? Kitchen's open, isn't it? Lasagne, and what did you fancy, Laurie?'

Laurie thought for a moment of her usual diet in London – sushi, Diet cola. 'Same for me,' she said.

When Graham came to take away their empty plates, Laurie was well on her way to merry. 'That was lovely,' she said to Graham, leaning back into the worn velvet seat. 'Thank you.'

'So tell me,' Patrick said, as Graham walked away. 'What's a woman like you doing in a place like Skipley?'

Laurie smiled. 'I don't know,' she said. 'I suppose everyone needs a break from their life once in a while.'

She took a sip of her drink. 'What's your excuse, Patrick? Are you from here?'

'From the village? No,' Patrick said. 'It's a long story.'

'And we're in a hurry?' Laurie glanced up at the clock and realised it didn't even matter what time it was. There was no reason to rush in Skipley.

'OK,' he took a sip of his drink and shifted in his seat. 'I'm from an even smaller village, if you can believe it, just down the train line, you probably passed it on the way in. Just a couple of houses and a corner shop. I applied for a job in a bank in Leeds and got it, so I moved. The money was good – I had my own flat and life, friends over there.'

Laurie raised an eyebrow. 'It sounds like you had it made. So what changed, what brought you . . . ?'

'Jack,' Patrick said.

Oh no. He's gay, Laurie thought, her heart sinking. No wonder. It had all seemed far too perfect.

Patrick must have clocked her disappointed expression, as he quickly filled in the gap. 'My brother. Jack's ten years younger than me but we've always got along. He's chilled, easygoing, funny. Or, at least, he used to be.' Patrick had a distant look in his eye.

'With my new job in town I wasn't seeing him that much, and last year when he was sixteen he went through a break-up that hit him really hard. He started drinking a lot and stopped going out, stopped looking after himself. One night he just disappeared. The police looked for a while, but then just seemed to give up, they said they couldn't help if he didn't want to be found. But I knew deep down that he did. That he needed us. So I took some time off work and started looking.'

'How did you know where to start?' Laurie asked.

'I didn't. He'd fallen out with most of his friends, so there were no leads there. I had a gut feeling he would have come near to where I was, so I started with the inner-city homeless shelters in Leeds.'

'And . . . ?' Laurie prompted.

'I found him,' Patrick said. 'In the shelter Andy runs now. It wasn't a pretty picture, Jack had been drinking heavily and sleeping rough for weeks – but he was safe, thank God. Andy helped us get access to a support programme for Jack – it took a year, but now he's in his own place and working part-time.'

Patrick paused, took a breath, shook his head slightly at the pain of the memory.

'And I take it you never went back to the bank?' Laurie asked.

'No I didn't,' Patrick said, shaking his head. 'Everything looked a bit different after that.'

'And do you see Jack much now?'

Graham rang the bell and Patrick turned towards the sound. 'Looks like it's last orders already. Shall we have one for the road?'

'How did that come around so quickly?' Laurie said, struggling to do up the buttons on her duffel coat. It seemed like just a few minutes after last orders, but the pub had emptied out and Graham had started to drop heavy hints that it was time to go.

Outside the thick snow crunched as Laurie and Patrick stepped in it. In the moonlight the countryside glittered prettily. 'Walk me home?' she asked, tipsily.

'It would be my pleasure,' Patrick said.

Laurie linked her arm through his. They walked together and he held on tight to her as she clambered over a stile. The physical closeness reminded her of being with Jay, but the only way to dull those memories was to make new ones, she decided. As they neared the cottage Laurie rooted round in her handbag for the key.

'Come in for a coffee?' she said. He nodded yes, and she dragged him by the elbow into the cottage, laughing as the heavy wooden door slammed shut behind them.

As Patrick turned her around to face him, Laurie's laughter finally slowed to a stop and the cottage fell silent. His blue eyes burned into hers and her heart raced as he drew her closer. Gently, he kissed her on the mouth. Laurie kissed him back, losing herself in the sensation and pressing her body into his. She wasn't sure what she was doing, but it definitely, definitely felt good.

The phone next to Laurie's bed rang, breaking into her dream. With her eyes still closed, she scrambled for it and answered with a bleary 'Yes?'

As she spoke, she opened her eyes and glanced around. Rumpled sheets. A trail of clothing leading up her bed. Oh God. Patrick. She hadn't. Already?

She wasn't naked, was she? She glanced under the covers at the Take That T-shirt she was wearing and frowned. It was one of Rachel's. Perhaps naked would be better.

'Laurie, darling, it's me, Mum.' Her excited voice broke into Laurie's thoughts.

'Mum, hi,' Laurie said, rubbing her eyes and trying to sound more awake than she felt. 'How are you?'

'Good, thanks, sweetheart. We are having the most gorgeous spell of hot weather out here, you wouldn't believe it's December ...'

Laurie brought the duvet up closer around her and squinted at the bright winter sunshine pouring in through the windows. Patrick wasn't in the bathroom, was he? She sat up to check – no, all clear.

'Mmm-hmmm,' Laurie said, only half-listening.

'Yes, beautiful – warm enough to eat outside, I went with Ana to the square yesterday and we had a lovely lunch there. And how are you, darling, are you having a good break?'

'Hi. It's good, Mum, yes. Enjoying it.'

Then Laurie spotted it, a note on the pillow next to her. She quickly scanned the piece of paper.

Morning Laurie,

Great evening with you. You seem pretty out for the count, so I'm getting a taxi – but let's do it again sometime?

Patrick. 09234 939384

P.S. A Take That fan? I would never have guessed ☺

Laurie breathed a sigh of relief. So Patrick hadn't stayed – and somehow, she didn't seem to have blown it. He wanted to see her again.

'Mum, listen ...' Laurie said, her head starting to throb with the effects of last night's wine. 'I've actually just woken up. Is it OK if I call you back later?'

'Yes, darling, of course.' Her mum sounded a little hurt. 'Let's speak later.'

Laurie approached the morning with her usual Sunday hangover routine: doorsteps of buttered toast, a bath and a copy of *Grazia*, which, thank God, the local newsagent had stocked just for her. As she sank down into the bubbles she thought about Patrick's note again. Was it really a good idea to call him? Or was she just setting herself up for a fall?

She thought back to the summer, with Jay. But things had changed. With work off the agenda, there was space in her life to care about someone else. She was stronger now.

She wanted to give it a chance. So Patrick wasn't her usual type – he was younger than her, for starters – but she felt good with him, relaxed. She shampooed her hair and thought back to when Patrick had touched it, recalled the excitement she'd felt. Jay had moved on, and now she was ready to do the same.

CHAPTER 20

Tuesday 12th December

'There's still no change,' Rachel said, on the phone to Laurie.

'Oh God, Rach. I'm sorry to hear that.'

'It's pretty tough, seeing Bea like this, it just makes you feel so powerless. All we can do is keep talking to her and hope that somehow she's listening and getting stronger. Laurie – I'm sorry to have to ask this, but would you mind if we stayed on another week or so, maybe longer?' Rachel went on, 'It's hard to predict exactly when, but until the 20th, maybe? We could book into a hotel after that. It's just – we want to be here with her.'

'Of course. Please stay, and take whatever time you need,' Laurie said. 'Don't worry about me, I'm just fine up here.'

'Hi, guys,' Jay said, putting his head around the door to the living room. Zak looked up from the dinosaurs he was colouring in, and Milly from her homework.

'Great, nearly a full house,' Jay said. 'Now, are you up for a challenge?'

Milly narrowed her eyes, suspicious. 'What sort of a challenge?'

'A surprise for Lily,' Rachel said, taking a seat on the sofa and motioning for Jay to sit down.

'A surprise!' Zak said, jumping up.

Jay sat down next to Rachel and Zak perched on the arm of the sofa. 'Yes. We're going to fix up her flat and make it beautiful.'

'Do you remember, Zak,' Rachel said, 'how the wallpaper was all peeling off? And the floor?'

'Yes,' Zak nodded. 'Lily was sad about that. I saw her.'

Rachel turned to Milly to explain. 'The council did some electrics work and haven't got round to tidying it up yet.'

'I've been trying to get her to let me fix it,' Jay said. 'but she keeps insisting there's no need. Now she's away for a couple of days, looking after a friend who's just got out of hospital. I've got the keys to her flat – we all keep spares just in case. I've had a whipround and everyone in the block has put in some money so that we can get some decent wallpaper for her. I've been making some furniture to replace her shelves, so we can get those put in too.'

'Anyway,' Jay said. 'What we really need right now is more hands on deck – and a little interior design expertise. Plus a big, colourful banner to welcome Lily home. Do you think you could help?'

'Sure,' Milly said. 'We can do that, can't we, Mum?'

Milly, Rachel, Jay and Zak looked around Lily's kitchen and living room. Milly pointed at the areas of ripped wallpaper. 'I don't know if we'll find an exact match for the sunflower print. It's really nice, but it looks quite old, doesn't it? But we could keep some in the alcove, as a feature, and get some new wallpaper in a plain colour, or a print that works with it.'

'A warm red could work,' Rachel said, glancing around at Lily's bright colour scheme. 'We could paint the skirting to match, and, if there's any money left, get a couple of cushions to match and tie it in. Jay, will the new shelving go here?' she asked, pointing to the battered wooden unit.

'Yes,' he nodded. 'It's a little bigger, but it will make more of the space, and there'll be an extra shelf to display her photos on, but the width will be the same.'

'What about the floor?' Zak said, pushing back the ripped lino with the toe of his trainer.

'I know a discount flooring place,' Jay said. 'And this colour should be an easy enough match.'

Milly pulled the hood on her grey marl sweatshirt up over her head and the sleeves over her hands. 'Right, shall we hit the shops?' she said. 'It's freezing in here.'

'Right, cups of tea and then let's get going,' Rachel said, putting on the kettle.

Milly and Jay put down the bags of shopping, and Zak sat down at the kitchen table. 'We bought loads,' he said, with a smile.

Rachel and Milly had found a good-quality red wallpaper on sale at the local department store – and, with what they'd saved, had bought a roll of patterned yellow trim to complement the sunflower print.

'This was an absolute bargain,' Milly said, bringing out a golden-yellow rug. 'And it should warm things up a bit in the living room, keep the heat in better than the floorboards.'

'The snake's my favourite,' Zak said, pulling an animal-shaped draft-excluder out of a carrier bag. Rachel had spotted it in a charity shop – it was almost new and the perfect size to block the gap under Lily's back door and stop the icy breeze.

Milly put on an apron and started laying newspaper down. 'I texted Nikki and she's coming to join us after school.'

'Great,' Jay said, taking Lily's cookbooks off the set of shelves that the council workmen had dented and damaged. 'Wow,' he said, taking one from the pile and opening the front cover. 'So this is her secret.' He held it up for Rachel and Milly to see. '*Lily's Caribbean Christmas*,' he said, reading the words on the front cover.

Milly looked over at her mum, her eyes shining with tears, and Rachel gently took her hand.

At around midday Jay and Sean brought the new set of shelves from Jay's workshop. They were made from a warm, hazelnut-shade of wood, and sanded to a really smooth finish. 'Let's put them over here for now, while we're still working,' Jay said, nodding over to the living room.

Zak was crouched on the floor making a banner for them to hang by the door. Rachel had pencilled the letters for him to colour in. 'Welcome Home, Lily!' Sean, Nikki's dad, read out the message. 'She's going to love that.'

Zak smiled. 'Yellow's her favourite colour, so that's why I've done a lot of it.'

Nikki and Milly were chatting to one another as they scraped away at the wallpaper. Rachel got up from where she had been crouching down putting in the new tiles and went over to see the new furniture. 'That's gorgeous,' she said, running a finger over the wood. 'Are they your own design?'

'Thanks,' Jay said, 'yes. The idea is that no two pieces of furniture are quite the same, I make them to fit the house and suit the people who use them.'

'Do you ...' Rachel said, an idea forming in her head. But her thoughts trailed off as she caught a snatch of the conversation going on behind her.

233

'So, Milly, have you heard any more from that guy?' Rachel heard Nikki whisper. 'The one back home.'

'Yes,' Milly said, under her breath. 'Loads. But shhh – my mum's only over there. I'll tell you about it later, OK?'

Rachel's brow furrowed. A guy – back home. So she'd been right to think that something must be going on. But why hadn't Milly said anything about it?

CHAPTER 21

Wednesday 13th December

'How about a walk today?' Patrick said.

'Sure,' Laurie said, trying to play it cool. While she wasn't normally keen on walking unnecessarily, she couldn't wait to see Patrick again. Plus she'd also started to go slightly cross-eyed sewing clothes for the fashion show on Saturday – a break and a bit of fresh air would do her good.

'Great. There's a path that runs up to the ruin of a windmill,' he said. 'with a view of the village where I grew up. The snow's melting a bit now, but it still looks lovely out there. I could come by yours at midday?'

Laurie hurriedly put together an outfit that said 'country chic' and that she'd actually be able to walk in. She'd gone for skinny jeans, wellies, and a tight, black cashmere jumper with a fake fur gilet. Underneath she was wearing her favourite red lingerie.

Patrick arrived at noon. He leaned in to give her a kiss on the lips hello. Couldn't they just – she turned to look at the stairs, it was such a short distance upstairs to the bedroom. But no, she told herself, just because his touch, his kiss, his smell, melted her – it was still probably better not to rush things.

She glimpsed Patrick's silver Audi parked in the driveway out the front.

'So we're driving to the walk, are we?' she asked. Good, but bad – people only drove to walks when they were going on really, really long ones.

He looked over at her and smiled. 'Yes, it's a little way away,' he said. A sharp bark came from the front seat and Laurie saw that the sheepdog from the pub was in the back seat. 'I borrowed Gadget,' Patrick said, 'to keep us company.'

Laurie raised an eyebrow. Gadget was fine, for a dog. But dogs and mud and her designer jeans seemed like a recipe for disaster. Couldn't they just go somewhere normal for this date, like for lunch?

'The walk's beautiful,' Patrick assured her. 'You'll enjoy it, I promise.'

As they got into the car Patrick said, 'So, sounds like you have a busy weekend coming up. How are the preparations going for the fashion show?'

'Fine, thanks,' Laurie replied. 'Still loads to do, but we're on track. Are you going to Diana's drinks on Friday?'

'Definitely,' Patrick said. 'Love a Christmas party.'

Patrick didn't say a word as they drove out of the

village, and neither did she, but the atmosphere in the car was calm. Around them, the snow had started to melt, but the trees and fields still had a thick dusting of white, with a sprinkling of black birds on them. Laurie glanced back at Patrick – he must have practically poured her, drunk, into bed the other night; she thought of the trail of clothes she'd left. Normally she'd be mortified, but for some reason she wasn't. It just didn't seem a big deal – perhaps this was what relaxing felt like?

They stopped and parked in a lay-by near the top of a hill. They let Gadget out of the back seat, and Patrick led Laurie by the hand to a look-out point by the side of the road. Snowy fields and hills stretched out for miles around. It was the perfect Christmas scene.

'So that's where we're headed,' Patrick said, pointing at the ruins of a windmill on a faraway hill. 'From up there you can see my village.' Laurie took in the expanse of fields, threaded through with a stream, that lay between where they were standing and the ruins of the windmill – their destination.

'That speck?' Laurie said, squinting. 'It looks like it's a hundred miles away.' She reached into her bag and took out her Gucci shades, putting them on to dull the glare of the winter sunshine on the remains of the snow. Patrick challenged her with a look. 'OK, I trust you,' she said, smiling and holding her hands up. 'If you say it's going to be fun, then I believe you.'

And it was fun, at least at first. They'd walked across the first field in a leisurely way, arm in arm, the cool air sharp but refreshing, and chatted easily as Gadget padded along beside them. But as they crossed the fence into the next field, Gadget spotted a stray sheep and dashed over, barking at high volume to terrorise it. As Patrick ran after him, Laurie continued on and got one wellie boot stuck in a frosty, muddy ditch. She couldn't lift it out without her sock-clad foot coming out, so was, essentially, glued to the spot. 'Help!' she yelled.

Patrick got Gadget on the lead, and returned to Laurie, helping her keep her balance while he prised her stuck-fast boot out of the ditch. 'Countryside hazard,' he said, putting her boot back on. 'Don't let it put you off.'

The next field sloped down, and they began to descend into a valley. A partially frozen stream, lined with trees, lay at the foot of the hill. They passed a robin perched on a fence post, who flew away as Gadget bounded towards it.

Patrick took her by the hand again.

'Race you to the water,' he challenged her.

Before Laurie could protest, Patrick had set off. She ran after him, crunching over the grass and picking up speed as the incline got sharper, until, metres from the stream she passed him by, holding her hands up and letting out a celebratory cry. Without a means to brake, she crashed victoriously into a tree trunk by the stream, then bent over in breathless laughter.

Patrick caught up with her. 'Hey,' he said, panting, as she slowly got her own breath back. 'You're pretty fast.'

'Used to running away from boys,' Laurie joked, swinging her hair, her back to the tree.

'Oh yeah?' Patrick said, moving closer and pinning her arms gently against the rough bark.

He pressed his body against hers. 'I'd like to see you try and get away from this one.'

She half-heartedly attempted to make her escape, and Gadget barked by her side. Then, looking up, she suddenly felt the closeness of Patrick's face, his mouth, his lips just inches from hers.

He leaned in and kissed her, lingering on her lips. As Laurie stopped her play-struggle and reached a hand up to his hair to pull him closer she kissed him more deeply, not wanting it to end.

'So tell me one thing,' Patrick asked, as hand in hand they began the ascent up a sweeping mud path to the windmill. 'How is it that you don't have plans, this close to Christmas?'

'My mum lives in Spain,' she said.

'And don't you have any other family? What about your dad?'

Couldn't they just go back to kissing? Laurie thought. Were all these questions really necessary?

'Not an option,' she said, bending down to pick up a stone in her path, and turning to throw it back down the hill, towards the stream.

As she walked up the hill with Patrick she thought back to the time, nearly ten years ago, when she'd last seen her dad. Back then she'd still thought that they could fix things.

That Christmas Eve, Laurie had clutched her umbrella and walked with purpose down the unfamiliar west London street, the address she'd found in the Internet records clear in her mind. As she passed the big, semi-detached houses the enormity of what she was doing began to sink in; she would be seeing her dad again, after years of not talking. After he'd left her mum when Laurie was thirteen, she'd sworn this day wouldn't ever come. But in her twenties, she'd begun to hope. She peered into the windows, saw the tall Christmas trees in high-ceilinged living rooms and felt a pang of envy. These were the kind of houses she had always wanted to live in. Like Rachel's family home.

When Laurie reached number fifty-six, she took a deep breath and rang the bell. But when the door opened, it wasn't her dad, but a boy of about ten, who stood there staring at her.

'Is Duncan Greenaway in?' Laurie asked, summoning up her courage.

'Dad!' the boy called out over his shoulder. 'There's a woman here to see you.'

A woman with dark-red hair, about twenty-five, the same age Laurie was then, stepped forward into the hallway. 'He's helping Mum with the car, Andrew,' she said to the boy. She looked up at Laurie and smiled. 'Sorry, my dad's busy with something, can I help?'

As Laurie's eyes met hers, she saw her own features echoed in the other woman's face.

'God, it's pouring out there,' she went on, 'would you like to come in?'

Instead of Laurie's dark colouring, the woman in front of her had her dad's eyes – clear and blue.

'No,' Laurie said, pain building in her chest. 'I won't stay.' A wave of intense shame overwhelmed her. 'But thanks anyway.' Laurie turned and walked away.

'So here we are,' Patrick announced. 'We made it.' He draped an arm around Laurie's shoulders as they reached the ruins of the windmill. She fought back the tears the memory had brought to her eyes.

'And there,' he continued, 'is my village. No place like home, is there?'

CHAPTER 22

Wednesday 13th December

'What's all this about?' Lily said, laughing as she put a hand up to the spotty scarf that was covering her eyes. 'What you up to, blindfolding an old woman here?'

Jay led her gently into her own flat, and as he untied the scarf and let it fall away, she opened her eyes and took in the scene.

Lily was silent.

The moment seemed to last for ever – Rachel wondered if they'd done the wrong thing – they'd come into her flat without asking, and changed things. Zak gripped on to her hand, waiting for a response. Lily was staring right at the banner he'd made.

Lily's eyes moved from the banner, to the kitchen and living-room walls that had been damaged, now freshly wallpapered and painted. Her gaze dropped to the floor, where the lino had been replaced with new tiles, and there was a bright new rug in the living room. As they drifted finally to the set of shelves, her hand went to her mouth. 'Oh my,' she said. 'Oh my, my, my.' She bit her lip and looked as if she might start crying.

As she looked up at the banner again a huge smile spread over her face. 'Did you do that, son?' she asked Zak, pointing. He nodded. She held her arms out and he dashed over for a hug. With her arm still around him she looked at Rachel, Milly, Jay, Sean and Nikki. 'And all this,' she said, sweeping her arm from the walls to the new cushions on her sofa. 'This was you?' They nodded.

'My home. It looks like my home again. All ready for Christmas.' She walked around and saw the snake-draft excluder. 'Ooh,' she said, 'I've been wanting one of these!'

'But this must have cost . . .' She accusingly narrowed her eyes at Jay.

'Don't even think about it,' Jay said, holding up a hand. 'You've been looking after all of us for years. Just let us look after you for once. This is from all of your neighbours.'

'Well I think I better say thank you then,' Lily said, smiling at everyone in the room. 'Thank you.'

Nikki turned the music up on Lily's stereo, and Rachel poured out lemonade and Cava for everyone in the room. Lily was sitting on a sofa in her living room, holding up the cushions to inspect them, and talking with Milly about which things she'd done.

A knock came at the door, and Zak answered it. 'Hope we're not too late?' Siobhan said, stepping into the room and revealing Aiden behind her. 'Of course not,' Lily said, waving them in. 'Come and join the house-warming. The bar's open,' she laughed, pointing to Rachel.

'This place looks terrific,' Siobhan said to Nikki, admiring the yellow trim on the walls. 'Did you and Milly help do this? Wow, perhaps it's you two who should be running Art Club.'

'Great job,' Aiden said to Rachel, as she passed him a glass of fizz. 'This must have taken you hours.'

'There were a few of us,' Rachel said. 'How was it at the hospital?' she asked.

'The same,' Aiden replied. 'I read to Mum a bit, the story Milly started. But then I got a call from Simon and had to handle that. I let the client know that we were behind on the interiors due to that damaged delivery, and while they understood, they weren't at all happy. We should still be able to get them in for Christmas, but the furniture's not going to be there – we really need to give them something extra as a sweetener.'

'I see,' Rachel said. 'That's interesting. Come over here, there's something I'd like to show you.'

She led Aiden over to the customised shelving Jay had put in. He ran a hand over the top shelf, and crouched down to look at the drawers and cupboards at the bottom, nodding appreciatively at the smooth way they opened. 'Is this hand-made?' he asked.

'It is,' Rachel said, motioning for Jay to come over. He arrived as Aiden got to his feet. 'And here's the man who made it.'

'Jay,' Aiden smiled in surprise. 'Would you be up for taking on a new commission?'

Rachel and Aiden had found a cosy table for dinner in the corner of Capelli's, a nearby pizzeria. Zak and Milly were sitting opposite them.

'So, what do you think?' Rachel asked Zak as he bit into a slice of American Hot.

'Delicious,' Zak said, wiping a hand roughly over his mouth. 'Why can't we go out for pizza every day?'

'Well, it would give us a break from cooking,' Rachel said, reaching over to wipe away some tomato sauce with a napkin that he flinched away from. 'But I think you'd get tired of it.'

'I could never get tired of going out in London,' Milly said, fiddling with her hoop earring. After the high of the party at Lily's, she seemed to have slumped into a bad mood. 'It's better than being buried alive in Skipley.'

Rachel raised an eyebrow.

'I'm serious,' Milly protested. 'Did you know you can walk around it in half an hour? The whole place.

Kate and I did it the other day. We timed ourselves. To prove that we really were living in the smallest, most boring place on earth. Look around you, Mum. London is so much better. Nikki's always doing cool things. There's stuff happening here –' she waved an arm towards the window, to point out the overflow of people from a Thai café opposite – 'Can't you see it? Laurie says London is the best city in the world,' Milly said.

'Oh, she does, does she?' said Rachel.

'Yes, and she said if I'm serious about wanting to work in fashion I should come and do some work ex-perience down here.'

'Right. Rachel thought back to what she'd overheard Milly say about a boy back home. 'And do you talk to her a lot, Laurie?'

'Yeah, sometimes,' Milly said, with a shrug. 'We email. She's pretty easy to talk to. She's not like other adults; she's interested in the same kind of stuff that I am. You know, its like she's younger. She's fun. She's not like you.'

Rachel glanced over at Aiden for support, but he was emailing on his iPhone, probably updating Simon on the situation with the furniture. His half-eaten pizza had been forgotten.

'People know how to dress here,' Milly went on, motioning with a dart of her eyes at the group of girls laughing and chatting at the table next to them, layered in scarves and accessories, with perfectly styled hair and make-up. 'It's not like back home where you've just got Doris's boutique.'

'Milly,' Rachel said, sternly, 'I've had just about enough of this. You don't know how lucky you are. Stop complaining and finish your pizza.'

'Thanks for the support,' Rachel said to Aiden, as they walked home. Milly and Zak walked up the street ahead of them.

'What?' Aiden said, putting his phone away and looking up. 'What support?'

'Exactly. Did you even hear what Milly said back there?'

'Something about Skipley?' Aiden said, still looking distracted. 'I had to let Simon know about Jay's furniture, send over his website so we can start to look at a time frame.'

'She hates it. And on top of that, she seems to think I'm the most boring mother in the world – nothing like Laurie, apparently.'

'I guess Laurie is quite young, isn't she, in her way?'

'What do you mean?' Rachel snapped.

'I just mean I can see why Milly gets on with her, admires her or whatever. And there's the whole fashion thing they have in common.'

Rachel ignored his comment. 'There's a boy,' Rachel said, 'someone in Milly's life – I heard her talking with

Nikki about it. I'm wondering if that's why she's been acting differently.'

'A boy?' Aiden said.

'Yes—' Aiden's phone rang in his pocket and he took it out and answered. Rachel sighed.

'Simon, hi – yes, what do you think? The finish is outstanding. I'm thinking if we offer them some quality bespoke pieces, they might forgive an extra few days on the schedule. Jay says he can work quickly . . .'

From: Millypede@gmail.com
To: Carter@yahoo.com

Hi Carter,

I've thought about what you said and I'm sorry if I upset you. I didn't fancy any of Nikki's friends, I promise! I guess it was stupid of me, writing that message. I should have seen you could take it the wrong way. But I haven't been thinking about anyone but you. Here's my mobile, by the way: 07834 384347.

I hope you are OK.

Milly x

The next day, Thursday, Rachel poured Zak some Rice Krispies and milk into a bowl and made a pot of strong coffee. She flicked on the kitchen radio, and turned it up.

'Ten shopping days till Christmas,' the DJ announced jauntily. 'How ready are you feeling?' Rachel poured coffee into her mug and took a seat next to Zak. 'Here, to get you in the mood, is a little song by Slade . . .'

'When are we going home, Mummy?' Zak said, loading up his spoon. Rachel had known the words would come at some point, but as he looked at her, wide-eyed, there was still a tug at her heart. 'It's nearly Christmas, isn't it?'

She thought of what they'd be doing if they were back in Skipley – they'd have bought a tree by now, and would be decorating it as a family.

'You like it here, don't you?' Rachel said, taking a sip of coffee and trying to lighten the mood. 'And we've still got the dinosaurs to go and see.'

'I do like it,' Zak said. 'And I guess I do want to see the dinosaurs. But we don't have a Christmas tree. It's not really much like Christmas.'

'I know, darling,' Rachel said, touching his arm. 'I'm sorry. I know it's not like usual. We're going to go home just as soon as we can. But Granny Bea needs us down here right now.'

A knock came at the front door and Rachel got up

to answer it, giving Zak a kiss on his head. She opened the door to find a young delivery man on the landing in front of her, holding a bunch of silver helium balloons.

'Balloons for you,' he said with a smile, holding out an electronic pad in Rachel's direction. 'Could you sign for them please?'

'Oh no,' she said, smiling in surprise. 'I mean, yes, of course I can sign for them, but they're not for me – they must be for my mother-in-law.'

She signed the pad and handed it back. The delivery man took it and checked his clipboard.

'"For Milly", it says here.'

'Milly?'

'Yep, that's what it says. Merry Christmas,' he said, passing the silver-ribboned bunch of balloons to her.

'And to you too.'

Confused, Rachel took the balloons to her daughter's room. She thought again of the snatch of conversation she'd heard between Milly and Nikki. There was 'a guy', someone in Milly's life, that she wasn't telling any of them about. And this was the proof. She tried to recall any names Milly had mentioned, boys at her new school – no one came to mind.

Milly answered the door, bleary-eyed with sleep. 'Balloons,' she said, looking at them in puzzlement.

'They're for you,' Rachel said, passing them over. They bobbed against the ceiling and Milly searched among the ribbons for a note. She finally found the envelope and opened it, reading the note inside.

'Who are they from?' Rachel asked.

'No one,' Milly replied.

'No one?' Rachel said.

'What, Mum?' Milly snapped. 'Why do you have to be so nosy?'

Rachel felt a flush rising to her chest. Anger and hurt competed inside her. 'You used to tell me things, Milly,' she said. 'I know you need your space, but do you have to shut me out all the time?'

'It's none of your business,' Milly hissed, slamming the door in Rachel's face.

Milly, Did you like your balloon surprise? Cx

Yes, thank you x

From: Carter@yahoo.com
To: Millypede@gmail.com

Pretty short text – maybe email was better after all . . . So are you coming home soon? I want to see you on Christmas Eve.

Carter

Aiden was in the shower. Rachel sat down on their bed and pulled her folded pyjamas out from under her pillow. On autopilot, she took off her jewellery and got undressed, throwing her clothes in the laundry, and slipped into her pyjamas. Pulling off her hairband, she shook her hair loose, then brushed through it quickly, then massaged night cream into her face. She thought of the way Milly had spoken to her. It still stung. Had she pushed things too far? Should she be giving Milly more privacy? Without Aiden to talk to about it she'd lost all perspective.

Perhaps just a chapter or two of a novel, to help her nod off, she thought. She scanned Laurie's shelves; *The Great Gatsby* and *One Day* jostled for space among *Vogue* annuals and art books. Then she spotted that, tucked away, lying horizontally across the top of the other books and pushed towards the wall, incongruous with Laurie's minimalist style, was a battered paperback copy of Jilly Cooper's *Riders*.

Rachel pulled it from the shelf, smiling to herself as memories flooded back. She and Laurie must have been about fifteen, around Milly's age, when they'd read it – old enough to know better, but young enough to giggle over the naughty bits. Laurie had found it on her mum's shelf and brought it into school, laughing at the cover – a woman in tight white riding trousers, a man's hand on her buttock. Rachel was pretty sure it was the same copy – Laurie had hung on to it all this time. They used to sneak off to the girls' toilets and read sections of it there. Hadn't they scribbled some notes on the inside cover?

The noise of the shower stopped. Rachel opened the cover – they'd not only turned down the page corners, but given each sex scene a mark out of ten. She remembered how the metal doors of the other toilet cubicles had clanked shut again and again in the time that they'd been locked away in their own, reading.

Rachel flicked through the pages, a warm rush of nostalgia coming over her as she saw underlined phrases. When she got to the back page, she saw that there was a white envelope wedged in there. As she went to take it out, the bathroom door opened and she hurriedly tried to shove the book back on to the shelf. She felt like a naughty schoolkid. As she struggled to get the book back in place, the envelope inside fell to the floor.

She bent to pick it up from where it had landed on the carpet. Purple writing and hand-drawn hearts covered the back of it, and as she flipped it over, she instantly recognised Laurie's rounded teenage hand-writing, the 'i's dotted with little circles. Her breath caught as she read the name there: Aiden.

Rachel lay in bed next to Aiden in the darkness, her heart racing, until she finally heard his breathing deepen. Slowly, she lifted the duvet, crept out of bed and went back to the bookshelf. She reached for the envelope she'd hidden in a rush.

She took it out to the kitchen so that she could read it in the light. As she saw Aiden's name again, she tried to convince herself that there could still be an innocent explanation.

She undid the flap and took out the letter inside, two pages of lined A4 filled with Laurie's teenage handwriting. It was as familiar to Rachel as her own: she'd received dozens of notes passed to her and 'mysterious' Valentine's cards in the same neat, round hand, often in the same purple ink. Her eyes rushed over the words – and the hope she had been clinging to, that she might have jumped to the wrong conclusions, slipped away completely.

'*Hi Aiden,*' Rachel read.

I'm in Geography and you're sitting right in front of me. Mr Evans has just told you off for messing around with Brandon, and writing on the desks. Now you've turned around and caught my eye, given me a smile. I love your smile. It brightens up my day. I can see how much you want to be alone with me, and well, I want that too – you're nearly close enough to touch right now, but in this classroom we can't do anything – it's driving me crazy.

Rachel wanted desperately to be able to stop – her heart was thudding in her chest. But she couldn't put the letter down. She had to read it all.

But it's nearly the weekend, and I'll see you at Sally's house party. We can sneak away, find somewhere quiet. I can't wait to be with you ...

Then, finally, Rachel reached the end, Laurie's signature and a row of hearts and kisses underneath.

Dazed, Rachel put the note away, and the envelope to one side on the counter, then sat down at the kitchen table. Through the fog that had settled in her mind, she tried to make sense of what she'd read, struggling to understand what had happened, and when. Had Laurie and Aiden been together before he'd been Rachel's boyfriend – or, her mind raced and she bit her lip – had Aiden been with them at the same time?

Rachel battled to stay in control of her emotions. She and Aiden had a marriage, two much-loved children together – and whatever had happened with Laurie took place over twenty years ago, she reasoned. It was Rachel and Aiden's marriage, not the teenage longing in the letter, that was real now. But however Rachel looked at it, the two people she'd thought she could trust most had lied to her, and it felt like the ultimate betrayal. Memories flashed back – the parties

Laurie had gone to, which *her* parents hadn't let her go to – the Geography class Laurie and Aiden had both been in. She remembered how, shortly before their GCSEs, Aiden and Laurie had come back from a school field trip in Wales, both full of stories about it – had they been together then?

The letter twisted everything Rachel had thought she knew. Aiden had mentioned, more than once, how good Laurie was looking, hadn't he? How glamorous she was? And they'd had that evening alone together in Skipley ... he'd hardly told her anything about it.

Eventually, with her head still spinning, Rachel forced herself to go back to bed. She hid the note back in the bookshelf where she'd found it and looked at her husband in bed, his chest rising gently as he slept. With Bea still in a coma, how could she confront him with what she'd read? She'd have to try and forget about it, for now at least. But, she thought, as she climbed into bed beside him – feeling a new distance from the man she loved – the thought of Aiden with someone else, not just anyone else – Laurie – was almost too much to bear.

No reply – again? I'm getting tired of this, Milly ... We need to talk face to face. Don't mess me around. If you do, you know I can let people know what you're really like – I could do that pretty easily. C

CHAPTER 23

Friday 15th December

Laurie looked through her suitcase for something suitable to wear to Diana's drinks. Patrick was going to be there – and she'd spent so much time slopping around in mud on their walk the other day. She was going to have to up the glamour level to compensate.

Most of her city clothes looked wrong in Skipley. But she remembered she had brought one thing with her, for emergency party use. It was a burgundy dress with sparkles on the deep V neckline. She slipped on sheer stockings and then tried on some matching shoes with towering heels – skyscraper high. Including them in her luggage had been serious wishful thinking – but she could get away with them tonight.

She couldn't wait to see Patrick again. They'd talked a couple of times on the phone since their walk together on Wednesday. Her head and heart were at odds – her heart told her to let go, trust him, but her head told her to take things slowly, this time, get to know Patrick more before taking things further. While a few times she'd pretended otherwise, the truth was that she really, really wasn't that great at one-night stands. That empty feeling of not being called the next day, intimacy disappearing in an instant – she knew it, and she didn't want it again.

She brushed her sleek bob and fringe until her hair lay perfectly flat. Almost ready – but there was something missing. She scanned Rachel's dressing table for some jewellery, and in a little wooden box found some long, silver drop earrings. Rachel wouldn't mind, she thought, as she hooked them through the holes in her ears. They'd always borrowed each other's stuff at school – it had been like having two wardrobes.

She applied liquid eyeliner in thick swooshes, and then layered mascara on to her already thick lashes. She took a step back and looked at herself in the full-length mirror. Not bad. She smiled.

Down in the kitchen Laurie found the plate of gingerbread Santas she'd made the night before. That week, with a few empty evenings in front of her now that she was staying longer in Skipley, she'd set herself the challenge of making one thing a day from Bea's book. With the fire on, and Christmas tunes playing, baking was the perfect way to spend the time, she realised. It was strange – over the years she'd convinced herself she needed constant stimulation, parties, work, travel – that was what made her happy. But it wasn't true after all. Home alone, with peace and quiet, and time to do things she enjoyed, she felt calm and content.

The kitchen was quickly filling up with stars and chocolate wreaths, and she'd even managed a Yule log – covering herself and every surface in chocolate in the process. Chocolate always made her break out in spots the next day, but as she'd licked the bowl she couldn't have cared less – that was what concealer was for, she told herself. She placed a few of the ginger-bread Santas carefully in cellophane and wrapped them with red ribbon, ready to take to Diana's, together with a bottle of Baileys.

First party of the season, Laurie thought to herself, here I come.

Candles in glass jars lined the pathway up to Diana's front door, and the Christmas wreath hanging on it was now woven through with delicate red lights.

As Laurie clattered up the path in her heels, Diana swung the front door open. 'Hello!' Diana called out, holding out a glass of champagne to greet her guest. Laurie took it gratefully and kissed Diana hello.

As Laurie stepped into the house, it was the warm, distinctly Christmassy, cinnamon and pine smell that hit her first. As she cast her eye around the house she let out a gasp of admiration. The staircase was garlanded with holly and ribboned with red lights just like the wreath on the door. Twirls of gold voile framed the fireplace and decorative branches woven with more lights were placed in pots around the living room and hallway. Diana's home looked absolutely stunning.

Trays laden with pigs in blankets, mini Yorkshire puddings with beef and horseradish, blinis with smoked salmon and cream cheese lined the table in the living room. She spotted Joyce over in the corner and headed towards her. Joyce was wearing the top Laurie had customised for her, albeit with a tinsel headband that lowered the classy tone a bit. Laurie smiled and pointed at the top. 'Suits you,' she said. 'I love the bow you sewed on,' Joyce said, looking down and holding the fabric bow out. 'It makes me feel all sort of princessy.'

'Impressive spread,' Laurie said, looking around at the plates of food. Joyce laughed. 'Our Diana's never been one to do things by halves,' she said. 'And she's invited half the village along tonight.' Laurie looked around the room and saw that it was nearly full: she recognised a couple of faces and spotted Ben from the café loading his plate with mini sausage rolls. She glanced around the room to see if Patrick had arrived yet.

'Nice tradition,' Laurie said. 'Having a party like this.'

'Oh, nothing of the sort,' Joyce said, and as she spoke Diana swept up by their side and topped up their glasses with more champagne. Joyce turned to her. 'You see, Diana's never had a party like this before, have you, dear?'

'First time.' She smiled. 'It's rather fun, though, isn't

it? Never got to do anything like this when *he* was around.' She stuck her tongue out, making a face, then started to laugh. 'So I thought I'd take the opportunity now.'

'Well here's to new starts, and more parties,' Laurie said. 'Now that's something worth drinking to,' Diana agreed, and they clinked their champagne flutes together.

Laurie looked over at Diana's nephews as they sped through the house, racing toy cars over every surface. In the corner of the living room Diana had set up a little table with materials for making cards and paper chains. Some of the older children were Pritt-sticking happily over there.

'Are you the fashion designer?' Laurie jumped in surprise and turned to see an older man in a tweed suit who'd joined them. 'That's me,' she said.

'I keep hearing about you,' he said, with a grin. 'My wife Sandra's not stopped talking about this fashion show you're having tomorrow night. She's on about how she's a model these days, and I should be the one making the tea. You've caused quite a stir.'

'Delicious,' Patrick said, taking a bite of a hot mince pie before Diana or Laurie could stop him. His hand went straight to his mouth. 'God, *hot*,' he said, laughing. 'I think I burned my tongue. But anyway, still worth it.'

Patrick had arrived just after eight. He followed Laurie

261

into the living room and as they stopped to talk to some of the women volunteers Patrick draped his arm around Laurie's waist. Laurie hadn't invited it, but it felt sort of nice. When the ladies made their excuses and headed over to the buffet table, Patrick pulled her closer and gave her a squeeze. 'You look,' he whispered in her ear huskily, 'absolutely irresistible tonight.'

Laurie wondered how much longer she'd be able to wait. The cottage – and her big, comfortable, warm, empty double bed, were only metres away. She took a sip of mulled wine and imagined for a moment what it would be like – to have his hands on her, to see that body she'd been admiring under clothes. The tension between them seemed to grow each time they spoke, and Laurie was only human – when he spoke to her like he had just now it was as if she ... dissolved.

She excused herself to go to the bathroom. Central heating always played havoc with her hair – so she'd brought some serum with her to smooth it down. As she made her way to the stairs, Ben came over to her.

She smiled hello, then moved to go upstairs to the bathroom. 'Laurie, isn't it?' he said, with a smile. They'd only spoken that one time, when she'd first arrived, but he'd been a friendly face back then, when she'd really needed to see one. 'Ben, hi,' she said, stopping on the bottom stair.

'You look nice.'

'Thank you,' she replied, politely.

'Are you ...' he started. 'Is Patrick your boyfriend?' Ben asked. Laurie hesitated. She didn't know herself what the answer was, but she was fairly sure she didn't want to be broadcasting it via the neighbourhood gossip.

'None of your beeswax,' she said, playfully dodging the question.

'It's just ... well, nothing. I don't really know him.' Ben shrugged.

'Right,' Laurie said, furrowing her brow as she tried to read his expression. 'So, forget about me. Who are you going to be cornering under the mistletoe, Ben? Any ladies on the horizon?'

'No,' he said, looking down shyly.

'Aha!' Laurie said. 'Now the shoe's on the other foot. Who is she?' she whispered, leaning closer. 'Go on, you can tell me.'

'All right,' Ben said. 'But promise you won't blab?'

'I promise,' she said, crossing her fingers behind her back.

'Her name's Milly.'

CHAPTER 24

Saturday 16th December

Laurie, hammer in hand, was ready to start the auction. Her eyes scanned over the crowd. She'd suspected there was a gap to fill in the Skipley social scene – but she'd never expected this. The community centre was packed to the rafters. She spotted Patrick in the crowd, looking more gorgeous than ever in a navy V-neck sweater. He winked at her. She didn't know how she'd managed to resist the temptation of sleeping with him after Diana's party. But now, she reasoned, she'd waited long enough. Tonight, yes. Tonight felt right.

The women had worked hard to get everything ready on time – whether it was decorating the set with red drapes, tinsel and fairy lights, getting drinks for the small bar, or doing last-minute sewing – they had stopped at nothing to make the event special. Even when hems still needed sewing that morning, just hours before the show was due to start, they had all kept the faith – and now the community centre was all set up for the auction.

Joyce was the first one up on the makeshift catwalk – modelling a long-sleeved cocktail dress with slashes of silver, and striding into the crowd like she was born to do it. Some of the women had been nervous beforehand, but not Joyce – she'd made it clear that at sixty-eight, after a lifetime as a wallflower, she was ready for her fifteen minutes of fame.

Wolf whistles came from the crowd. Laurie recognised a few faces from around the village, and Diana's party – there was Sandra's husband, the woman from the bakery, Graham from the pub, Ben, and Andy, the manager at the homeless shelter.

'Do I have forty pounds?' Laurie asked, motioning to Joyce on the runway, 'for this stunning one-off piece?'

Laurie spotted a policewoman, still in uniform, raising her hand.

'Fifty pounds?'

The woman from the bakery put her hand up.

'Sixty pounds?'

Hands flicked up with increasing speed until the policewoman was the only remaining bidder at a hundred and twenty pounds.

'Sold to the lovely lady in uniform,' Laurie said, banging her hammer. She didn't want to jump the gun, but at this rate, they would have the costs of the charity Christmas dinner covered in no time.

Diana was due up next. Laurie glanced down at

where she was standing, nervously fiddling with her hair, and gave her a wink. Diana walked up on to the stage. She was in a Christmassy number, a strapless black dress with a band of scarlet silk across the top and a tailored scarlet jacket. The result was dazzling – simple and bold and seriously sexy. As she took tentative steps down the catwalk, a couple of the local men stared at her, jaws on the floor. One man in particular – Graham – was staring at Diana in unveiled admiration. Music pumped out, and Diana's confidence slowly grew – she twirled at the foot of their hand-made catwalk and the crowd let out a roar of approval.

'Diana, that's nearly four hundred pounds from the entry donations alone,' Laurie exclaimed, as she went through the figures, 'and we're looking at close to eight hundred for the dresses and suit jackets people bid for. Not bad at all for a night's work!' Laurie high-fived Diana, who looked a little startled.

As more fizz and wine had been drunk, the bids had crept higher. The jacket Diana had been modelling went for eighty pounds, and Pam's outfit, a party dress with cap sleeves and lines of sequins sewn on it, had gone for a hundred and fifty. Now that the crowd had finally dispersed, mostly shifting down the road to Graham's pub, Laurie and Diana were able to count up the money they had made.

'Andy's going to be delighted,' Diana said. Then,

suddenly seeming more coy, she continued, 'And something else interesting happened tonight.' Laurie raised an eyebrow in question. 'I got a phone number,' Diana admitted, passing Laurie a card with Graham from the pub's contact details on it.

'Graham,' Laurie said approvingly. 'Good work. But forget the phone, why don't we both go down there now? I said I'd meet the other girls, and Patrick is over there too.'

'I don't normally go to the pub,' Diana said, wrinkling her nose as if the whole notion embarrassed her.

Laurie gave Diana a stern look. 'Right,' she said. 'And I suppose you normally get up on the catwalk, do you?'

Diana couldn't deny it – it was plain to see that stepping out of her comfort zone hadn't done her any harm so far. All she needed was a little more encouragement.

'Come on,' Laurie said, filling up a glass with the remainder of a bottle of Cava on the bar table. 'I made a leap of faith coming here, and I'm so pleased I did it. Get this down you and then let's head up the road.'

Laurie and Diana could hear the singing even before the pub came into view. There was what sounded like a very drunken chorus of 'Last Christmas' coming from the isolated pub, but rather than putting Diana off her mission, it seemed to be attracting her like a magnet. She was already singing along.

'I haven't been out since Richard left,' Diana said. 'I mean not like this, to a pub. He always told me pubs were tacky – can you believe it?' she said. 'From a man who's now partying it up in Ibiza?'

Laurie pulled her coat tightly around her and looked forward to getting inside the warm pub. The temperature had continued to drop, with thicker snow falling through the evening.

As they opened the pub door, the ladies inside let out a cheer. 'Our star model,' Pam shouted out, raising her glass in Diana's direction. 'And to the woman who made it all happen,' she said, looking at Laurie. Laurie felt a warm glow build up inside her. It had been a hard slog, with late nights along the way, but it had all been worth it. She ordered drinks for her and Diana, who was happily chatting away to all and sundry, and glanced around the bar for Patrick. She spotted him over on the other side of the pub, chatting to a couple of women in the corner – he saw her looking and waved over.

Laurie handed Diana her drink. She and Graham were now deep in conversation, and Diana looked relaxed and happy. Gadget the sheepdog was standing nearby, in a pair of red antlers, batting them with his paw and trying to pull them off, and Alfie was barking crossly at them. Their owners were looking on and laughing.

Laurie made her way over towards Patrick. 'Hello,' she said, snaking a hand around his waist.

'Hi, gorgeous,' Patrick said, leaving his conversation and enveloping her in a hug. 'Congratulations.' He pulled back and kissed her hello.

'Thank you,' she said. It had felt good to have him there in the crowd. 'Listen,' she whispered in Patrick's ear, 'I was wondering if you might be available to help me celebrate tonight ... in a private party at the cottage?'

Patrick smiled. Laurie was glad she'd decided to take the leap and ask him – the idea of finally spending the night with him just felt right.

He leaned in towards her ear, and whispered back, 'I'd be delighted to. I feel like all my Christmases have come at once.'

Laurie laughed and squeezed his hand. She took a sip of her drink and then, seeing a mobile on the table, a memory came back to her. Damn – she'd had a text from Rachel the other day and had meant to call her back. She'd been so caught up in planning the auction it had completely slipped her mind. She looked in her handbag for her phone, but saw it was empty apart from her wallet and keys.

'Patrick,' she said. 'Can I borrow your phone a second? I think I must have left mine at home. I need to make a call.'

He handed her his iPhone. 'Sure, babe, here you go,'

She moved through the crowd out towards the window, where reception was always better. As she went to put in the digits of Rachel's number, which she'd committed to memory years ago, a message beeped and the start of it appeared on screen. She caught a glimpse of the first two words: 'Hi there'.

She shouldn't read it. Of course she shouldn't. It was a private message to Patrick. And she had absolutely no right to be . . .

Too late. The whole first line of the text was visible, and Laurie caught sight of it.

> Sorry I didn't get back to you earlier. I do want to meet up.

Laurie felt a rush of jealousy. She stopped herself – she shouldn't jump to any conclusions. It could be a colleague, a friend, his brother.

She would call Rachel and— No, she couldn't ignore the message, not now that she'd read some of it. She needed to put her mind at rest. She would read the rest and then explain to Patrick that she'd opened it by accident. It was easy enough to click an on-screen text open in error. Taking a deep breath and looking up to check that Patrick was distracted in conversation, she touched the little blue box and read on.

> Christmas Eve I'm normally with my family, but I'll see if I can get out of it, for a bit at least Mx

Laurie furrowed her brow. Christmas Eve? M, with a kiss? Was Patrick already lining up dates with another woman for when she was gone? A wave of shock and indignation rose up in her.

Then she looked up at the sender's name. She wasn't sure how she'd missed it earlier: Milly

In one crushing moment, the truth hit her.

Laurie walked back through to the bar. It seemed hotter and more crowded than before, and she felt dizzy. Patrick was getting a round of mulled wine for a couple of the older ladies, who were laughing heartily. He looked over as she came closer and gave her a wink.

Laurie handed him his phone back without saying a word. The Christmas music whirled and throbbed. Laurie was straining to breathe properly, she needed to get outside into the fresh air. She grabbed her coat from the coat-stand and turned to go, but as she did, Patrick caught her by the elbow.

'You going?' he said.

She didn't even want to look at him. As Milly's emails came back to her, and she remembered the advice she'd given, she felt sick – Laurie realised she was partly responsible. She turned and quickly walked away through the revellers. Patrick weaved through the crowd to the door, following her, and as she reached for the handle she felt his presence behind her. He put his hand over hers. 'Laurie,' he whispered in her ear. 'Wait.'

'Don't touch me,' she hissed, before slipping away from him out of the pub door.

Outside, wooden tables and chairs formed an empty pub garden, the grass around it frosted. Laurie inhaled deep lungfuls of cold air and tried to calm her racing thoughts. Patrick caught up with her again and took hold of her arm.

'What's going on, Laurie?' he said, spinning her round to face him. 'What was that about? Were you just going to walk out and leave me?'

'Patrick,' Laurie said, fury rising up in her. 'Tell me something.' Her head was spinning.

Adrenalin coursing through her veins, she took a deep breath and spoke. She had to know the truth. 'Milly Murray,' she said. 'Does that name mean anything to you?'

'Milly . . .' he said, shaking his head. 'Nope.'

'Really,' she said. He reached out to touch her hair and she smelt his familiar aftershave.

'Yes, really. Can we go back in now, please?' he said. 'It's freezing out here.'

'Are you absolutely sure?'

She looked at Patrick again. This handsome man with his sparkling eyes and nicely fitting jeans – who'd been so tender with her. Did she really know him at all?

'Pretty girl,' she continued, 'tall, with dark-red hair?'

Patrick shrugged his shoulders, his stare remaining steady. 'Doesn't ring a bell.'

Laurie knew now that she had to see it through. Her resolve hardened. 'Oh, but you'd remember a girl like that, wouldn't you, Patrick?'

'Look, I'm sure,' he said, irritated now, 'I don't know anyone called Milly. What is this, Laurie? What's going on with you?'

'The thing is,' Laurie said, trusting her gut, 'I don't think I believe you, Patrick.'

Silence hung between them. After a long moment, he broke it. 'OK,' he said, 'now you mention it, I do think I may have met a Milly. This girl lives round here, right? I imagine I'll have seen her around – Skipley's a small place.'

'Seen her around?' Laurie said, her voice rising as anger welled up inside her. 'Or texted her, asked her out? Because there's a difference, Patrick.'

Patrick hesitated, then spoke again. 'OK, look, yes, I do know her,' he said, holding his hands up as if under attack. 'I've spoken with her. But she's just a kid, Laurie. It's got nothing to do with us. I mean nothing even happened.'

'You're right there, she is just a kid,' Laurie said, 'she's fifteen years old, Patrick,' Laurie continued, feeling sick to her stomach as she said the words. 'And if nothing's happened, it's not for want of trying, from what I've heard.'

'Oh Christ,' he said, putting a hand to his forehead. 'I mean, I met her in a pub,' he said. 'Woah, she looks much older than that. I thought she was eighteen or something. Look, Laurie, I was confused,' Patrick insisted. 'I'd seen Milly around, but I only talked to her once, before you even got here. As soon as I got to know you, I knew this – us – was something much bigger. But I didn't want to hurt Milly, so I was letting her down gently, saying we'd still meet up for a friendly drink when she got back. It's you I care about. This doesn't have to affect things between us.' He reached out to touch her shoulder. She flinched and his hand fell away.

'Oh yes it does,' she roared.

'Come on, Laurie,' he implored her, 'I really like you.' Laurie stepped further away from him. 'You're the one I really want. Come back to mine tonight.'

'Oh, yeah, right,' Laurie said, rolling her eyes and letting out a laugh laden with contempt. 'Because that's how much respect I have for myself, and for my goddaughter. Because you know that's who Milly is, Patrick. Come back to yours . . .' she laughed wryly. 'I've half a mind to report you to the police right now.'

Patrick's face fell and he looked like a child who'd been caught out.

Laurie leaned in towards him. 'Tell me, was any of what you told me true?' she asked. 'All that stuff you said about your brother, your family?'

'Yes, of course it is,' he snapped back, looking towards his feet.

'I don't believe you, Patrick,' Laurie said, kicking herself for falling for his lies. 'Milly deserves far, far better. Don't you dare go near her again. Or I will go to the police. You can count on that.'

Laurie left Patrick there and turned on her heel to walk back in the direction of the cottage in the heavy snow, thinking only of the phone call she urgently needed to make.

CHAPTER 25

Saturday 16th December

It was past midnight when Rachel saw the cottage land-line number flash up on the screen of her mobile. Laurie. She reached for the red button and cut off the call.

But from where it lay on the coffee table, her phone taunted her. She knew, instinctively, that it would ring again.

Moments later it did, beeping insistently.

'Aren't you going to answer that?' Aiden said, looking at the flashing screen.

The thoughts – and the images, all those horrible images, of Aiden and Laurie, flooded her mind again. She'd tried to carry on as normal, but now the anger and confusion was rising to the surface, and the feelings were even stronger than before.

As Rachel stared at the ringing mobile she realised she needed to hear the truth. She got up and took her phone into the bedroom, away from Aiden and the noise of the TV, closing the door firmly behind her. This time she answered the call.

'Rachel,' came Laurie's voice. Calm, Rachel thought. Oblivious to the fact that she'd torn someone else's world apart.

'Yes,' Rachel answered, numb.

'Hi. Listen,' Laurie said, sounding more flustered than she had at first. 'I need to talk to you about something, it's important.'

'Oh, really?' Rachel said, steeling herself, worried her voice would crack. 'Well you know what? There's something I wanted to ask you, too.'

'There is?'

'Yes.' Rachel sat down on the edge of the bed. She had to keep her nerve. She had to ask – or she would never know. She took a deep breath, then spoke.

'Laurie, I've just found a note you wrote when we were at school.'

'A note?'

'To Aiden.' Rachel forced herself to continue. 'I found it in your bedroom. It fell out of one of your books.'

'Oh God.' Laurie's words came slowly.

'What, Laurie?' Rachel said, her voice thickening with anger now. Laurie's guilty tone was all the confirmation she needed.

'Rachel, I'm so sorry,' Laurie began, her voice so quiet it was as if it belonged to someone else. 'I know I should have been honest. I should have told you,' Laurie said, hurriedly. 'I mean—'

'Laurie – you knew I was in love with him. All those

277

evenings we spoke about him, you listened to me go on and on, analysing every conversation the two of us had. Then – when you went to those parties – Laurie, you'd report back to me. Telling me who Aiden was with, who he was talking to.' Rachel felt her grip on the past she knew slip with every word. 'What was that?'

'Rachel, let me explain . . . Look,' she said, hurriedly. 'I need you to trust me, and to listen to me now. There's something I need to tell you—'

'Trust you?' Rachel said, her rage building. 'Are you serious? I don't need explanations, Laurie. Not yours, not even Aiden's. Nothing is going to make this go away.'

'But—'

'It's been a really hard time, Laurie, and I needed a friend. But now I'm even wondering, was there another reason you wanted to swap homes?'

Laurie was silent at the other end of the line.

'Did you actually want to help?' Rachel thought of Aiden, of Milly, the fact her daughter was talking to Laurie instead of her. 'Or was it because you wanted my life?'

'No, Rachel, listen . . . you've got to—' Laurie protested.

'Laurie, I don't want to talk to you, and I don't want you talking to Milly either. Goodbye.' Her hand was shaking as she slammed the phone down.

CHAPTER 26

Sunday 17th December

On Sunday morning there was a brief, blissful moment when Laurie couldn't remember anything about the night before. Then the memories flooded back – the best night she'd had in ages had turned into a nightmare.

She showered quickly, dried her hair and threw on jeans and a hoodie. She looked out of the front window to check the weather. The flurry of snow last night had settled thickly, and, unable to find the coat she'd taken off last night, she pulled on a sheepskin jacket from the hall closet before going outside. Pulling it tightly around her, she crunched through the snow to Diana's cottage.

Diana opened the door still in her dressing gown. 'My God,' she exclaimed. 'You look like the Abominable Snowman! Come in and out of the cold.'

Diana brought over coffee and buttered crumpets. Laurie let herself be distracted by Diana's tales of the night before.

'He asked me to stay after closing,' Diana said. 'We had a – what did he call it? A lock-in. Just the two of us.'

Diana's eyes were bright and she had a new flush in her cheeks. She and Laurie talked through all the essentials: what exactly Diana had talked about with Graham, how they had left things (they both seemed keen), were there kisses (yes) and were they any good (oh yes), and who was going to make the next move (Graham had Diana's number).

'Graham was saying last night how nice it is that you and Patrick got together,' Diana said. 'But you left early, how come?'

'I knew I wasn't the best judge of character when it came to men,' Laurie said, shaking her head. 'But it's really off the chart this time.'

'Patrick?'

Laurie nodded.

'But he seemed—'

'Like such a nice guy?' Laurie finished Diana's sentence. 'Yep, that's what I thought too. But no, he's a total creep,' Laurie said, picking up another crumpet and taking a bite. 'I can't believe I fell for everything he said. He was flirting with someone else when he was seeing me, setting up dates with her,' she said. Diana's jaw dropped. 'But it's worse than that. The other girl was my own fifteen-year-old goddaughter.'

Diana gave a horrified gasp. 'Not Milly?'

'Yes, Milly.'

'Un-be-blimmin-lieve-able,' Diana said, eyes wide.

'I know. Pathetic, isn't it?'

'Worse than that,' Diana said, her face hard with disapproval. 'She's underage! It's disgraceful. Well, he's not going to have many friends around here in a week or two. You leave that one with me. What a toerag! Does Rachel know?'

'Not yet,' Laurie said, thinking back to the disastrous phone conversation the two of them had had.

'She's not going to be happy about it. Poor Milly, I mean, she's a smart girl ... and you can't blame her for getting sucked in by him. I mean, we all did.'

Laurie couldn't shake the feeling that she should have known better. Why had she not been able to suss Patrick out from the start? Had she really been that desperate not to be alone at Christmas?

As she left Diana's house and walked back to the cottage, Laurie reran the conversations she'd had with Patrick in her mind. When he'd talked about himself, she realised, he'd rarely given details, and what he had said – well, maybe none of it had been true.

As she let herself back into the cottage, Laurie knew it was time to leave Skipley. She looked around the living room – the window seat, scattered with cushions, the photos of Rachel, Aiden and their family, their CD collection, books. Being here, living here, she'd felt almost like part of the family. It had made her realise she missed having Rachel in her life and that she wanted to be a better godmother to Milly.

Instead all she'd managed to do was damage their lives and ruin her relationship with both of them. Yet the one thing Rachel had asked for – for Laurie to steer clear of her family – Laurie knew she couldn't do. Milly was still in contact with Patrick, hearing the same lies she'd heard, and was planning to see him in just a few days. Whatever it took, Laurie had to make sure Milly knew the truth.

If Rachel refused to answer her calls, she'd find another way. She went upstairs to start packing.

CHAPTER 27

Monday 18th December

Rachel got up at 6.30 a.m., when it was still dark outside. With the radio on quietly, she made gingerbread snowmen and candied fruit and nut wreaths. By the time her family woke up the flat was heavy with the scents of ginger and baking. She was still feeling empty and raw from the argument with Laurie. But she dealt with it in the way she often dealt with her problems – by baking. Aiden came into the kitchen to make tea. 'What's that cooking?' he asked, breathing in.

'Biscuits,' Rachel said. 'I want Christmas to be just like it always is,' she said, looking up from the mixing bowl. She took a breath as the reality of the situation sank in. 'Wherever we are for it.'

'Right,' Aiden said, distractedly.

'We'll work it out,' Rachel said, taking some biscuits out of the oven and putting them out to cool on a rack. 'Would you like company at the hospital today?'

'Yes,' Aiden said. 'I would. Let's all go together.'

*

'So, when I got to Level 3 the monster came and started to breathe fire at me,' Zak explained. 'You can't go past him, you have to get up and over him. But I found the coin that makes you bigger and—'

Zak had been talking to Bea for about ten minutes about his latest computer game. At first he'd been shy about talking to her, hadn't known what to say, but now, after a week and a half of it, he seemed completely comfortable with his unresponsive audience.

That morning, Dr Patel had only repeated her advice that they should be patient. 'Ten days,' Aiden whispered to Rachel, when the doctor walked away. 'Surely they should know something by now.'

Rachel took his hand gently. 'It sounds like they don't. I suppose she doesn't want to give us false hope – she's said from the start that it's a case of waiting.'

'And then, whoosh, I was over it, Granny –' Zak's face was gleaming – 'and through to the waterfall round. It's true. You can ask Milly.'

'It's true,' Milly said, perching on the edge of the bed and stroking her grandma's arm. 'He made it through to Level 4. And in Zak-world that's like winning the lottery or something.'

Rachel looked at Milly. When she was with her grandmother, her tough front disappeared.

'So, Granny,' Milly said, taking over the conversation. She looked around the room for inspiration and her eyes rested on a snow globe sitting on Bea's bedside table. It was one of Milly's favourite decorations from the cottage – inside was a tiny Eiffel tower. 'It's a week till Christmas. Only a week. And you won't be surprised to hear that we're not at all organised without you. We don't even have your *Countdown to Christmas* to help us. Zak and I have some chocolate Advent calendars, and we're opening those every day, but we don't have a tree or anything.'

'But it's OK. Mum found some nice branches and we've decorated them with fairy lights, so the flat looks pretty. Zak's made some paper chains. And this morning Mum started baking, she's made those fruit and nut wreaths, and some gingerbread snowmen. The flat smells like your cottage when you're baking.

'Do you remember that year, Gran, when you first let me bake with you? It was after Grandpa had died, and you said you didn't want to make the gingerbread house on your own? We sat down together and you showed me how to decorate each piece. Granddad has always been the best at doing it, you said, but then when I got started you told me you saw part of him in me.' Milly's voice started to crack. 'I miss Granddad. We all do. And I know you said that day that you wanted to join him, that all you wanted was to be with him, in heaven. So if that's what you really want, Granny, then do that, go.

'We'll be OK.' Tears started to fall on Milly's cheeks, and Rachel reached a hand around her shoulders. Zach started to let out small sobs and clutched Milly's other hand tighter. Rachel looked over at Aiden and saw tears in his eyes.

'But know that if you do, we're going to miss you so, so much,' Milly said. 'Because you're the best gran in the world. And Christmas won't be right without you.'

The bedside fell silent, and the only movement was in the ward, beyond the curtain. Trolley wheels rolling, nurses calling out.

'I think it's time to go,' Rachel said, giving Milly's shoulder a squeeze. Aiden nodded. Milly and Zak got to their feet slowly, and Rachel pulled back the curtain and turned to leave.

'No,' came a quiet voice. Rachel turned around to see Bea moving her head roughly from side to side, repeating the word. 'No, no, no.' A shiver ran over Rachel's skin, and Aiden dashed over to Bea. Accelerating beeps came from the machines around her. Milly and Zak's gaze was fixed on their grandma's face. 'Call for the doctor, Rach,' Aiden said, and Rachel looked around for Dr Patel, who was just a couple of beds away. Rachel beckoned her over. Adrenalin coursed through her veins as she turned back to Bea's bed, the sound of Dr Patel's footsteps heading in their direction.

Slowly, surely, Bea started to stir. 'I'm not ready to go,' she said, her eyes flicking open. And, taking in all of their faces, she sank back into her pillow, closing her eyes again. 'Oh no, I'm not ready at all.'

CHAPTER 28

Tuesday 19th December

'Wish I had a chance to say goodbye to all the ladies in person, but, you know . . .' Laurie said to Diana.

'I completely understand,' Diana said reassuringly. 'Don't worry. We're all grateful to you, you know. Particularly Andy at the shelter – he says thanks to the auction they'll be having their best Christmas dinner yet.' Despite the heaviness in her heart, Laurie smiled.

'And leave Patrick to me,' Diana said, a determined look on her face. 'I'll sort him out.'

As she went back to the cottage, Laurie cast one last glance around. When she'd arrived, it had all looked cluttered to her – the photos, the cushions, the overflowing bookcases. But now she saw it – it wasn't cluttered at all, it was homey.

She shut the heavy wooden door behind her and dragged her suitcase out to the waiting cab.

On the train from Leeds to London, Laurie thought over her plan. She'd called her Aunt Clara from the cottage and arranged to spend a couple of days with her and Andrea. It wouldn't be right to go back to her flat, and staying on at the cottage, with everything that had happened, would have felt even more wrong. Her aunt had seemed pleased to hear from her; she'd stay there until the time came for Rachel and her family to go home. Laurie thought of Aiden's mother and hoped there would be good news soon.

Laurie got out her iPad and went online, and her finger hovered over the apps. Facebook, Twitter . . . her email. She hesitated for only a moment before switching it back off and looked instead at the wintry scenery that was passing her by. Whatever she might have missed could wait.

The train was due in to Kings Cross at five. As they passed through the outskirts of London Laurie saw Christmas street lights twinkling, fairy-lit trees in people's windows, shops bright with decorations. With the announcement that they'd reached the station her fellow passengers started to get their things ready, taking down bags packed full of brightly wrapped presents and talking excitedly about their plans to meet family, see Christmas shows.

Hauling her luggage off the rack above, Laurie narrowly avoided knocking the head of a guy in an Arsenal shirt. 'Watch it, love,' he said, in a gruff London accent. Laurie stepped out on to the platform and felt around inside her handbag for her Oyster card. It seemed like a hundred years since she'd last swiped it at a ticket barrier and bustled through. A month ago it had been as natural as breathing, but now she was just like one of those tourists who stand maddeningly in front of the barriers, blocking the way as they work out how to use them.

With a deep breath, Laurie pushed her way through the barrier. Her break from reality was over. She wheeled her case through the station, got a takeaway coffee and searched the departure boards for the next train to Bromley.

When it came to Christmas, Aunt Clara never held back, and the illuminated fat Santa in the front yard showed that this year was no exception. The front room was heavily laden with gold tinsel and the artificial tree up in the corner was weighed down by vast amounts of baubles. On the top, as always, was a fat angel with rosy cheeks, tipped slightly forward. Presents were piled high underneath.

The TV blared in the background. Laurie saw it was *The X-Factor*. 'Is it the semi-finals?' she asked, realising she hadn't caught a single episode while she was up in Skipley.

'Yeah,' Andrea replied. 'It's been rubbish this year. But there's this one girl who, they say—'

'Laurie,' Clara said, coming back into the room, and interrupting them. 'Ah, Laurie, Laurie, Laurie,' she said, in her loud, singsong way. She arranged the mugs of tea on the coffee table and put down a packet of Mr Kipling's mince pies. She sat down next to her niece and put a hand on her arm sympathetically. 'Now, I'm glad you're here, darling, don't get me wrong. But don't tell me, is it because you're going to be all alone at Christmas again?' Clara said, looking Laurie directly in the eye and then shaking her head in a way that suggested faint despair. 'No boyfriend, like Andrea?'

'Mum!' Andrea said, eyes wide, before looking pleadingly towards her cousin for forgiveness. Laurie's silence was obviously all the answer she needed.

'I tell you, you have to think about your life outside work too, you know. You and your cousin, honestly, I worry so much about Andrea sometimes ... In your thirties, you two,' Clara said. 'Your mum and me, we both had babies by the time we were your age. You don't have for ever, you know ...'

Andrea rolled her eyes at her cousin, bringing a wry smile to Laurie's lips.

'Anyway,' Clara said, turning back to the table, oblivious, 'your mami. Have you spoken to her? You should call her. She misses you. She can't understand why you insist on spending Christmas alone.'

Laurie took a big sip of tea and tried to remember why she'd thought it was a good idea to come to her aunt's house.

'Why don't you call her, darling,' Clara said, pointing to the kitchen where the phone stood on a side table. 'We get cheap calls to Spain, it's practically free. You should call her.'

Laurie nodded and got to her feet. Anything was preferable to her aunt's incessant guilt trips.

'Ooh, you put on some weight, Laurie,' Clara said, tapping her on the bottom as she moved past, 'getting big, this.'

'I guess I have,' she said, with a shrug. 'Actually, I think it suits me.'

She could hear Clara whispering her approval to her daughter in the front room. It was only slightly quieter than Simon Cowell's crushing analysis.

Laurie took a deep breath, picked up the receiver and dialled her mum's number.

'Mum,' she said as her mother picked up, greeting her in Spanish. She could picture her mum on the balcony of the villa, with its view out towards the pool. 'It's me.'

'Sweetheart,' her mum exclaimed. 'What a lovely surprise. How are you?'

She thought of the texts and calls from her mum that had gone unanswered for too long. It dawned on her that she'd allowed everything in her life to become more important than her own family.

'I'm fine,' she said. It was never too late, though, was it? An idea came to her, and she decided to go with it. 'Listen, I've been thinking. Do you have any plans for New Year? Because if you don't, I'd love to see it in with you.'

Laurie and her mum talked for about twenty minutes while Clara and Andrea prepared dinner. Laurie told her about Skipley, the charity auction, the new recipes she'd tried out. She didn't say anything about Patrick, and her mum didn't mention anything about her own love life. But Laurie felt a new connection and an understanding between them. Her mum was living the vida . . . well, not that loca after all, by the sounds of things. She pictured her mum, streaks of grey in her brown hair now, and her petite figure a little rounder with each passing year. Yes, she'd had her troubles, but she'd always tried her best to be a good mother. Laurie thought back to the painful truth she knew, but had never shared. The house in west London where her dad had made his new life.

'You're going to Spain!' Aunt Clara exclaimed, delighted to hear the news. 'Well, don't make another move until I've spoken to Liliana at the flight company. You know the deals she can get. Internet schminternet,' Clara said. 'Nothing can beat my friend Liliana Gomez.'

Five minutes later, Clara was back. 'Twenty-five pounds one way!' she announced triumphantly as she stepped back into the room. 'Ah, no need to thank your Auntie Clara,' Clara said, coming to give Laurie another smothering hug.

'Thank you, Aunt Clara,' Laurie said.

'You leave on Christmas Day, in the evening,' Clara said, looking at what she'd noted down on a pad, 'and you'll come back on the tenth of January. Seeing as you say you don't want to do anything for Christmas, you may as well take advantage of the cheap flights, eh? It'll be a nice break for you, darling.'

Laurie sat down for Aunt Clara's famous paella. As she smiled and laughed and talked about what she would do when she got out to Spain, what she would eat, what the weather would be like, she felt excited about the trip. But a thought nagged at her conscience. After dinner, she would do it, she thought. There was one more phone call she had to make.

CHAPTER 29

Wednesday 20th December

'Mills,' Rachel said, knocking on her daughter's bedroom door, 'I'm just going downstairs to deliver the Christmas biscuits. Are you sure you won't come too?'

'I'm all right, Mum,' Milly said, opening the door a crack. 'See you in a bit.'

Rachel stopped by Siobhan's flat first, and knocked on the front door. She could hear giggling, music and voices, one of which sounded decidedly gruff and manly. So this must be the P.E. teacher Siobhan had been talking about, she realised. It was probably best not to interrupt. She left a package of biscuits on the doormat outside the flat with Siobhan's card.

Next she popped downstairs to the ground floor, to Lily's. Zak, who had gone down there earlier, opened the door. He was beaming. 'We got Lily's family on Skype,' he said.

As Rachel stepped into the flat, she saw the kitchen table and counter tops were full of food and drink that Lily must have bought in for Christmas Day.

'This way, Mum,' Zak said, pulling Rachel's hand and leading her through into the living room. Lily was leaning into her laptop, smiling and waving. 'Hello, Rachel,' she said, looking up, 'come and see how wonderful this thing is. Meet my grandchildren – look, you can see their little faces!' Rachel walked around and peeked over her shoulder to look at the screen. A boy and two girls' faces were crowded into the screen and they were all talking over each other excitedly. Zak stood back from the screen, smiling proudly.

'Oh,' Lily said, looking away from the screen. 'And Zak's just told me the good news about your Bea!' she said, smiling at Rachel. 'What a Christmas present that is. You couldn't ask for more, could you?'

Rachel put a hand on Lily's shoulder. 'Thank you, Lily. Your support has meant the world to us.'

Lily turned back to her grandchildren. Rachel passed her son the Christmas parcel she'd put together, not wanting to interrupt. 'Will you give this to Lily when she's finished?' Zak peered through the cellophane at the festive treats inside. 'Don't worry,' Rachel said, 'I saved you some. Just come back upstairs when you're done here.'

Rachel looked down at the one remaining Christmas parcel in her hand. Saying goodbye to Zak and giving Lily a wave, she headed back out of the door. She walked up the stairs towards Jay's flat. The last present was for him.

'Bea's woken up,' Rachel said.

'That's amazing!' Jay replied, a wide smile on his face. 'Come in, sit down. Tell me everything. Let's open these now and have some over coffee,' Jay said, taking the biscuits into the kitchen.

Rachel nodded. A few moments wouldn't hurt. The treats made a gentle clattering sound as Jay put them on to a plate.

'I've just been downstairs at Lily's,' Rachel said. 'She's been doing a lot of preparing for Christmas Day. Looks like you guys are going to have quite the feast in store.'

Jay spooned ground coffee into a cafetière. 'Oh yeah?' he said. 'I can't wait.'

The kettle boiled. 'Just a shame that you guys can't be there. You'll be back at your house by then, won't you?'

'Yes,' she said. 'It looks like we might be.' Rachel was only just starting to believe it.

Jay's mobile buzzed on the kitchen table. 'Sorry, do you mind if I get this?' he asked. Rachel nodded that it was fine and he picked up, stepping away and walking into the living room as he answered.

Rachel went back to her coffee and gazed out of the kitchen window. Jay's telephone conversation drifted through the doorway.

'Actually, it's funny you should ask that,' she heard him say to the person at the other end. He walked back into the kitchen and looked directly at Rachel. 'Because she's here with me right now.'

'Thanks for coming, Rach,' Laurie said.

The fact that she was there didn't mean anything, Rachel thought to herself. She would give Laurie half an hour and that was it. She checked the clock on the wall. Five-thirty p.m. She'd be back at the flat by 7 p.m., in time to make Milly and Zak dinner.

Perhaps this had been a bad idea. But when Jay told her that Laurie was back down south and desperate to meet up with her, it would have looked childish to say no. They'd arranged to meet at a pub in Clapham Old Town, one full of people just out of the office, winding down for the holiday with glasses of wine.

An awkward silence hung over their own table. Laurie's blouse was crinkled, her hair flicked up on one side, and she looked tired.

'I came because I wanted to update you,' Rachel said, her tone businesslike. 'Bea's woken up from her coma, she's getting better. So you can have your flat back.'

'That's wonderful,' Laurie said, putting her hand on her heart and smiling. 'It must be a huge relief.'

'Yes, it is,' Rachel said. 'It really is.'

'I'm sorry I wasn't honest at the time,' Laurie said. 'About, you know.'

Rachel bristled – an apology wasn't going to fix things this time.

'Rach, I can't stand this . . . this distance with you,' Laurie said, looking her in the eye.

'That's not fair,' Rachel said, finally snapping. 'I'm allowed to be angry with you, Laurie. Give me that, at least. You lied to my face every day of our friendship.'

'I didn't,' Laurie said, wounded. 'I just didn't tell you the whole truth, all the time.'

Rachel thought of Aiden, pictured Laurie and him together, the image she hadn't been able to push from her mind since finding the note. She'd thought she couldn't face hearing the details, but not knowing them was even worse.

'I have to know, Laurie. What happened with Aiden?'

'What *happened*?' Laurie said, furrowing her brow.

'Yes. When you were together, for how long – whether it was while—'

Laurie cut her off, shaking her head. 'Nothing happened, Rach.'

'Nothing?' Rachel said, feeling numb.

'Nothing,' Laurie repeated.

'But—'

Laurie stepped in to explain herself. 'But I still should have told you that I had a massive, crippling, cringe-inducing crush on Aiden too,' she said, wrinkling her nose before continuing. 'It wasn't fair to listen to you talk about him and pretend I was a disinterested party. Because the truth is, if he'd shown the remotest interest in me back then, I would have gone for it. Sisterhood or no sisterhood.'

Rachel listened, but couldn't join the dots. Yes, it was supremely weird to think of Laurie fancying Aiden. Even twenty years ago. But that wasn't the story she'd been expecting. She was still waiting – for the Laurie-and-Aiden-together part.

'So you were never,' Rachel forced herself to ask, 'you know . . . ?'

'What?' Laurie asked.

'You never, you know, kissed him . . .' Rachel's mind was racing. 'Nothing ever happened?'

Laurie shook her head rapidly. 'Oh God, Rach, no. No way.' She laughed, dismissing the thought with a wave of her hand. 'I never stood a chance in hell. You know how it was for me at school –' she pulled her face into an awkward, geeky expression, her teeth goofy, eyes crossed, and in spite of herself, Rachel smiled – 'I was desperate to be accepted, liked. Aiden was nice to me. I carried on being a bit stalky for a while. I'd write him all these little notes about how much I loved him, sometimes as if we were really going out, then I'd hide them. I never actually had the guts to tell him. The letter you found must have been one of those. Eventually, Brandon – you remember Brandon, don't you?' Rachel remembered Aiden's cocky, short-tempered friend from school. She had to admit she hadn't shed a tear over leaving him behind in Bromley.

'What a charmer he was,' Laurie said, voice heavy with sarcasm. 'He found the notes in my desk and told me straight away how pathetic and deluded I was. Ha. That it was you Aiden fancied. It hurt, but of course he was right – a couple of weeks later Aiden asked you out.'

Rachel took in Laurie's words. All the things that had run through her head, last night and on the way over here – none of them were real. Her marriage was still solid. Her oldest friend hadn't betrayed her, or at least not in any way that really mattered. The tight ball of tension in Rachel's stomach started, slowly, to release.

'You two are meant for each other, Rach.' Laurie smiled. 'Aiden was devoted to you then, and I'm sure he is just as much now. You're the one he's always been in love with. I saw that the moment you got together. Aiden had made his choice; it hurt, but I understood. After a couple of weeks – OK, to be honest, after a few months –' she laughed, wryly – 'I stopped obsessing about him and moved on.' The ghost of a smile appeared on her lips. 'And on . . . and on.' Rachel smiled back. In the Upper Sixth Laurie had blossomed physically and hadn't held back in enjoying the attention, working her way through the best-looking guys in their year. 'But I still wanted so badly to be you.'

Rachel looked at her friend in disbelief, 'Really?' she asked. Rachel had never been anything special. She hadn't been to college, had a career. Not like Laurie – independent, go-getting, glamorous Laurie. Rachel paused for a moment. Rachel might not be Laurie, but she'd achieved a few things in the past month, hadn't she? She thought back to Lily's flat, the redecoration she'd helped to do – she'd enjoyed every minute of it, and the end result looked really good. Maybe she could do something for herself after all. Diana had always had faith in her abilities. But until now, she hadn't believed in them herself. She realised that she wasn't Laurie's less successful opposite – she was a strong and capable woman ready to start her own working life.

'Forgive me?' Laurie asked, hopefully.

Rachel took Laurie's hand across the table and held it. 'If you'll forgive me, for doubting you.'

Laurie squeezed her hand gently and smiled. 'Well, thank God for that,' she said, 'because there's something else I need to talk to you about. And we're going to need some wine for this one, believe me. It's about Milly.'

Rachel flagged down a black cab on the high street, near to Clapham Common. She gave the driver the address of Laurie's flat and climbed inside. She'd said goodbye to Laurie at the tube, and the two of them had hugged. What Laurie had told her about Milly had come as an enormous shock, but with Laurie's support and advice she felt strong enough to try and deal with the situation. Everything else had been forgotten as the two of them focused on what mattered most – making sure that Milly was OK, and that she didn't get hurt.

The taxi made slow progress down Clapham High Street, braking as Christmas shoppers dashed out into the road, hurrying over to M&S for festive booze and food. Rachel willed the road to clear. The short journey dragged, and the meter clicked up – but Rachel couldn't care less about the money. All she cared about was getting back to Milly, and talking to her.

When she got back, she went straight to Milly's room.

'Milly,' she whispered. Then, hearing her daughter's 'Yes', pulled the door open.

Milly was lying on the bed in a pair of tracksuit bottoms and a white T-shirt, her head buried in one of Laurie's *Vogue* magazines.

'Love,' Rachel said, 'have you got a minute?'

'Hi, Mum,' she said. 'Sure. What's up?'

Rachel took a seat on the edge of the bed.

'Is it about Granny?'

'No,' Rachel said, taking off her boots, 'nothing like that. Your granny's recovering well.'

'OK,' Milly said, sitting up cross-legged on the bed. 'Good.'

'I went to see Laurie.'

'Did you? But – how come . . .' Milly said. 'If she's down here . . . how come we're not . . .'

'She's staying with her aunt for a few days, while we wait for Granny to get completely better.'

'OK,' Milly shrugged. 'Weird that we're still here, but whatever.'

'Milly,' Rachel said, taking a breath. 'I know it's not been an easy time, and me and your dad have been caught up worrying about Granny.' Rachel thought back on the times Milly had seemed withdrawn, or even upset, and Rachel had just let her go to her room. 'Is there anything that you want to talk about, Mills?'

'No,' Milly said, closing the magazine and putting it down on the carpet.

'Are you sure? I'm not just talking about here in London. Is there anything back home—'

'Mum,' Milly snapped. 'I'm fifteen. I'm not a kid any more.' She gave her mother a glare. 'I don't have to tell you everything.'

'Mills, I don't want to pry. But I want to help you, if anything's going on.' Rachel saw that her daughter's eyes were watery with tears. But Milly seemed determined not to say a word.

'Milly – who were the balloons really from?' Rachel asked gently, pointing to the wilting metallic cluster in the corner of the room.

'Why are you hassling me again?' Milly said, wrap-

303

ping her arms around her knees and pulling them up towards her.

'Because I care about you. And so does your dad,' Rachel said, putting a hand on Milly's arm and looking her in the eye.

A flush rose in Milly's cheeks. 'OK. They're from a guy. From home. Who likes me.'

Rachel braced herself. She needed to go on, but she didn't want to push Milly away.

'And do you like him?'

'I don't know,' Milly said, looking down. 'I thought I did. But now I'm not sure. I've only met him once.'

'Milly, this guy,' Rachel said. 'He's quite a bit older, isn't he? I don't think—'

'How . . .' Milly said, her cheeks flaring red. 'How do you know that? Have you been snooping in my things?'

'No,' Rachel said, 'I would never do that.' She tried desperately to back-pedal. She couldn't risk Milly shutting down. 'It's just I've heard—'

'What business is it of yours . . .' Milly started, then tears began to spill over her bottom lids. 'What do you mean? What have you heard? What did Laurie tell you?'

'I need to know,' Rachel said, trying to stay calm. 'Are you planning on seeing him again?'

Milly's voice trembled. 'I don't know. I mean I liked him when I met him,' she said. 'He seemed nice. But now – I don't know. There's something weird about him. He's been really pushy about meeting up. Kate and Emma told me he's been asking them stuff about me. It's started to freak me out. I think I might have made a big mistake,' Milly said, biting her lip.

'It's OK, darling,' Rachel said. 'You haven't done anything wrong.' She put her arm around Milly as her daughter's tears started to fall.

Milly deserved to know the full story, Rachel decided, and so when Milly had calmed down Rachel told her what had happened with Laurie.

Milly's jaw dropped. 'The total, utter . . .' she started, indignation taking the place of her tears.

'Obviously Laurie had no idea he'd been in contact with you. But then she saw a text from you on his phone.'

'God, that's so out of order,' Milly said, her face colouring. 'It's embarrassing. What a freak.'

'I agree,' Rachel said. 'But Mills, I'm confused. The thing I'm wondering is what was a smart girl like you doing with a guy that much older in the first place?'

Milly shrugged. 'He didn't tell me his age.'

'But you met him in the pub, apparently? When have you even been to the pub?'

'I went with Kate, once, before we came here. Look, I told you. I'm bored in Skipley. There's nothing to do there – and now I'm at my new school I don't even get to see Kate unless we go out. I met this guy and he offered to drive me to places, I thought maybe I could go somewhere outside the mind-numbingly dull village we have to call home.'

The words struck at Rachel's heart. It was as if Milly really hated the place.

'I want to get out, Mum,' Milly said, 'and I thought this guy might be the answer. But it was stupid. It was never really him I was interested in, Mum. I just wanted something exciting to happen to me for once. I've tried to tell you and Dad how bored I am in Skipley, but you always just gloss over it.'

It was true that Rachel hadn't taken Milly's protests seriously. She'd dismissed them as Milly being spoiled. But, by ignoring her daughter's frustrations, she'd made things worse.

'OK,' Rachel said. 'I can see your point. I should have listened earlier – it was easier for me to tell myself that you were fine, rather than accepting things are different now. You're growing up, and maybe we haven't adjusted to that yet. Once your dad's back, I think we should all talk about this.'

Aiden got home late from the hospital and tried to get into bed without waking Rachel. She heard him and instinctively moved towards him, touching his shoulder. 'How's your mum?' she asked him, still half-asleep.

'She's good,' Aiden whispered. 'Amazing, actually. Good old Mum, from the look of her you'd never know what she'd been through.'

'That's great,' Rachel whispered back. In her sleepy mind she knew that there was something else she should mention to him ... but the thought drifted away. It could wait until the morning, whatever it was.

'I love you, you know,' she said, curling in towards him and feeling the warmth of his chest, touching his hair. He kissed her gently on the mouth. 'I love you too, Rach.'

CHAPTER 30

Friday 22nd December

Aunt Clara and her family had a cherished annual tradition – Christmas karaoke. It was one of the reasons that Laurie had stopped visiting her aunt during the festive season. But this time, there was no way out.

Laurie was staying with Clara and that meant playing by her rules. The twenty-second of December was karaoke night – all the women from Clara's beauty salon, Andrea's schoolfriends and the neighbours from their street were called upon to shout their lungs out to eighties Christmas hits at the local karaoke bar. The one saving grace was that at least it had private rooms, minimising the risk of Laurie being spotted by anyone she knew.

Laurie felt a pang of regret as she thought of what would be happening over in central London that same night. It was the Seamless Christmas meal, and Danny and Laurie's colleagues would be at Nobu, her all-time favourite restaurant. She'd wondered yesterday about calling Danny and seeing if she could still come along – but it didn't feel right. He'd made her take a break, and she wasn't going to go crawling back just for the sake of a slap-up meal.

After dinner, she and Andrea got ready and Clara called friends to arrange last-minute details. She'd put her Santa hat on over roller-perfect curls and her flashing Christmas tree earrings, even though she was still in her dressing gown at this point.

'Do I really, really—' Laurie protested.

'Yes, you do,' Andrea said, in a tone that made it clear there was no room for argument. 'This is my life, Laurie – I do this every single year. And just this once you can make it slightly – slightly – more bearable for me. There's no way you're getting out of this one.'

Laurie wrinkled her nose, then rifled in her handbag for her make-up.

'Stick this gold glitter gel on you and it'll make Mum's day.'

Laurie reluctantly put a little glitter on her shoulders and collarbone. Andrea took it off her and mischievously plastered it all over her cousin's cheeks.

Aunt Clara peeked around the bedroom door. 'Wow – you look pretty!' she exclaimed.

Laurie glanced in the mirror. She looked like an actual bauble. Well, if you can't beat them, she thought to herself, join them.

*

However, after a few Raspberry Margaritas, Laurie turned into a total microphone-hog. Her sultry rendition of 'Baby, It's Cold Outside' brought on a roar of applause and whistles that were near to deafening. From that point onwards there was really no stopping her – Blondie, Tina Turner, Cheryl Cole, she was strutting around to all of them.

'Give it to me!' she shouted, laughing and grabbing the mic from Andrea, who had been dithering for about five minutes about what to sing.

'We're all glad you're enjoying yourself,' Clara said, physically restraining her. 'But snatching's not really in the Christmas spirit, is it, darling?'

By the end of the evening, Laurie had nearly forgotten Patrick Carter even existed. She leaned on Andrea's shoulder in the taxi home, trying to stop everything from spinning. Skipley had been about more than him – she had done it, she had finally learned how to relax. Her mini gap year had worked: Laurie had found herself.

'That was funnnnn,' she shouted out to the three women in the cab. 'Where are we going next? Clubbing? Let's go clubbing! YAY!!'

A message came through on her mobile, she slurred an excuse to the others as she read it, squinting to focus. It was from Danny.

Laurie, Merry Xmas. We're all missing you tonight.

'Ha, good,' Laurie said out loud, to no one in particular. She read on.

Quick work update – the new Navajo bags were only held back a few days – total hit with the Christmas market. Exceeded our expectations. And the faulty bags – well, get this. Someone in-house leaked a photo and it went viral – people thought the logos were an anti-capitalist protest?? There was a rush on our Dalston sample sale and we sold the lot in a morning. Gillian's saying something about anti-branding being the new branding . . . But, listen, it's been crazy without you. We need you. Gillian asked just now if we could talk about you coming back sooner. Start of Jan? What do you say? Dx

Laurie thought about her plane tickets to Spain. How much she'd learned over the course of a month about what she really wanted. She tapped back a short reply.

Hi Danny. Thanks for the offer, but you were right – I do need a break. See you in Feb. Merry Christmas. Lx

She pressed SEND. Her spinning head felt suddenly clearer. When she went back to work, she thought, it wouldn't be like before – working all hours, weekends, evenings. She was in control now, and things were going to change.

CHAPTER 31

Saturday 23rd December

'I still can't believe it,' Bea said, as her family crowded round her bedside. 'They said I'll be home for Christmas – and, touch wood –' she reached out and tapped what was almost definitely a cheap veneer on the side table – 'plenty more to come.' She had a wide grin on her face, an expression none of them had seen for quite a while. Bea really looked fine – only the dressing on her head and a shaved patch of hair gave an indication of what she had gone through, and, typical Bea, she'd already found a sparkly headscarf of Milly's she could cunningly cover it up with. Everyone agreed that it suited her.

Milly gave her gran a big hug. 'I'm so happy you're well, Gran.'

'Me too,' Zak said, reaching in to join their cuddle.

The ward, which had looked so bare, cold and unwelcoming each time they'd come to visit Bea, now seemed to be bathed in a warmer light. From Bea's bedside you could see a fairy-lit Christmas tree and make out the glimmer of decorations hung up and down the corridor.

Aiden's head turned as Dr Patel came in through the curtain.

'All the family here to see you, Mrs Murray?'

'Yes, Doctor, they're rather a lovely bunch, aren't they?' she smiled. 'Don't know how they put up with me sometimes, but I'm happy they'll have to do it for quite a while longer.'

'Yes, they certainly will,' Dr Patel said. 'You gave us all quite a scare. Unfortunately any operation like this carries risks and you were very unlucky. But I'm pleased to tell you that the surgeon managed to remove all of the tumour. The chances of it recurring are small, but of course if you do notice any symptoms returning – please don't ignore them. We'll need to do some tests on your hearing before you leave here, and your GP back home will follow up on those checks. You'll need to rest over the next couple of months, and no driving either.'

'When do you think we'll be able to take her back home?' Rachel asked tentatively.

'She should be fine to go in a few days,' said Dr Patel, with a smile. 'So you'll be home in time for Christmas. Just remember to rest when you get there, Mrs Murray,' she said, with a look at her patient that showed her suspicion that Bea was unlikely to sit still for a moment after the enforced bed rest she'd already had.

Rachel felt a wave of relief. As she joined the children in their hug, she reached around and held Aiden's hand. She caught his eye and felt a missing piece of her heart slip back into its regular place.

'Half an hour and we're out of here,' Rachel called out, as she cleared the breakfast bowls. 'Go on, scram – pack up your last bits of stuff,' Aiden said, as Zak popped back and opened his mouth to ask another question – it was his classic delaying tactic.

Aiden caught Rachel's eye and smiled. 'It's almost like . . .' His words trailed off.

'Just what I was thinking,' she said, and touched his hand. His brow furrowed, but his smile remained. 'Go, on,' Rachel said, 'you're allowed to think it now, you know.'

'It's almost like normal,' he said. 'Mum's the main thing, of course,' Aiden added, bringing Rachel in towards him and kissing her head. 'But it's more than that.' He leaned back against the counter, a dazed smile on his face. 'Everything just seems to be coming together, Rach. The first two pieces of Jay's furniture have arrived and Simon says they were a real hit. I still can't quite believe it – we've pulled off the Westley barn job, and more than that – the clients are thrilled. I've spoken to that furniture showroom about us promoting Jay's designs and they've agreed – so it looks like we'll be able to carry on working closely together.'

'That's fantastic,' Rachel said, Aiden's exhilaration blending with her own sense of relief.

'John and Sue, the Westley-barn owners, have recommended us to some friends of theirs – a couple who have bought a church in Giggleswick and want to convert it into a family home. We've never worked on a church before, but you know I've been wanting a challenge like this – and it could open up a whole new market for us.'

Rachel gave Aiden's arm a squeeze. 'I've got a good feeling about next year,' she said, with a smile.

'Me too,' he said. Then he leaned in and gave her a kiss.

Bea was in the passenger seat, so she got to listen to *The Archers* at top volume. Granny's prerogative, she said.

Rachel was crammed into the back seat with Milly and Zak, and the boot was overflowing with their luggage.

'Is it nearly over, Gran?' Milly whined. 'I mean seriously, what even happens in *The Archers*? It's the same every single time.'

'Oh, you're wrong there,' Bea said, turning around in her seat. 'Quite wrong. Have you forgotten when that chap fell off the roof? You can't miss it, Milly. It's too important. Something like that might happen again.'

Milly let out a groan. Rachel was squashed up against the car door, with a teenager, a six-year-old boy, pillows and soft toys surrounding her. The only thing keeping Zak quiet was chomping on a bag full of gummy E numbers she'd probably live to regret giving him when the hyperactivity kicked in.

Rachel didn't like goodbyes, and even though she was looking forward to getting home, their farewells to Jay and Siobhan had made her feel sad. At least she knew she'd see Jay again soon – he would be coming up to Yorkshire in the New Year with more furniture for the barn, and to install everything with Aiden.

Lily had tried hard to convince all of them to stay and sample some of her Christmas-Day feast. 'It's the least I can do after what you did, making my home so beautiful again,' she had said. 'If it weren't for all of you, I wouldn't have such a pretty home to show off at the party. I insist. I've got pull-out mattresses,' she'd said.

In the end she'd given in, sending them away with a mini Caribbean Christmas cake and a bottle of rum. 'You all have your celebration,' she said. 'But then, on Boxing Day, have this, and remember your old neighbour Lily.'

Zak and Milly had given her hugs goodbye and Zak pulled out a hand-made Christmas card. 'We can Skype,' Zak said, and Lily smiled.

'Of course, son. Thanks to you, I know how to do it myself now.'

Aiden had gone ahead to check that the car was working OK and it was with a wave of relief that Rachel heard the engine start up. 'That's our cue,' she said.

Then another sound, purring, like a quiet motorbike, came from around Lily's feet. Zak and Milly swung around. Mr Ripley crept past Lily's legs and towards them, putting up his head to be stroked.

As Rachel looked at her family, it was hard to believe they'd only been away from Skipley for a month. Life had been turned upside-down for each of them, and yet here they were, heading back home. But they were closer than ever. Yes, Christmas would be a little thrown together this year – she hadn't reserved a turkey and none of the normal preparations had been made. Who knows – they might even end up eating pizza – but it just didn't matter. She had all of her family together and happy and that was what mattered.

As the Ambridge theme tune played out and Bea agreed to put on a CD, Rachel called out that she had a request. She located the CD in the holder stuffed into the passenger-seat pocket and passed it forward. Bea put it on, and Milly was the first to recognise it and start to sing, the whole family joining in:

'We're driving home for Christmas ...'

Back at the cottage, Rachel brought down the box of baubles and tinsel from upstairs, and Zak and Milly emptied it in an instant. Milly sifted through the decorations, picking out her favourites. They'd been lucky enough to find a tree for sale on the high street as they drove through it on their way home, and Aiden and Rachel had strapped it to the roof.

Rachel went to get them all drinks, humming along to the carols on the radio. They'd made a family decision that their unpacking could wait until later. As she walked towards the fridge she noticed a Christmas card on the counter top.

She ripped open the white envelope to find a reindeer-shaped card inside.

'*Murrays!*' Laurie had written at the top.

Thank you for letting me stay in the cottage. Have a wonderful Christmas. I've reserved a turkey for you at the butcher's, it'll be ready for collection on Christmas Eve.

Love,
Laurie x

P.S. There are a few things for you in the fridge.

Rachel opened the fridge door, full of curiosity. There were various Tupperware boxes and packages in there. She took them out and put them on the side.

She opened the first one – cranberry sauce. The next – mini Christmas wreaths.

'Aiden,' she shouted over, 'come and look at this.'

Opening a lid at a time, she saw that each box was filled with something from *Bea's Countdown to Christmas*. A smile swept over her face.

'I thought you said Laurie wasn't big on cooking?' Aiden said, draping his arm around Rachel's shoulder.

'Well, it looks like people can change,' Rachel said proudly. 'Doesn't it?'

It was 10 p.m., Zak was in bed and Milly was up in her room, reading. 'Do you think it's safe?' Aiden asked, with a smile on his face, looking around the living room as if someone might pop out of a broom closet.

'I reckon so,' Rachel said, taking out the bags of presents that they still needed to wrap. Aiden got the wrapping paper, ribbons and tape out of the top drawer of their wooden chest, and the two of them sat down on the living room rug.

'Bubbles?' she asked, cracking open a bottle of Prosecco before he could answer and filling glasses for them both. Aiden put on the Christmas-carol CD they always listened to while they were wrapping presents. They'd done it every year since the first one they were married. A precious slice of time alone as a couple before the mayhem started. It was a tradition they'd sworn never to let go.

Aiden was wrestling with the tape dispenser. 'This thing's attacking me,' he said. As he took the glass from Rachel gratefully with his other hand, Rachel untangled him from the sticky tape.

'You're free,' she said.

'Where would I be without you?' he smiled.

They chinked their glasses and Aiden pulled her close for a kiss. 'And as well as being heroic and helpful, you also look beautiful tonight.'

Rachel accepted the compliment, and, for once, believed it. She had on her favourite glittery black dress with long silver earrings. She'd looked in the mirror earlier and seen that the stress had fallen away from her face. The creases between her eyebrows had disappeared and the colour had come back into her cheeks. A slick of red lipstick was all she needed to feel glamorous that night.

'Can we relax now, do you think?' Aiden said.

'I think so,' Rachel said. 'Once we've got these presents wrapped anyway.' She put Milly's new hair straighteners down sideways and wrapped them in silver paper.

'No, I'm being serious. Are we sure this guy's gone?' Aiden asked. 'The creep who was talking to Milly?'

'Oh God, yes,' Rachel said. 'Put it this way, would

you hesitate if Diana put her mind to running you out of town? Actually he legged it pretty soon after Laurie left town. Apparently he's not even from round here. He's a drifter, who the charity took on as a van driver, that was all the work he actually did for them – but he made everyone think he was a proper employee. He seems to have fooled a lot of people around here.'

'Unbelievable,' Aiden said. 'What a nasty piece of work. If I saw him now . . .' He shook his head. 'Well. Just best that I don't, really.'

'I know. But hopefully something good's come out of this whole horrible situation. At least Milly seems to be telling us the truth now. We have her – I think – back on side. We're all talking properly again. Or at least starting to.'

'You're right,' Aiden said. 'And as much as I would love to throttle this Patrick guy, I think coming face-to-face with an irate Diana was probably the worse punishment.'

Rachel laughed.

'Listen, Aiden,' she said, taking another sip of Prosecco. 'Talking of Diana.'

'Mmm-hmm,' Aiden said, distracted, as he tried to bite off a piece of Sellotape with his teeth.

'Not like that,' Rachel said, intervening with a pair of scissors. 'There's something I wanted to talk to you about.'

'Fire away,' Aiden said.

'Before we went to London, Diana suggested something to me. The time away gave me some space to think about it. She wants me to come on board with her interior design business. You know the sort of things she does – she's planning to branch out into children's bedrooms. She likes the way I decorated Zak and Milly's – and, well, I really enjoyed doing that. She said perhaps together we could build up that side of things. She'd pay to train me up.'

Rachel felt nervous. Not because of what Aiden might say, but because to say it out loud made it seem like a real possibility – up till now it had been no more than a dream. 'I know I've never done anything like it before. But I've realised I'm ready for a new challenge.'

'And working is something that you want?' Aiden asked. 'Because if it is, then you should go for it. I've always said you've got so much to give.'

A smile crept back on to Rachel's face.

'But you're not doing it because you're worried about money, are you, Rach? I'm really hopeful that next year is going to be a good one for the business.'

'It's not that, sweetheart,' Rachel said. 'Although of course I want to contribute too. But it's more than that – now that the kids are older, I want to do something for me.'

'Well, then you should do it, Rach,' Aiden said. 'I know you'll make us all proud.'

CHAPTER 32

Saturday 23rd December

Laurie turned the key in the front door and stepped inside the hallway of her apartment block. She was still a little tired after the night of karaoke, and braced herself to lug her suitcase up the stairs.

'Hey,' came a familiar voice. She looked up and saw Jay walking towards her across the hall. He wore a dark jacket with a scarf around his neck, and a pair of jeans with dark-brown brogues. 'Can I give you a hand with that?'

'Hi,' she said, still a little startled by his sudden appearance, and by the way her spirits had immediately lifted at the sight of him. 'Yes. Thank you. Unless you're on your way somewhere?'

'It can wait,' he said.

Laurie tried to stop herself thinking about where he was going.

Jay reached down for the suitcase and winced theatrically for a split second as he lifted it. 'Have you got a dead body in here?' he asked, laughing.

'I'm smuggling in a St Bernard,' she replied, then,

in a hushed voice, 'I know Siobhan's not a dog-fan, so keep it on the down-low.'

'So how was it?' Jay said, as they walked up the stairs together. 'The countryside?'

'OK,' Laurie said, 'I liked it, in some ways.'

He tilted his head and picked up the bag again, taking it up the final flight of steps before bringing it to rest in front of her front door.

'Really?'

'Yes. It wasn't *all* bad,' she said, a smile creeping on to her lips. 'Although it's good to be back, I must say.'

'How did you manage to get so long off work?'

'Long story,' Laurie said. Jay waited for her to say more. 'I got sort-of temporarily sacked,' she said.

'What?' he replied, incredulous. 'But you run everything there.'

Jay was so close to her she could almost feel his warmth. She couldn't think about anything other than how much she wanted to kiss him. It was torture having him right there, nearly close enough to touch. She'd been fooling herself to think she could start something with Patrick – even when it was going well, those feelings had paled in comparison to what she still felt for Jay.

'Actually Danny texted me last night and asked me to come back earlier. But I told him no. I'm not ready to go back just yet. There's more to life than work.'

'Sounds like you did some thinking while you were away,' Jay said, after a long silence.

'Yes, I did. And I hear you've been busy too. Rachel told me about the furniture you've been working on for Aiden's barn conversion.'

'It's a great opportunity,' he said. 'I'm grateful to Aiden for taking a chance on me.'

The conversation stopped again. Jay's eyes drifted down, and then back up to Laurie. 'It was quiet without you, you know.'

'I'm not sure how to take that,' Laurie said, laughing. 'Good quiet, or boring quiet?'

Jay's eyes lingered on hers. 'Boring quiet,' he said, with a smile. 'Definitely.' She felt a rush of excitement and pleasure. Wasn't that a bit like saying that he'd, sort of, missed her?

She hesitated for a moment, deciding whether to ask him in. A coffee – it was a normal, neighbourly invitation to make.

His eyes had flicked down towards the stairway window, where sleet was battering against the glass pane. 'Right – I'm going out in that now.'

Oh. Of course, she thought. Coffee was probably a stupid idea anyway. She'd probably only say something to ruin things. 'Rather you than me,' she said, with a nod at the window. 'Bath, wine, bed – that's my plan.' She opened the door to her flat and pulled her suit-case inside.

'Well, I'd better be going,' Jay said, 'but welcome back, Laurie.'

'Thank you,' she said.

She closed her front door behind her and leaned back against it, breathing out. What was it about him? She felt like a snow globe that had been turned upside down and shaken up.

Christmas was only two days away, and she hadn't even asked him about it, she realised. She wheeled her suitcase through to her bedroom, and then went into the kitchen to put the kettle on and put on the radio, which was, as she flicked between the channels, blasting out Christmas tunes on every one. She glanced around. There was something strange about the flat. It felt different, but she couldn't put her finger on why. Then she spotted the colourful paper chain around the kitchen doorway. She peeked out and into her living room – there over by the bay window was a beautiful display of branches threaded through with white lights, and holly and ivy were draped over her living-room mantelpiece. Paper chains were draped over the window frames and a pile of Christmas cards had been laid out carefully on her coffee table, next to one of those festive, red-petalled plants she could never remember the name of. Laurie's hand went to her mouth. Her flat looked more beautiful, and well – cared for – than she'd ever seen it.

She walked around the living room taking it all in.

There wasn't a tree – thank God, she hated pine needles – but the room was stunningly decorated. She saw a large card up on the mantelpiece with her name on it. She took it down and opened it, full of childlike anticipation.

Laurie read over the Murray family's Christmas message and a scribble from Zak: 'I made the paper chains'. On the left-hand side of the card was a note from Rachel: 'Look what we found!' Paperclipped to the card was a photo of Rachel and Laurie at school. Laurie smiled: she could even remember when it had been taken; the day after their last exam, when they'd driven to the coast. Laurie tucked it into the corner of her mirror fondly.

CHAPTER 33

Sunday 24th December, Christmas Eve

Bea had spent the morning supervising the making of her famous gingerbread house with Milly and Zak. Milly was putting the pieces in the oven, ready to bake.

'Give them twenty-five minutes,' she said, from her spot at the kitchen table, 'and next we can glue it all together with icing so that it makes a house. I can help with that part.'

Rachel looked across at Bea – she was like a different woman than she had been in the hospital ward. The colour had come back into her face, and her cropped blonde hair was once again perfectly styled. She wore a neat navy cardigan with a white blouse and tailored trousers.

'Can we put Smarties and gummy bears on it when we decorate it, Granny?' Zak asked.

'Of course,' Bea said, ruffling her grandson's hair. 'I've got some silver balls to put on it too.'

'And can we do the cinnamon stars afterwards?' he asked, a cheeky smile on his face.

'Can we?' Milly joined in, holding up a star-shaped biscuit cutter and peeking through it.

It was such a good feeling to have Milly home with them all on Christmas Eve. To think that tonight she could have been – Rachel stopped herself. It didn't bear thinking about.

'Don't let them wear you out, Bea,' Rachel said, getting to her feet. 'They'll have you baking till midnight if they get their way.'

'But the house is special,' Zak said. 'Milly talking about the house woke you up.'

Rachel and Bea smiled.

'Don't worry about me, Rachel, I'm just fine. It's good to be busy.'

'But the doctors said . . .'

'Oh pah!' Bea dismissed it. 'If I've learned anything from this, it's to enjoy life while you're here, and not waste a moment. And I always take what doctors say with a big pinch of salt.' She gave Rachel a wink. While Rachel and Aiden were insisting that she take it easy, Bea's social life had started coming to her. Joyce and Pam had already popped by to say hello and bring her Christmas presents.

'Did you hear about Diana?' Bea whispered to Rachel conspiratorially as Zak drifted over to the counter and pulled the wooden spoon out of the bowl to lick. Rachel shook her head, no. 'She's in love,' Bea said, her eyes bright with the gossip. 'With Graham, the pub landlord. Such a nice chap. Wouldn't have had him pegged as her type, not for a moment, but you just never can tell.'

'Wow. Now that is a surprise,' Rachel said. Diana had made man-hating a full-time occupation over the past few months. That was a pretty big turnaround in just a few weeks.

'And she looks good too,' Bea finished. 'In fact, come to think of it, I don't know what's been going on around here, but most of the ladies are better dressed than before. Joyce was wearing a lovely top with a big bow it on this morning. And wasn't she saying something about being a supermodel? Perhaps my head's still not quite right . . .'

'It's not your head. That'll be Laurie,' Rachel said, smiling to herself. It sounded like Skipley had been caught up in Laurie's fashion whirlwind.

'Well, I don't know what your friend did, but she certainly seems to have livened things up around here.'

As they sat around the fireside that evening, full of the chicken pie that Aiden had made, Milly turned to her parents.

'You know when we talked the other day,' Milly started, 'and you said I should be honest with you, about the things I want to do.'

'Yes,' Rachel said with slight trepidation, glancing over at Aiden. They'd spoken with Milly together, before leaving London, and promised that they would listen to her more in future.

'Do you think I could go down and stay with Auntie Laurie, in the Easter holidays, say? Maybe I could do some work experience with her at Seamless?' she said. 'See Nikki at the same time?'

Rachel looked over at her daughter – she seemed so grown up and self-assured. She and Aiden would have to get used to the fact that Milly was never going to be their little girl again.

'What do you think?' Aiden said, turning to Rachel, 'would Laurie would be OK with that?'

'I don't see why not,' Rachel said. 'Laurie's always said she'd love to have you come and stay with her. I don't know about the work experience, we'll have to ask – but if she's not too busy, I reckon she'll probably like the idea of you being her little protégé. Let's ask her when she's back from Spain.'

'Thanks, Mum and Dad, you're amazing,' Milly said, leaping to her feet and hugging both of them. 'I just know that next year is going to be totally amazing. I can feel it.'

Rachel hugged her back. She wasn't sure what she and Aiden were letting themselves in for, but trusting Milly with more freedom felt right.

After the kids had gone to bed, Aiden pushed a satsuma into the stocking Milly had hung on the mantelpiece.

'Funny, isn't it,' he said. 'That she's so grown-up now and yet there'd be a mutiny if she didn't get a stocking'

'Yes,' Rachel said, standing behind Aiden and putting her arms around his waist. She leaned close. He dropped one of his hands so that it was gently holding hers.

'Rach,' he said, turning around to face her. 'Come and sit down.' He led her over to the sofa where they both took a seat. 'I want to give you your present early this year.'

'Oh really?' she said, surprised. 'That's new. How come?'

He took out a wide envelope and handed it to her. 'Just because.'

Rachel took the envelope and opened it carefully. She gasped when she saw what was inside. 'Aiden, we can't . . . we shouldn't –' her hand flew to her mouth – 'two tickets to Venice?'

'Don't worry. Let's just say I called in a couple of favours. I booked us into a nice little family-run place, not quite five-star, but it looked beautiful. And Diana said she'd be happy to look after the kids for a long weekend, if Mum's not better by then.'

'But Aiden . . .' Rachel said, a lump forming in her throat. She pictured the canals, the gondolas, the palazzos – spending some time alone there with Aiden was something she'd always dreamed of. 'You know I've always wanted to go to Italy.'

'I do. And now this can be the honeymoon we never had.' He smoothed her wild hair back softly behind her ear. 'Milly put a bit of a spanner in the works the first time, didn't she? There's just one thing I'm going to need from you first,' Aiden said.

'Oh yes?' Rachel said, suspicious.

'Yes,' reaching behind him to the side table he picked something up and held it over their heads. Rachel laughed at the sight of the sprig of mistletoe with white berries.

'I think I can manage that,' she said, and as Aiden leaned in towards her she kissed him tenderly on the lips, feeling a rush of love as strong as she'd felt on the day they got married.

• ❄ •

From: Ben.groves@gmail.com
To: Millypede@gmail.com

Milly, hi.

Merry Christmas!

It's Ben, from school. Laurie mentioned you'd be coming back to Skipley around now, so I wanted to let you know I'm having a party for New Year's Eve. Do you fancy coming? It'll be fun (I promise). Nothing big, just a few friends. I thought it might be good for you to meet some people, given that you've not been at our school for long.

Anyway, hope you can make it.

Ben G.

From: Millypede@gmail.com
To: Ben.groves@gmail.com

Hi Ben,

Thanks for the invite – that would be great. Will just get the
OK from the olds, but as you're only round the corner I'm
sure it will be fine. OK if I bring a friend?

Looking forward to it.

Milly x

CHAPTER 34

Sunday 24th December, Christmas Eve

'Laurie, glad as I am to have you back, you know I hate shopping,' Siobhan grumbled as Laurie dragged her through Covent Garden. 'And on Christmas Eve?'

'I've got to pick up something special for Mum,' she said. 'And anyway, look. It's nice,' Laurie said, sweeping an arm to take in Christmassy stalls and brightly lit shop windows, rosy-cheeked shoppers loaded up with silver and gold boxes and bags.

'You've changed,' Siobhan said, scrutinising her friend's face to try and identify where this newfound Christmas cheer was coming from.

'Chestnuts?' Laurie asked, stopping at a stall to buy herself a paper bag of them.

'Yes, please,' Siobhan said, rubbing her cheeks vigorously to warm them up. 'Anything hot right now would be good.'

'But seriously,' Siobhan said, accepting the toasty paper bag and returning with Laurie to the pavement scrum, 'since when did you start feeling so festive? Last thing I heard, you weren't even going to come to Lily's.'

Laurie had been feeling a little Scrooge-like lately, it was true – and she was still planning on having a quiet celebration by herself this year, rather than going down to Lily's.

'I'm still thinking I might give that a miss,' Laurie said. 'Although I haven't told Lily yet. But I'm really looking forward to going out to Spain and spending some time with Mum – champagne and dancing in the square on New Year's Eve. Plus it's twenty degrees out there at the moment.'

'Can you pack me up in your suitcase?' Siobhan said, shelling another chestnut. 'I could really do with a bit of sunshine right now.'

'You look pretty glowing to me,' Laurie said, noting the flush in her friend's cheeks. Siobhan's smittenness was written all over her face. From what she'd told Laurie already it sounded like the stress and strains of secondary-school teaching were rapidly being erased by plenty of acrobatic sex.

'Thank you,' she said. 'It's so weird, Laurie. I mean it's all happened really quickly. And now Ed's inviting me along to meet his family. It's so early – I mean, what are they going to think of little old me?'

'They'll love you,' Laurie said. 'Everyone loves you.'

Siobhan gave her friend a gentle punch in the arm. 'Aw,' she said, wrinkling her nose a little. 'I never knew you cared.'

'Well, I do,' Laurie said, stopping at a jewellery stall by the side of the road. 'And I'm going to need you more than ever, now that I'm going on a proper man fast,' she said, picking up a necklace and holding it to her collarbone for Siobhan's inspection. 'What do you think of this?' she asked, the silver that backed the amber pendant cold against her skin. 'Just imagine me with darker, more olive-y skin.' Then she pointed to her hair. 'And a few more grey streaks.'

Siobhan peered in closer. 'I can already see some of those actually.' She zeroed in on a grey strand and pulled it out, holding it up for Laurie's inspection.

'Aargh,' Laurie said, wincing and swatting her friend away. 'No decent hairdressers up north. So, go on, is it nice?'

'The amber's gorgeous,' Siobhan said, 'but the turquoise is beautiful too,' as she lifted up a similar necklace with a smaller pendant.

'Turquoise for Mum,' Laurie said, smiling. 'And the amber for you.'

After they'd finished their Christmas shopping Siobhan and Laurie collapsed on Siobhan's sofa, watching *Serendipity* for what must have been the hundredth time. Siobhan had reasoned bad John Cusack in Christmastime New York trumped John Cusack in a decent film, so they'd put aside *Grosse Point Blank* to watch afterwards, to put the theory to the test. A tin of Quality Street was open between them, and brightly coloured wrappers littered the sofa and floor – purples and yellows on Laurie's side, gold and greens on Siobhan's. They were both immersed in the film when Siobhan's mobile rang.

'Hi,' Siobhan answered. It must be Ed, Laurie thought, noticing the flirty tone Siobhan's voice had taken. And judging by the way she was swiftly sweeping the sofa clear of chocolate wrappers, he was probably coming by.

'That was Ed,' Siobhan said, as she lay her mobile down on the coffee table. 'Holy crap, he's coming around, and he's only five minutes away.'

Siobhan dashed to the bathroom. 'Got to put some slap on,' she said. 'Stay and meet Ed,' she called out, her voice echoing off the tiles. 'You'll like him,' she said, poking her head out of the doorway. Laurie wasn't sure – the men Siobhan had dated before were wafty, Tantric-sex enthusiasts who smelled of incense – in short, not Laurie's idea of great company, and definitely not the kind of person she wanted to spend Christmas Eve with. But she owed it to Siobhan – and she'd said Ed was different.

The intercom buzzed and Siobhan let loose a tirade of swear words. 'Don't worry, I'll let him in,' Laurie called back. She tried to buzz Ed in, but he didn't seem to be getting the door-pushing timing quite right.

After a minute or so, he was quietly swearing as much as Siobhan had just been, seemingly oblivious to the fact that Laurie could hear his every word through the speaker.

'I'll go down and get him,' Laurie said. 'And you,' she took in Siobhan's silky dressing gown, 'get some clothes on in the meantime.'

Downstairs, Laurie opened the front door to find Ed standing out in the cold, a black wool coat pulled tightly round him. He was hard to miss – over six foot, with broad shoulders and short dark hair, his cheeks wind-reddened. The feature you couldn't miss, though, was a grin that seemed to stretch from one ear to the other.

'Tough entry policy here,' he joked, putting his hand out to greet Laurie. 'I'm Ed. You must be Laurie. Nice to meet you.' Laurie went to shake his hand, then kissed him on the cheek instead; it seemed more natural.

'It's good to meet you too. I've heard a lot about you.' Laurie beckoned him in.

As she turned around to walk back into the hallway, she saw that Jay was behind her, on his way out. He looked from Laurie to Ed. Was Laurie imagining it, or did his face fall a little?

'Merry Christmas,' he said, and with a nod to Laurie and then to Ed, he headed out of the front door.

*

Siobhan passed Laurie a piping hot cup of mulled cider and she wrapped her mittened hands around it. The gospel choir had just started their carol service in the square by Brixton Town Hall and a big crowd had gathered. They broke into a searing rendition of 'O Come All Ye Faithful' that gave Laurie goosebumps. Lily was in the front row, singing her heart out. It was a crisp, clear evening – kids ran and danced in front of the choir, their parents tucked into mince pies, and the grannies and grandpas were out in force. Siobhan nudged her. 'Worth getting off the sofa for, wasn't it?' Laurie nodded, and took a sip of warming cider. Ed put his arm around Siobhan and held her close.

OK, Ed was lovely. Laurie had to admit it. He seemed totally into Siobhan, laughed at all her crap jokes, and had even made Laurie feel like she wasn't a gooseberry. On the walk down he'd entertained them both with stories about the kids he taught, and bought them both sparklers from a guy in the square.

Fireworks went off and the choir sang even louder. Laurie found herself joining in with the song – all this Christmas cheer was getting a bit contagious.

CHAPTER 35

Monday 25th December, Christmas Day

'Look what I got,' Zak said, emptying his stocking out on to his parents' bed. It was 6.30 a.m. and Rachel groaned as she gradually woke up, then, seeing her son's gleeful face, found a smile.

Inside Zak's stocking, among the other small gifts, was a beetle that rattled across the floor in an alarmingly realistic fashion.

Later, over their breakfast of scrambled eggs and smoked salmon, he showed it to his grandma.

'Why, that's *lovely*, darling,' Bea said, smiling and then looking at Rachel with a raised eyebrow.

Aiden filled his mother's plate high and passed it over to her. 'Wow,' she said. 'That's a sight for sore eyes after all the hospital food, I can tell you,' she laughed. In a red cardigan with a holly leaf brooch on it, Bea was a picture of health. She had managed to sneak her presents in and under the tree without Zak or Milly seeing.

They all took their cups of tea over to the sitting

room area and cosied up under blankets. 'Can I be postman?' Zak said, standing tall in his blue pyjamas.

'Yes,' Aiden said, with a wink.

Zak delivered presents to all of them to open. Rachel opened one from Milly – a delicate green scarf. 'It's gorgeous,' she said, holding it up. 'Did you make this, Mills?'

'I found the pattern in one of Laurie's books,' Milly said, with a modest shrug. 'So do you like it, Mum?'

'I love it,' Rachel said, giving her a hug.

'Aha!' Bea exclaimed, as the paper fell away from the gift she was opening. She held up a DVD of *Out of Africa*. Aiden had bought it for her, thinking of the African memoir they'd read to her while she was in hospital. 'It's a fascinating story, this one.'

Bea looked as if she was about to say something, then paused. 'It's a funny thing, you giving me this, actually.'

'Is it?' Aiden said, puzzled.

'Yes,' Bea went on. 'There's something I've been meaning to tell you all.'

The CD came to a stop. Everyone, even Zak, waited for Bea to continue.

'When I was getting better in the hospital,' Bea said, cradling her mug of tea – Rachel's heart constricted as she recalled those dreadful moments when they'd been waiting for Bea to come out of her coma, wondering if she ever would – 'I had some time to think. And seeing as I seem to be OK, I want to make the most of the time I have.'

'The thing is,' Bea continued, 'while I've done a lot in my life that I'm proud of –' one hand went, unconsciously, to touch the locket around her neck, which held a small photo of David, Aiden's father, and looked over at her grandchildren, who were watching her with rapt attention – there are some things that David and I never got round to.'

Rachel felt confused. Bea had always seemed so content, going about her day-to-day tasks and caring for her grandchildren. She had her friends, and her bridge evenings, her activities in the community. It had never crossed Rachel's mind that Bea might want anything more.

'I want to go to Africa,' Bea announced.

Aiden nearly spat out his mouthful of tea in shock. 'You what, Mum?' he said, sitting bolt upright.

'I want to go on safari, with a tour group,' she said, pulling a brochure out of her bag. Zak leapt up on to the sofa next to her and peered at the photos of lions and elephants. 'Cool!' he shouted out, looking up with a wide grin on his face.

Bea's smile grew as wide as his as she pointed to photos of the African sunset and hippos in watering holes.

'But, Mum,' Aiden said. 'You're only just out of hospital – and the doctors said—'

'Don't worry,' Bea said, waving away her son's concerns. 'I'm not going to head off this minute. But I was looking through this brochure.' Rachel saw it was a Trailfinders one that had come through the cottage door weeks back. 'I remember Diana saying she wanted to go after her husband left, but with the business doing so well she decided to wait. Well, I've got no work to worry about these days, and I've got some savings still. David and I always talked about travelling together –' her eyes glinted with tears, but her smile remained – 'but we ran out of time.'

'I think David would be very proud of you doing it on your own,' Rachel said, her own eyes welling up.

'Me too, Granny. I think it's a great idea,' Milly added.

'Well, if you insist,' Aiden said, reluctantly. 'But make sure you give yourself plenty of time to get better first. And please promise to be careful?'

'Of course I will be,' Bea said.

'OK,' Aiden said, hesitantly. 'Well in that case, with all this news, I think it's about time we cracked open some champagne to celebrate.'

He went over to the fridge and got out a bottle, letting the cork fly with a pop.

'Four glasses this year, I think, don't you?' Rachel called out to Aiden, giving her daughter a wink. Milly smiled and gave her mum's arm a squeeze.

'Once a year, Mills,' Aiden said, as he got the glasses out of the cupboard, 'so don't go getting any ideas.'

After lunch – a plump turkey together with all the delicious treats Laurie had made for them, the Murrays were lying slouched across the couches in the living room. Zak was acting out a charade, and, shielding his mouth with his hands, unsubtly whispering the answer to his grandma.

'Charlie and the Chocolate Factory!' Bea called out. Milly groaned good-naturedly and shifted her position on the sofa so that her head was resting against her dad's shoulder. 'Every year, Zak. You can't keep cheating like that, you know. It's really obvious.'

Rachel got to her feet and picked up a box of chocolates from the sideboard. 'Chocs?' she said, passing them around. Eager hands reached out, and she passed the picture list to Bea, the most discerning chocolate eater among them. 'Shall we let Granny choose first? After all, she's not going to be able to eat many chocolates when she's on safari.'

'You know what, Rach,' Aiden said, with an expression of faux puzzlement. 'I think we might've forgotten one present. What do you reckon?'

'I think you're right,' Rachel said. 'Maybe something fell out of Santa's sack on the way to the tree?'

Zak swung his head from left to right looking for a present that they might have missed.

'There's something in your stocking, Zak,' Milly said, spotting a large red envelope poking out of the top of the emptied stocking which had been rehung on the mantelpiece.

Zak dashed over to retrieve it and bounced on to the sofa next to his sister. 'It's got both our names on it,' he said. 'Can I open it?' Milly nodded, and he ripped open the red paper with gleeful abandon. Inside was a cut-out card of a marmalade-coloured cat. 'What does it say?' Milly nudged him. Zak opened the card. 'Vou-cher,' he read slowly. Milly took over, reading over his shoulder, '"This voucher entitles the holders –" that's us, Zak – "to a . . ."' Milly's eyes lit up and her hand went to her mouth. Aiden turned to Rachel and gave her a wink as Milly finished reading, '". . . to a kitten of their choice."'

CHAPTER 36

Monday 25th December, Christmas Day

'Merry Murray Christmas!' Laurie called down the phone.

'And to you too,' Rachel said back. Laurie could hear Milly and Zak shouting hello in the background. It was a crisp day, and Laurie felt the chill even in her centrally heated flat. There was frost on her bay window and, she noticed as she peeked out, a glistening white coating on all the cars in the street.

'So, how's your day going up there?' Laurie asked.

'Good, thanks. Thank you so much, Laurie, for everything you did – all the cooking. We're absolutely bowled over.'

'No trouble at all. Least I could do.' Laurie felt a rush of warmth at the memory of cooking in Rachel's kitchen in Skipley. 'Just hope it doesn't poison you.'

'I think we're safe – and given how good it tasted it wouldn't be such a bad way to go.'

'So any good presents over there?' Laurie asked, imagining a room full of shiny, ripped wrapping paper.

'Well yes, actually. Milly and Zak have got a cat –

or the promise of one, I mean. Mr Ripley was a bit of a hit when we were staying at your place. Oh – and Aiden's surprised me with a trip to Venice.'

'How exciting,' Laurie said, 'and after the last month you guys really deserve a break.'

'I can't wait. And get this – Bea's just announced she's off to Africa.'

'Are you serious?' Laurie said, walking over to the kitchen.

'Yes. It's been non-stop this morning. Anyway, how are you? I thought you'd be down at Lily's by now. Are you going over there later?'

Laurie flicked on the kettle and got out a mug to make herself coffee. 'I don't know . . .' she said. 'Maybe.'

'Maybe?' Rachel said. 'I thought it was the event of the year?'

'It is . . .' Laurie bit her lip. She could hear music coming up through Jay's living room floor. She pictured him and his girlfriend exchanging gifts and having a festive love-in before going down together to Lily's flat. It's just . . .'

'You should go,' Rachel said. 'Lily will want you to be there. You'll enjoy it.'

'Oh, I don't know. Perhaps.' She quickly changed the subject. 'Oh, I got your email by the way, of course that's fine about Milly coming to stay. I'd love to have her here. And at Seamless, once I'm back at work.'

'You are going back then?' Rachel said. 'For sure?'

'Yes. But – don't ask me how – Skipley seems to have knocked the workaholic out of me, Rachel. I'm going back, but it's going to be different this time.'

Laurie got out her suitcase and put it on the bed. Spain. She'd help her mum get over her broken heart – and maybe, somewhere along the line, she thought, she'd forget about her own.

She held up her strapless platinum bikini – checking the material hadn't gone saggy. Nope – not really surprising, she hadn't had much of a chance to wear it over the last couple of years. She slung it in the suitcase, idly dreaming about sangria and swimming pools. She tried to choose between two pairs of strappy heels, then opted to pack them both. She placed a white cotton dress on top of her other clothes. She'd pack the rest later.

She thought about what Rachel had said, about going to Lily's, and checked her watch. It was only 3.30 p.m. – her flight wasn't until ten. She still had plenty of time. Going to her wardrobe, she pulled out a red dress, then put the shower on full blast, peeled off her clothes and stepped into the steam.

Laurie arrived at Lily's door holding a bottle of champagne and trying with all her might to keep her smile fixed in place. When Lily opened the door to her flat, reggae music drifted out. Lily took one look at her outfit and hooted with laughter.

'Well,' she said, 'it's certainly different.'

Laurie was wearing her V-neck red dress, but with a cardigan over the top, a brown and black one with a huge, three-dimensional knitted robin on the right-hand side. It was one she'd picked out of the rag bag in Skipley and brought back on a whim. There were rows of gold sequins down each arm.

'I know, it's dreadful, isn't it?' Laurie said, pulling the sleeves of her cardigan down. 'But Christmas comes but once a year, eh?'

Lily smiled, then took her by the hand and led her into the flat. 'It's good to see you, gal,' she said. 'We've missed you around here. Now, let me show you what they did for me,' Lily said.

Laurie walked past some guests chatting by the doorway as Lily led her to the kitchen. Laurie gasped as she saw the difference. The kitchen walls and some of the living-room ones had been repapered with a gorgeous print, and there was a stylish, homey set of shelves holding her cookbooks. The torn lino had been replaced, and the whole flat looked even better than new. 'Nice, isn't it?' Lily said, smiling. 'Jay made the shelves,' she said, running her hands over the wood. 'Talented man, that one,' she said, giving Laurie a wink. 'And your friend Rachel and her children, they helped out too. Bless them all,' Lily said, her eyes shiny with unshed tears.

All around her people were eating and drinking, laughing together. On the kitchen tiles, there was a middle-aged couple swaying to the music. Lily raised her eyebrows at Laurie in approval as she saw them grinding closer. 'Now there's the Christmas spirit in action,' she said, with a chuckle. Friends of Lily's from the neighbouring blocks were scattered around the table, along with their teenage children. Laughter filled the room.

As Laurie put some jerk chicken out on her plate, she caught sight of Jay. Or the back of his head, at least. He was outside in the back yard, just visible through the window, laughing and talking to someone just out of view.

Laurie had tried to mentally prepare herself for this moment, but still, her first instinct was to hide. She looked around – the sofa tucked away in an alcove was pretty much invisible from where Jay was. There was a guy sitting on it whom she recognised, but couldn't place. He was wearing a sharp blue suit and had long, greying dreadlocks. She went to sit next to him. He'd lifted a framed photo off the side table and was looking at it. 'Fine-looking woman,' he said, appreciatively. Laurie looked up in surprise, then saw he was pointing at a photo of Lily at a party. Laurie moved in closer to look at the photo. Lily must have been in her thirties, about Laurie's age now, dancing with a little boy on a crowded dance floor. Her face was turned to the camera with a wide smile.

'Still is now,' he said, looking up. Laurie took in his

lively brown eyes and caramel skin. Not at all bad-looking, for a grandpa. 'You're Bill the Bikeman, aren't you?' Laurie asked. 'It is Bill, isn't it?' Laurie had seen the sign he sometimes propped up next door, advertising his bike services in big chalk letters. There was always a queue outside it.

'That's me, yes,' he said with a deep laugh, dragging his eyes away from Lily and putting his hand out for her to shake. 'Pleased to meet you. Can I pour you another rum?' He reached over for the bottle and poured her out a glass, topping it up with ginger ale. Laurie took a bite of her chicken.

'You got something, just there,' Bill said, politely, pointing at the place in Laurie's teeth where some black jerk sauce had got lodged. Laurie, embarrassed, got it out and thanked him.

'Pretty good cook, isn't she?'

'The best,' Laurie replied, then followed Bill's line of sight back to Lily. 'You should talk to her, you know,' Laurie prompted him.

'Really, you think so?'

'Oh yes. I happen to know for a fact that she's single. Hot property.'

That was all the encouragement Bill needed. 'Well, in that case,' he said, 'will you excuse me for a moment?' Laurie motioned for him to go ahead, and he stood up, straightening out the fabric in his trousers. With just a brief backward glance and a smile at

Laurie, he made his way over to where Lily was standing talking to a friend.

Laurie scanned the room: there were a few familiar faces circulating around the table, but it didn't look like Siobhan and Ed had arrived yet. Laurie checked the clock on the wall. It was only four, she had hours still.

Her phone buzzed with a message. She clicked in order to read it, grateful for something to do.

Rachel.

One thing. You do know Jay's still in love with you, don't you? And that he's single? x

Laurie's pulse raced. She looked up and caught sight of Jay right away, in the kitchen. He had come in from outside. He wasn't talking to that girl, or in fact any girl at all, but to Sean from the basement flat. Jay saw her looking. Excusing himself from the conversation, he made his way over to where Laurie was sitting. Her heart started to race.

'You made it,' he said, a smile spreading across his face. She hurriedly tucked her phone away as he took a seat next to her.

'Wouldn't have missed it,' Laurie said.

'I'm glad you did,' he said, smiling. 'Merry Christmas.' Jay lifted his can of Red Stripe to clink it with her glass.

Laurie's mind went blank – with Jay so close she couldn't think of a word to say.

'I enjoyed meeting your friend Rachel,' he said, putting his beer down on the coffee table.

'Oh yes, you two got on?'

'Oh yeah,' he said. 'We're like this,' he laughed, crossing two fingers to show her. 'She even made it along to one of our gigs.'

'Siobhan told me about that,' Laurie said, feeling the tiniest pang of jealousy.

'Rachel made me think about a few things, actually.' He paused. 'God, I'm really not good at this stuff,' he said, raking a hand through his hair. 'But I feel like . . .'

Laurie's heart was thudding in her chest as she waited for him to continue.

'At the end of the summer it seemed like there was something there. Something special between us,' Jay said, 'and there still is. On my side at least.'

His words hung in the air. 'I think it's worth another try. A proper one. I think you're amazing, Laurie. I always have. That is unless that guy last night was your boyfriend . . . in which case—'

'Ed?' Laurie said, a smile creeping on to her lips. 'No. He's Siobhan's.'

'OK. Good,' he laughed. 'Glad we cleared that up. So, what do you think?'

As Laurie looked into Jay's eyes, summer didn't seem that long ago. She wanted it back – with Jay she felt different. Like a better version of herself.

'I'm sorry I was an idiot,' Laurie said. 'It must have seemed really selfish. I think I was scared. Because you and me ... well, it's a big thing, isn't it?' she smiled, then covered her face with her hands. 'God, this is hard, isn't it? Listen,' she went on. 'I've got a flight to catch in a couple of hours.'

'A flight?'

'Yes. Long story.' She took a deep breath and summoned up all of her courage. 'But if you want to continue this conversation,' she said, 'we could talk upstairs, while I finish packing?'

'Sounds good,' Jay said.

Laurie couldn't tell for sure if Lily had spotted Jay and her leaving – she was slow-dancing in the kitchen with Bill, to a reggae track.

Laurie's heart thudded as she walked up the stairs with Jay and walked into her flat with him.

'Wine?' she asked, going through to the kitchen.

'Yes, thanks.'

Laurie took a bottle of red from the side and opened it, pouring two glasses. He stood beside her and she was conscious of how close he was. She felt his familiar warmth, took in the smell of him that she'd missed.

'So, where are you going this time?' he said, taking one of the glasses and standing in the kitchen doorway.

'Spain,' she replied. 'Just for a couple of weeks. I'm seeing in New Year with my mum. A bit of mother-daughter time's long overdue.'

'Sounds good,' he said.

'Sure you don't mind keeping me company while I throw the rest of my shoe collection into my suitcase and try to close it?'

'Not at all,' Jay said, smiling. 'It would be an honour to sit on it with you.'

As Laurie walked towards Jay to pass him, he smiled and pointed to something above the doorway. 'What's this?' he asked.

Hanging there was a sprig of mistletoe, tied with a red bow. Laurie smiled. Rachel must have put it up.

She looked across the doorway at Jay. 'Because if it's a trap,' he said, 'I really don't mind.'

Jay moved his hand up her arm and brought her gently towards him. He smoothed back her hair, then cupped her chin with his hand. Looking into her eyes, he ran his thumb over her bottom lip.

Laurie closed her eyes as he kissed her, her whole body tingling at his touch. She put her arms around him. It felt natural, as if they were meant to be there.

As they kissed, Laurie forgot all about the flight she was about to catch. She thought instead of all the time with Jay she wanted to catch up on. The second chance they had now, to put things right, do it better this time.

And then there was room for just one other thought in her mind: *Thank you, Rach.*

I hope you enjoyed reading Meet Me Under the Mistletoe. Here are a couple of my favourite things to make at this time of year, to keep you in the Christmas spirit.

Zak's Photo Snowglobes

Drop your family into a Christmas scene! These pretty personalised snowglobes make perfect gifts for doting grandparents.

You will need:
A clean glass jar with a flat top
White glitter
A photo of a family member (smaller than the jar height and diameter)
Sticky-back plastic (or a laminator) to cover the photo
Distilled water
Small amount of glycerine (available from chemists)
Superglue or a glue gun
Waterproof Christmas decorations for the backdrop

Prepare your photo. Choose a photo of a family member and cut around the outline of their face or body. Then waterproof the image by laminating it or covering it in sticky-back plastic (on both sides) leaving a centimetre extra surrounding the image, so that the photo is completely sealed in.

Create your Christmas scene. The underside of the jar lid is going to provide the base for your Christmas scene. Bend the bottom centimetre of the photo over and glue it to the inside of the lid using glue-gun glue or superglue. Add waterproof Christmas decorations behind the image to keep it propped up, like a plastic sprig of holly, a Santa cake decoration, or a souvenir Eiffel tower. Leave enough space around the edges for it to screw back on easily.

Fill your jar with distilled water almost to the top, then add a couple of teaspoons of glitter and a dash of glycerine to help the snow to drift down slowly.

Seal it up. Put plenty of glue around the lid, and then screw it on tightly. Decorate the edge of the lid with glitter or a ribbon, for extra sparkle. Give jar a shake and enjoy watching the snow fall over your handmade scene.

Next up, some beautiful ribbon-tied Christmas tree decorations. These traditional biscuits will add a touch of class to your tree, and they taste twice as good as they look ...

Milly's Gingerbread Stars
Makes about 30 biscuits.

Ingredients:

340g plain flour	1 tsp baking powder
½ tsp salt	1½ tsp grated nutmeg
1½ tsp ground cloves	2 tsp ground cinnamon
3 tsp ground ginger	225g unsalted butter, softened
340g soft brown sugar	1 egg, beaten
75g crystallised ginger, finely chopped	

To decorate:

225g icing sugar

Silver balls to decorate

Preparation: Put some classic Christmas tunes on the stereo and pour yourself a glass of sloe gin.

1. Sift the flour, baking powder, spices and salt together into a mixing bowl.

2. Beat the butter and sugar together, and then beat in the egg gradually. Stir into the flour to make a dough, then add the ginger. Now reward yourself with a sip or two of the gin.
3. Place the dough between two sheets of cling-film, and roll out to the thickness of a pound coin. Pop it in the fridge for half an hour. Pre-heat the oven to 180°C, and put your feet up for a bit.
4. When the dough's ready, cut out the biscuits, and put on a greased baking tray. Cook them for about ten minutes, and, while they are still hot from the oven, poke a hole at the top of each one. Leave them to cool on a wire rack.

Decoration: Thread a ribbon through the hole at the top of each biscuit. If you're making your own icing, simply sift the icing sugar, and then mix to a stiff consistency with boiling water. Brush the icing over the biscuits and decorate them with silver balls. They can then go in an airtight container (they'll keep for a couple of weeks) or you can hang them straight on your tree.

Enjoy, and Merry Christmas!
Love,
Abby x

ACKNOWLEDGEMENTS

Huge thanks to my brilliant editor Jo Dickinson for her creativity, insight and guidance, and to agent extraordinaire Caroline Hardman for her support at every stage.

To the excellent team at Quercus – Jenny Richards for the lovely cover, Georgina Difford, Katie Gordon, Kathryn Taussig, David North and everyone else who has worked so hard on my book.

To Caroline Hogg, Emma Stonex and my mum Sheelagh, for their continuing encouragement and wise words. Thanks in particular to James, for his ideas, enthusiasm, and flair for Christmas tree decoration.

Finally, to the friends and family who make my festive season sparkle each year. Merry Christmas!